THE BENEATH

DON'T LOOK
BELOW the
SURFACE

THE BENEATH
S. C. RANSOM

DON'T LOOK
BELOW the
SURFACE

nosy
crow

First published 2015 by Nosy Crow Ltd
The Crow's Nest, 10a Lant Street
London SE1 1QR
www.nosycrow.com

ISBN: 978 0 85763 276 0

A CIP catalogue record for this book is available from the
British Library.

Printed and bound in the UK by Clays Ltd, St Ives Plc.
Typeset by Tiger Media Ltd, Bishops Stortford, Hertfordshire

Papers used by Nosy Crow are made from wood grown in
sustainable forests.

1 3 5 7 9 8 6 4 2

For Ellie, my inspiration

DON'T LOOK BELOW the SURFACE

CHAPTER 1

I slumped down on my usual seat at the end of the deserted platform, my phone stuffed deep into my pocket. As the Tube train finally rounded the corner I glanced down the tunnel. A figure was silhouetted against the headlights – it was a girl, her long hair streaming out around her, running fast. I watched in horror, drawn to the edge of the platform. She was still a long way back. Too far back.

The train driver saw her too, and the huge noise of the horn shook the walls. The noise quickly transformed into the squeal of brakes, but it was clear that there wasn't going to be enough time.

"Run faster!" I screamed as loudly as I could. "You have to run faster!"

The electrified rail was horribly close to her feet as she

sped along. She was going to die from either that or the train. The noise of the horn was constant, and the squeal of the brakes hurt deep inside my ears. At last I could see her face; she looked terrified, but she was getting closer.

"Come on! You can make it!" I leapt over the barrier near the end of the platform and leaned out towards her, reaching with one hand and holding on to the railings with the other. "Come ON!"

Her dark hair was whipping around her face as the wall of air being pushed by the train propelled her forward, and she nearly stumbled as she tried to wipe it aside to see. The face of the train driver was crystal clear in the cab right behind her, a face equally full of terror. I could see his arms braced against the impact – not that her thin frame was going to make much impression on that wall of speeding metal – and then I saw him close his eyes, not wanting to see her end.

The front of the train was almost on her, but she was so close! Her hair cleared from her face for a second and she reached out her hand towards me, grazing my outstretched fingers. Without thinking I grabbed her firmly by the wrist and pulled.

"JUMP!" I hollered, and yanked at her with all my might, throwing myself backwards as the train shot past just centimetres from my nose. The two of us fell on our backs in a tangle of arms and legs on the tiny piece of access platform that sloped down towards the tunnel, and the Tube train thundered past, screeching to a halt

halfway down the platform.

Before I could ask her what she thought she was doing she was on her feet, looking around her as if she was being hunted. She grabbed my hand and hauled me up, and then, reaching behind us on the smooth tunnel wall, she clicked something. A panel swung inwards, revealing a dark void. I could hear people running along the platform and the driver shouting. The curve of the platform meant that we were out of sight, but it was only going to be for a moment.

The girl grabbed my hand and looked into my eyes.

"Please?" she whispered in a strange accent.

Whatever the reason for her flight, I needed to know more. I was fed up hiding out on the Tube platform where the text messages couldn't reach me instead of going home. Jenny Tait was just going to have to find someone else to bully for a while. I stepped into the gloom and the panel swiftly shut behind me, leaving no trace of either of us on the platform.

The panel clicks shut and we are alone. I can't believe it. I'm in the Aboves' old tunnel. I'm in the Aboves' tunnel with one of them. A real one. But one who just saved my life.

I whisper to her to stay quiet, then hold her hand more firmly and walk further into the passage, making sure I avoid all the rubbish on the floor. I feel the excitement of being somewhere I've never been before, even though

I can see it in my mind's eye on the map and I've been drilled in how to get in and out. The place is really filthy, not like the tunnels at home. The dust and the muck sit around in thick layers and it's not really safe. But for now it will have to do.

I lead the girl down the steep steps and along the narrow access corridor until we get to the main platform. There is a single greenish light on, casting deep shadows across the walls. I hear her gasp, but her steps don't falter. She's brave then. All the time we walk along in the gloom my mind is racing. What am I doing? I still have my mission to complete – to find Lily Blackthorne and take her down to Dane.

But I can't resist the temptation to talk to the girl who saved my life. Near the light are some old seats. I stop and turn to look at her. She's looking around with her mouth open.

"Here, let's sit down for a moment."

It took me a second to realise what she was saying. Her accent was weird, but I was glad of what she was suggesting. I sank down on to the hard bench and tried to fathom out exactly where I was. We had been at the very end of the platform at the Tube station when I rescued her, and then she had pulled me through the wall. Now we were on another, completely different, disused platform. I could read the station name on the wall – Baker Street – but the advertising posters were hanging in shreds and too mucky to make out. I wondered how long it had been since someone was last here. The only sign of life was the eerie glow of the Emergency Exit sign. Without it I could have believed that she had whisked me into the past.

"Where are we?"

She shrugged, dropping down on to a seat further up the bench. "In a place no one uses any more. We'll be safe here for a while."

"What on earth were you doing on the track?" I sat up and turned to look at her. "You were almost killed!"

"I was trying to find my way, took a wrong turn and that was it. All of a sudden it was coming up behind me." She glanced briefly at me and then looked down. "Thank you for saving me," she continued in a soft voice.

"Any time. I was pretty sure that I was going to fail though. That train came so close – half a second longer and you would have been under the wheels, and we wouldn't have been having any sort of conversation."

"I can't believe that you managed to pull me out of the way. You don't look strong enough."

I couldn't help smiling. "Me too." I looked at my hands. "I didn't know I had it in me."

I realised that my heart was still racing, the adrenalin pumping through my veins. I took several deep breaths to try and calm down.

"Are you all right? Are you going to be ill?"

"No, I'm fine. I'm just a bit stunned with all of this." I

waved my hand around. "How do you know this place? How did you just open up a blank wall like that? What's going on?"

She leapt up from the bench and started to pace up and down, her arms folded tightly across her chest. She was thin, and, from what I could see in the dim light, was wearing a hippy-style cheesecloth shirt, unbuttoned to show a stretchy exercise top in lurid green underneath, and flared pinstripe trousers that looked as if they came from a 1970s man's suit. She was mumbling to herself, and for the first time I began to doubt the sanity of my decision to follow her. No one knew I was here, and if something happened no one would ever find me. My heart, which had begun to slow down a little, picked up pace again and I could feel the hair on the back of my neck stand up. What would Nan do if I just disappeared?

"Anyway," I said brightly. "I'm Lily. Are you from round here too?"

She stopped and stared at me, saying nothing.

I can't believe it. The person who I've been sent here to find is the girl who's just saved my life. Dane said she is always on the platform at this time of day but I didn't think for a moment this could be her. How am I supposed to complete my mission now? She's not what I expected, but then I never really thought of her as a real person, just as someone we need.

She is still talking.

"So, what's your name?"

"Aria."

"That's a pretty name. I've not heard that one before. Do you live close by?"

I can't answer so she carries on anyway. I don't know what to do, and walk up and down the platform wishing I could ask Dane's advice. But I know what he'll say, and I know what's expected of me. I have to get her back through the caves, where he is waiting for us.

"Look, Lily, I need your help. I need you to—"

A movement down the old, disused tunnel makes me freeze. Is it a figure in the shadows? I look around and see the mice on the track, and I feel as if I have been punched in the chest. I know what's coming.

Aria had stopped talking and was staring at something on the old tracks. I stepped forward to see what it was and then hurriedly stepped back. Mice were running along in the same direction, away from a noise that was becoming noticeable above the distant rumble of the trains. It was the sound of far-off slithering, low and somehow menacing. It electrified Aria. She ran the few steps towards me and grabbed my hand again.

"We have to go. Now. There's no time to waste!"

The noise was getting louder. I couldn't work out what might be making it, but as we started back towards the place where we had come in I was conscious of something big moving across the floor in the tunnel ahead of us. It was too dark to make it out but I could see the shadows shifting. Aria stopped dead and whipped round, dragging me with her. We sprinted towards the other end of the platform, but the noise coming from that direction was worse. It was the same slithering sound as before, but with a distinct undertone of scratching. We skidded to a halt in a small cloud of dust. The mice on the tracks were in a frenzy, running to and fro, then trying to bury themselves in whatever small space they could find. Aria looked from tunnel to tunnel, fear on her face.

"What … what do we do now?" I whispered, as the hideous scratching noise got even louder.

"There's no other way out," gasped Aria. "They've got us surrounded. This is it."

"Why don't we just go out of the exit?" I asked, edging towards the white and green light.

The shadows in the dark at either end of the platform were beginning to take on a long, low shape, and a musty, dead stench filled my nose, making me want to gag. Whatever creature smelled like that, I didn't want to meet one.

"What exit?" she asked.

"The one right here," I shouted as the noise increased.

Grasping her hand tightly, I pulled her through the archway under the sign and up the stairs in front of us. But the further up we went, the darker it became, and at the top we could see nothing. The noise was coming closer and Aria seemed almost paralysed with fear. I

pulled her round to face me and shook her sharply.

"We need to find the door!" I hissed.

I can't believe that the Crop has come this far up. Did it follow me through the tunnels or has the Farmer sent it to finish me off? I don't understand where she's taking me. How does she know the way? We only have minutes before the end, just moments before the Crop makes it up the stairs and we'll be cornered. We're both going to die.

Lily is shouting from further along the dark corridor.

"I can see light under a door – this is the way out, come on!"

I turn and run, but know from the sudden smell that the Crop has made it to the top of the stairs. I hate to turn my back; I don't want to die like that but I have to run. I can hear Lily at the door, fighting with the handle. With a final grunt she wrenches it free and it opens up with a rusty squeal. Light floods the far part of the corridor, but not where I am. Running into the light will mean that the Crop can see me, but I run towards it anyway. As I reach the door she grabs me and pulls me through, slamming it shut behind us. The door shudders as the Crop throws itself at it, angry at missing its prey.

"What the hell was that?" *she asks, turning to look at the door.*

I hope that it will hold. It seems to be all right; it's not budging. I finally notice where we are standing. It's one of the Aboves' walking tunnels. It's light and clean, and the walls are covered with pictures in startlingly bright colours, most of which seem to be of girls kissing boys. There are people too, some wearing tiny clothes that show all of their arms and legs. No one seems to be taking any notice of us.

"Come on, this way," she says. "I want to get as far away from whatever that was as possible, and then you can tell me what it was – or they were."

I drag my eyes away from a picture and we walk quickly down the tunnel, but there are more and more people showing their legs. I don't know where to look. The fear tightens in my chest – this can't happen. I was supposed to get her and take her through the caves, not go running around with the Aboves in their tunnels. But I don't know what else to do so I follow her. We can't go back.

Finally we get to the end and walk into a big chamber. There are dozens of people here, coming out of tunnels, some going into others. But what takes my breath away is at the end of the chamber. Lots of metal steps are leading up, up an impossible distance, almost as far as I can see, and they are moving. The people are just standing on them and the steps are carrying them towards the light. Other steps are carrying people down towards us. Lily grabs my hand again and pulls me on to them – steps that are flat at first, and then suddenly lift us up. On the walls are small squares with moving pictures. I'm staring at them, trying to work out what they can be for, when I hear a noise, a thumping on the wall of the moving steps right next to me. Surely it can't be the Crop? Can it have got out from the old tunnel and be beneath this stairway? Is there any other way for it to get out?

Lily hears the noise too, and looks at me.

"It's nothing, just a banging escalator. This one does it all the time."

"How can you be sure?" I ask.

She shrugs. "Maybe we should run then," she says.

We set off up the steps as fast as we can. I nearly miss the top, where the steps suddenly go flat, and I stumble as I find myself on solid ground again. Lily drags me towards a low wall that runs across the room.

"We're in luck," she tells me as she pulls me through a gap. "The ticket barriers aren't often left open."

And suddenly everything is gone. There is no roof, no ceiling and the light burns my eyes. For the first time in my life I am Above.

DON'T LOOK BELOW the SURFACE

CHAPTER 2

I don't think I had ever been so relieved to get out of the Tube and into the late afternoon light. The rush hour was gathering pace along the road towards home and the noises I could hear were all ones that I could place – no more unseen creatures. That had been one of the scariest moments of my life, and for a fraction of a second I wondered if I had been set up, if the strange girl had actually been messing with me. I glanced sideways at her, as she'd barely said a word since we escaped from that disused platform.

She was standing stock-still on the pavement, the crowds jostling around her, staring up at the sky. I called her name but there was no response.

"Aria?" I tried again, reaching for her arm. "Are you OK?"

She didn't look as if she had been messing with me. There was a bemused expression on her face and she still didn't appear to have heard me. She seemed to be squinting in the daylight, even though it was pretty overcast, holding her hand up to protect her eyes. We were getting in the way of the people wanting to get into the Tube station, so I gripped her arm more firmly and pulled her to one side.

"I think you need a coffee, or sweet tea or something," I muttered as she followed, still looking upwards. "Come on, this way."

I could see the café on the far side of the road, and glancing both ways at the traffic I led her over the pedestrian crossing. Halfway across she let out an almighty shriek and ran back towards the Tube entrance. The large double-decker bus, which had been slowing to allow us to cross, sped up again, the driver shaking his head.

"What's that?" she gasped, pointing at the retreating bus. "It was about to hit us both."

"Not on the crossing," I said, taking a tighter grip on her. "Come on, let's go."

She let me steer her over the road, but it was like trying to lead a skittish pony. Aria flinched as cars went by, and she was so engrossed in watching them that she nearly walked into a lamppost. We were attracting more than our fair share of curious looks. I could see another bus coming and felt her back stiffen, so swerved her into the café as quickly as possible and sat her down at a quiet table.

"Phew, I don't want to be doing that again in the near future. Right, I need coffee. What would you like?"

Her eyes were as wide as saucers as she looked at the display of cakes and sandwiches, and I could see her fingers gripping the table as she leaned towards them.

"Where did you get all those?" she whispered, her gaze never leaving the counter.

"You do ask some daft questions. Do you want something to eat as well?" I did a quick mental rundown of the contents of my purse. "Want to split a muffin?"

Aria said nothing, but just continued to stare at the food.

"Would you like something to eat?" I asked again, not sure if she had heard me.

She nodded mutely.

"What about a drink – what would you like?"

I hoped that she wasn't going to choose one of the super-expensive hot chocolates with all the trimmings. For some reason the question seemed to confuse her.

"What?" she asked. "Water, of course."

"OK, wait here and I'll get it."

I left her at the table, still clutching the top as if her life depended on it. Soon I was back with one plain coffee, one double-choc muffin and a glass of tap water, which left me with about fifteen pence. She gasped as I put the muffin down on the table and her hand darted out towards it – then stopped. I pushed it towards her.

"Go on, you have it. I'm not really hungry."

She shot me a glance that seemed pathetically grateful and, holding the muffin almost reverently, started picking at the top with her long, thin fingers.

I sipped my coffee and watched, almost embarrassed, as she ate. Her skinny frame was hunched over the table, the long dark hair falling forward, but not enough to cover her high cheekbones and perfectly straight nose. The dark eyes that continued to dart around the room were completely free of make-up. There was no doubt that she could be beautiful with a decent haircut and some proper clothes.

She devoured every last speck of the muffin. I'd never seen anyone eat with so much obvious enjoyment; every single chocolate chip was savoured, no crumb overlooked. I thought at one moment she was about to eat the paper case as well, but in the end she just scraped all the bits off it. There didn't seem much point in trying to get her to talk while she was eating, so I nursed my cooling coffee and waited. Every few minutes I felt the phone in my pocket vibrate, but for once I felt strong enough to ignore it. Today I had better things to do than to read Jenny's snarky comments.

Finally every particle of the muffin was gone, the only evidence remaining being a small smear of chocolate on Aria's chin. She sat back, eyes half closed, and breathed deeply.

"Thank you," she murmured.

"No problem. You, um, looked as if you enjoyed that. Have you not eaten for a while?"

She lifted her eyes and looked directly at me for a few moments. Twice she looked as if she was about to speak, before thinking better of it.

I couldn't stand waiting any longer. "Look, it's obvious that something is going on. What were you doing in the tunnel? What on earth were the things that were chasing us?"

"I can't tell you exactly. I just know that they are really dangerous."

"In what way?"

"They'll kill you if they catch you."

"Sounds as if we were pretty lucky then," I said, more and more convinced that I had picked up someone with a severe personality disorder.

Aria slumped back in her chair, her hands falling into her lap.

"He'll kill me anyway," she said, playing with a button on her shirt.

"Who? Who would do that?"

"The Farmer. He obviously knows that I'm up here, and that's not allowed."

"I don't get it. What's a farmer got to do with anything?"

Her dark eyebrows knitted together. "I don't understand you. There's so much up here I don't recognise. I didn't think it would be this difficult."

She was beginning to wind me up with her non-answers, but I didn't want to give her a hard time, not if she was in need of some sort of professional help.

"OK, Aria, let's do this one question at a time. Where do you live?"

"With the Community."

"And where exactly is that?"

She lifted her dark eyes, and the intensity of her gaze startled me.

"Underground. We live underground, below your tunnels, below your world."

I tried to keep the surprise from my face, and wondered if she was actually living with the homeless people who shelter in the Tube.

"So," I said, choosing my words carefully, "have you been down there long?"

"No one knows. There are stories, but we don't know exactly how long. It must be hundreds of years."

I nearly spat my coffee across the table. "Hundreds of years?"

"If not longer. We have stories that go a long way back, but only the Elders are allowed to hear most of them. I'll never hear them all now."

From the wistful tone to her reply it was clear that she believed everything she was saying. But could I?

"So, you are part of a community that lives underground, right?" She nodded. "How many of you are there?"

"Not so many now, not after all the troubles. Maybe a few hundred."

Every answer she gave me raised more and more questions, so I went back to the one that was most obvious to ask.

"And why are you here? Are you running away?"

I can still taste the sweetness of the cake on my tongue. I've never seen so much cake – more than enough for everybody, and she didn't even bother to have one. Maybe they are as greedy and wasteful as the Elders say. I look around. No one is tucking into the huge platefuls of food, even though it is all just sitting there on the side. About half of them look pretty miserable. Most are drinking cups of a bitter-smelling brown liquid, including Lily. The room is so brightly lit that it hurts my eyes.

Lily is still looking at me. Shall I tell her the truth? I take a deep breath.

"I've just been told how I was going to be Assigned, and I don't want to be what they want me to be."

"What does that mean – 'Assigned'?" she asks.

She doesn't understand – why should she? She has even less knowledge of our world than I do of hers.

"In the Community, when you reach fifteen you find out the role you will take for the rest of your life."

"What, like a doctor or a teacher, that sort of thing?"

She is leaning forward with her arms on the table and a frown on her forehead, struggling to make sense of it all. I nod, not wanting to say too much, but enough to convince her that this is the real reason I'm here.

"And when do you start doing that?"

"On your sixteenth birthday."

"And you do that forever? That is way too harsh. I'm not surprised that you've run away."

She leans even further over the table and drops her voice. "So what was it that you didn't want to be? What was so awful that you had to run away from your entire life?" she asks.

I am surprised as the tears come, tears that I've not shed since Carita was Assigned years before. I agreed to join Dane's mission when it was clear I was heading for the same fate. Whatever happens now, there is no way they will keep even that Assignment. I am a lost cause.

I feel a touch on my arm, and flinch before I realise that it's gentle – a touch of kindness. Her voice is gentle too.

"Please don't cry, Aria. Whatever it is you don't have to tell me. I was just curious, that's all."

I hear her leave the table for a moment and return a second later. She presses something soft and papery against my fingers.

"Here, wipe your eyes with these."

She is kind and brave, this stranger whose life I have invaded. What would she think if she knew the whole truth?

I sat back and looked at the weeping girl opposite me.

She seemed at a loss with what to do with the napkins, so I took one and dabbed at her cheeks, mopping up some of the tears that were making tracks down her face. The waitress, who had been about to come over and clear our table, did a swift about-turn and tried to look busy somewhere else.

It wasn't going to be possible to stay in the café all evening, so I had to work out what to do with her. I couldn't make up my mind if I believed her or not. After all, living underground seemed pretty unlikely. But I couldn't abandon her either – I had to make sure she was OK. I glanced surreptitiously at my watch; the café would be open for another couple of hours, but I had no more money. She didn't look as if she had anything on her, so we were going to get thrown out soon enough. And in half an hour or so I was going to be expected home for tea.

"So where are you heading to now? I'm going to be off soon."

"I … I don't really know," she said, finally taking the napkins and wiping her face before sniffing loudly. "Can I come with you? I have nowhere to go…"

What on earth was I going to do? I could hardly turn up at home with a complete stranger. Leaving her here was my only choice. I might have saved her from the track but that didn't make her my responsibility. Anyway, I had more than enough problems in my life without inviting another one in, especially one who seemed so utterly

clueless about what was going on around her.

I was about to get up to go when my phone vibrated again, and Aria jumped. I hesitated before fishing it out of my pocket, feeling my stomach clench. Would it be a mundane one from Nan asking me to pick something up for tea, or another vile anonymous one? It still made me feel sick every time I turned the phone over. I took a deep breath and glanced at the screen.

It was from Nan, and I felt my shoulders sag with relief. She was popping out so we weren't going to be having tea for a while. I was just about to reply when the phone buzzed again. Without thinking, I glanced at the little screen.

The spiteful message hit me like a punch, making me cry out loud. Aria jumped up, knocking the table and rattling the empty cup and saucer. She tensed as if ready for a fight, looking around her wildly.

"What's wrong?" I asked, leaning over to put a calming hand on her wrist.

"You saw danger. I heard you. I just don't know what the danger is…"

Her eyes continued to dart about, searching for something that wasn't there.

"Sit down," I said in a low voice, glancing at the café manager, who was staring over at us. He clearly thought we were up to no good. "Now!"

Aria sat back down with a thump, looking even more confused. "But you shouted. Why did you do that?"

"It was just a text."

That made it sound harmless, but every day Jenny found another way to hurt me, to dig in the knife so expertly.

Aria stared at me blankly, and I knew I had to explain a bit more. "The text is a horrible message that I'm pretty sure is from one of the girls in my class, although she's far too smart to send it from her own number."

That was the problem. The teachers at school said bullying was unacceptable but unless you had actual proof there was no point in telling them. All it would do was land you in more trouble. I just had to put up with the hate mail. It could only be from Jenny, and I was the easy target to pick on now. She seemed to know everything about me and my dull life with no family, few friends and no hope of a boyfriend. It gave her plenty of ammunition for her texts.

Aria was still looking bemused. "What message?"

"On my phone," I said, trying and failing to keep the incredulity out of my voice. "You know – a text message. See?"

I turned the phone round to show her, but it didn't change the confused frown on her face. She took the handset and ran her fingers over the surface.

"That's the sort of stuff she's been saying." I pointed to the screen where Jenny's latest thoughts, this time about my weight, were still partially visible.

"I don't understand," she said in a small voice.

"Read it from the beginning," I sighed, leaning over to scroll back up to the top of the message. Aria let out a small squeal as the characters moved, and dropped the phone.

"How does it do that?" she whispered, whipping her hands under the table as if she was expecting the phone to bite her.

"Do what?"

"How do you make the picture move? I mean, I've heard about moving pictures from the Listeners, and I saw the funny ones on the moving stairs, but I don't understand what they're for."

"What picture? And what's a Listener?"

"The squiggles on there – *the picture*," she said, bringing one hand up to point at the screen.

"But that's just a text. It's not a picture." At that moment the screen saver kicked in, showing a photo of Beanie looking cute in her little collar. "That's a picture…"

Aria looked as if I had electrified her. Her hand whipped away from the phone again, and she actually hissed.

"What's that?"

"It's my cat, actually, or she was, until a little while ago."

I looked at her soft little face, tiny paws and friendly eyes. Who was looking after her now, I wondered for the thousandth time, and were they making her happy? For a moment I could almost feel her soft fur under my hand, and I had to fight a sudden choking feeling in my throat.

It wasn't helpful to think like that.

I turned the phone face down and sat back. Aria was looking at me with horror.

"You like that thing?" she asked, pointing at the phone.

"Do you mean Beanie? Of course I like her. She was my cat. Well, kitten really, but she's … she's gone now." I paused for a second, gathering myself. "I'm guessing that you're not a cat person then?"

"Of course not! No one likes animals. Why would they?"

"Well, don't sit on the fence then!" I said.

Every time I thought of Beanie my eyes still filled with tears. Luckily Jenny didn't know about that or it would have become yet another thing to ridicule me about. I had last seen my little cat when she was about eight months old – bigger than a kitten but not a proper cat, and still happy to play all the kittenish games. Her favourite was chasing a torch beam across the floor, and we had played that so often that I emptied half the batteries in the house. Dad had been especially cross about that, but then he had been annoyed about a lot of things, and I still felt guilty that I missed my cat more than I missed him. For a moment into my mind flashed the twins, my little brothers. I missed them more than anything, but couldn't afford to let myself think about them.

I blinked hard to keep the tears back, not daring to

look up. Maybe I didn't want anything to do with this girl, not if she was an animal-hater. The thought that I might be with someone like Jenny stiffened my resolve. I sat back and stared at her, but was instantly taken aback. Rather than the scorn or disgust I was expecting to see on her face, there was only puzzlement.

"I'm sorry," she faltered. "Have I upset you? It's just that where I'm from, well, we don't like animals. I didn't mean to offend you."

There was no doubting the sincerity in her voice.

"It's OK," I said. "If you don't like cats, you don't like cats. It's not as if she's around any more."

"So much up here is strange. I didn't realise … I always imagined that I would know enough to get by…"

"Get by? What are you doing here, Aria?"

As I asked the question the phone vibrated against the table and I looked down.

My fist clenched around the phone as I read Jenny's latest message. It was a new low, even for her.

"What is it, Lily? What's the matter? Are you cross?" Aria asked.

I looked up at the stranger sitting opposite me, a stranger who needed help, and who wanted to be my friend. My decision was suddenly easy.

"Come on, Aria, let's go. I'm taking you home with me."

DON'T LOOK BELOW the SURFACE

CHAPTER 3

We are leaving the place with all the food and walking now, walking along the edge of the walls. I try not to look up, because nothing is there and it feels so wrong. The light is bright in my eyes and I have to screw them up tightly so that I'm not blinded. Everything is so big and so loud. Huge machines are roaring past, and their smell is terrible. There are hundreds and hundreds of people and all of them seem to be in a hurry. They come in all shapes and sizes and in different skin colours as well, and a few have pale-yellow hair. The smell of the people is terrible too, but Lily doesn't seem to notice. We are leaving behind the stairs that lead back to my life. Turning round I can see people pouring through the entrance, only pausing to pick up the folded papers from the big racks. As we turn a corner I wonder if I can find

my way back. And if I can, what will be waiting for me?

It was a slow walk home: Aria kept stopping dead to stare at people, which was a bit embarrassing. I couldn't understand her. She was certainly behaving as if she had been underground for her entire life, but I really didn't see how that was possible. Surely whole communities of people couldn't be living under the city?

I kept close to her as we walked down the street, calming her when a siren made her jump and when the cars on the street stopped in a queue next to us, engines racing. We were nearly home when Foggy bounced round the corner, dragging Will behind him. Foggy was a lively dog, mostly golden retriever but with a fair few other things thrown in. He immediately leapt up to say hello.

"Hi, Lily, how are you?" asked Will, smiling. "Get down, Foggy!"

He wrestled with the huge, hairy dog but quickly gave up. Foggy continued to slobber over me.

"Oh, hi, Will. Um, great, thank you. Hi, Foggy."

I rubbed Foggy's ears before pushing him away with as much force as I could muster, and he finally dropped back to the floor. I brushed the dirt from my sleeve and tried to think of something interesting to say.

I'd known Will forever, from the time when we were both young and I came to visit Nan, but since I'd moved in with her I'd realised how gorgeous he had become.

He was very friendly but I worried that he just thought of me as a kid. He was only a year ahead of me at school though, so I was doing my best to get him to see me as potential girlfriend material. Finally my plans seemed to going in the right direction, and he smiled at me again as he hauled in Foggy's lead. I smiled back and turned to introduce Aria.

She was pressed back against the window of the launderette, her face a picture of terror. Foggy, sensing fun, dived for her. Aria let out a blood-curdling scream and he froze. She was scrabbling to get away, hands reaching behind her across the smooth glass. Her eyes stayed fixed on the dog, and he bolted as she screamed again. Will was yanked across the pavement on the end of the lead.

"Easy," he said, calming down the dog, who was now shaking with fear behind his knees. He glared at Aria. "You've frightened him."

Aria gulped but said nothing, her lower lip quivering. Will turned to me.

"What's her problem?" he asked under his breath, his glorious dark eyes flashing. "I'd better get going – the noise has upset Foggy."

And with that he was gone – another wasted opportunity to actually talk with him. I watched his retreating back for a moment, before sighing and turning back to Aria, who was shaking so much it looked as if she might be having a panic attack.

"You're OK, calm down. It's only a dog and he's gone now." I tried patting her on the arm to see if that helped, but it made her jump again. "Look, nothing much can really hurt you out here unless you leap into the road in front of a car or bus, OK? There's no need to scream."

I took her arm and led her the rest of the way down the street to the place that was now my home. Nan lived in the ground-floor flat of an old terraced town house. Outside, the whole row was shabby and dirty, the stairs to the flats below covered in old newspapers and Burger King wrappers. She had been there for decades, obsessively cleaning her windows so that she could watch the passing world. She wanted to be on the top floor to get a better view, she had told me, but her arthritis had been giving her trouble for some time and it was all she could do to climb the four short steps up to the front door. She kept the brass-work on it gleaming too, but that and her windows were the only bits of the entire building that weren't covered in a thick layer of London grime.

I had been living with her for about six months, crammed into a tiny box room that really wasn't designed for the job. I had had to part with most of my stuff; only those belongings that really mattered were finally allowed across the threshold. There was absolutely no space for another bed, so I pushed aside the thought about what I was actually going to do with Aria and mentally filed it as a problem for later. *Something will come up*, I told myself, hoping to get back the bravado that had made me invite her home in the first place.

Still holding Aria by the elbow, I steered her up the steps.

"This is it – I live here with Nan," I muttered, horribly aware of just how grubby and unappealing it looked.

She was still jumping at every noise, and then it started to rain. Fat drops fell on to the step and I could feel them hitting my head and hands. Aria went rigid, and I could see old Mrs Mallion next door twitch her curtains. I fished the key out of my bag and almost shoved Aria through the door, grateful that Nan was out for the moment.

I expected a comment about the rain, but Aria was standing in the small hallway, mesmerised.

"You put coloured fur on the walls!" She reached out to touch it.

"Are you taking the mickey?"

"I don't know what that means," she replied, running her hands gingerly across the red flock wallpaper. Nan had told me it was ironic. I just thought it looked like an old curry house.

"It's beautiful," breathed Aria, continuing to gaze around in wonder, her fingertips never leaving the surface. "I've never seen anything like it."

Lily's home is unbelievable: so much space, and so many pretty things! I'm glad to be inside, away from the brightness and the sky. I know that's what it's called, but I didn't expect it to be so far away. It makes me feel nervous. I understand now why the Listeners have to learn so much before they can come Above. I'm sure Dane would have explained more of it to me, but I'm not supposed to be here; I was only supposed to be in the tunnels. Everything here is bright, even inside, and it makes my eyes and head hurt.

Lily leads me through lots of different rooms to one she says is just for her, with no need to share at all. Lily and her family must get very lonely in the night if they can't whisper to each other.

I've never seen anything as lovely as Lily's room. She has her own window and an unbelievably soft bed with a really thick cover. On the walls are pictures of boys and at the end of the bed a cubbyhole full of things that make me gasp. I look at them closely, hardly daring to believe what I'm seeing. There is a long line of colourful strips, some with glittery writing, each attached to the side of a rectangular-shaped object, like a thin box.

"Go on," she says. "You can take one if you want."

I run my fingers along the edge and then carefully pull one of the prettier ones. It slides out noiselessly. There are glittering swirls on the front, and I lift the cover to see if it is a box, or if I am right.

"That's one of my favourites too," says Lily with a smile, throwing herself down on the bed. "You've got good taste in books!"

"It is, isn't it?"

"What?"

"A book? These are all books?"

Lily's mouth opens into a round O, but she says nothing. I carefully turn the page, looking at the words I can't understand. I am actually holding a book. I never thought that would be possible.

"Why are you allowed to have them?" I whisper, looking back at the rows of others.

"You've never seen a book before?"

Her voice has gone oddly squeaky. I shake my head.

"I know that they exist and I think that the Community has a few, but we're not allowed to see them."

"WHAT?" she splutters. "You're not allowed to see books? How did you learn to read?"

I laugh at her mistake. "I can't read – I'm a child! They don't teach us that."

I stroke the pages gently, feeling the softness of the paper and the slight roughness of the words. There are hundreds of pages. I know that it contains secret information, and habit forces me to whisper again.

"What secret does this one tell?"

She waits for a moment before speaking, a look on her face that might be pity, but then she whispers back.

"There's no secret in there; it's just a story about a girl falling in love."

What Lily is saying makes no sense to me. There can't possibly be a book that doesn't tell a secret.

"You mean like a fairy story?" I ask. "The type of thing

we tell to babies?"

Lily seems puzzled again. "No – well, maybe. It is fiction – made-up stuff – but it's not a fairy story. Most of them are stories set in real life."

I hold the book closer to me and let my eyes wander over all the others.

"Are they all stories?" I ask eventually.

Lily smiles. "Yup – every one! Would you like to hear one?"

I nod speechlessly and she jumps up to choose. "Make yourself comfy on the bed and I'll find us a short one, otherwise we'll be here all night."

She picks a book that is bigger and heavier than the rest, with a bright, shiny cover.

"OK, I know exactly which one you'll like," she says as she casually turns the pages of the book. Suddenly she looks up at me, frowning. "Did you just say that you can't read because you're a kid?"

"Of course. What would be the point? Only a few of us will need to read to do our tasks when we're Assigned, and almost none of the girls get to read. I can't think of one who can." I pause for a moment, wondering if I can ask such a question, then decide that I must. "Why has your leader allowed it?"

"Do you mean my dad?"

"No, not your father. The leader. The one who is in charge and decides what you must do."

Lily sits back on the bed with a thump, and after a

second of silence begins to laugh. Then, just as quickly, she stops.

"I'm sorry, Aria. I didn't mean to do that, but really…"

"I don't understand. Again."

"I know, and I'm sorry." I see her struggling and failing to keep the incredulous tone from her voice. "It's just that here – in my world – everyone can read. And no one will tell me what I can do with my life! I'll make my own decisions, and as soon as I'm old enough and out of school I won't even have to listen to Nan."

I see it in her eyes, the passion and the honesty. She has no master, no one directing every detail of her existence. The girl I was supposed to capture is freer than I will ever be.

Aria had definitely answered one of my big questions: she was not making everything up. She really did live underground in a secret community with leaders who refuse to let the children learn. It was positively medieval. There was no way I was going to be able to send her back, even if there was a way to get past the creatures in the tunnels. I couldn't send her back to a place with no books, where she wasn't allowed to read. It was absolutely out of the question.

CHAPTER 4

There was no time to lose. I had to come up with a plan –
and quickly if it was going to have any chance of working.
Snapping the book of short stories closed I turned to
face Aria.

"OK, so here's what we are going to have to do. The
story will have to wait until a bit later. Nan's out at the
moment but she'll be back before too long." I sneaked
a glance at my watch. "Oops, not long at all actually. I
can let you stay here tonight, but as you can see there's
not a lot of room so it would be weird for you to stay
longer." I could see her start to ask a question. "Don't
worry, I've got something in mind for tomorrow. I just
need to sort out the logistics, that's all. Right now we
need to come up with a story that Nan will swallow and
you can remember."

A grateful look flashed across her face before the worried frown replaced it again. "Do I get to meet Nan then? What will I say to her?"

"Try and say as little as possible, I think; just listen. I'll tell her that you are terribly shy – that will stop her being suspicious. And don't call her Nan; that will be odd."

"Isn't Nan her name?"

"Of course, but it's because she's my old nanny, so only I'm allowed to call her that. You can call her Mrs Wakefield, or Mrs W, perhaps. Elizabeth – or Lizzie – Wakefield is her full name, but I wouldn't risk that just yet."

"Old nanny – what's that?"

"When I was little she helped my mum to look after me," I explained.

"And is she old?"

"I guess so. She won't say exactly, but she must be well into her sixties by now. She's not that healthy either, so that makes her seem older."

"Over sixty…" Aria shook her head. "No one in the Community is that old. All our Elders are in their forties. No one gets to be sixty…"

She tailed off, staring into space.

"Really?" I asked, appalled. "What happens to everyone? Here people usually live until they are seventy or eighty, and sometimes much longer."

"Eighty?" she squeaked, eyes widening in surprise.

"Sure. Some get to be a hundred. Why do you all

die so young?"

She avoided my gaze.

"That's … that's just the way it is. What else do I need to know about your home then?" she added, as if she was keen to change the subject.

I thought about the flat and how it might appear to someone from what amounted to a different world.

"Let me give you a quick tour," I said. "I don't want you screaming at things again."

I held out my hand to help her up from the low, squishy bed and she took it gingerly, letting go as soon as she was upright.

"OK, I have no idea about how you live, so let me just point out a few things and if you know how they work, then fine. Is that all right?"

Aria nodded, so I started my tour.

"Electric lights?" I asked, flicking the switch on and off.

"We have those, but not so bright, and we don't get to turn them on and off." She pressed the switch a couple of times, testing it.

"OK, one to you then." I looked at my laptop. "Computer?" Aria shook her head. "No time to explain that right now." I wondered how on earth I was going to describe the Web to her. Nothing else in my room seemed too challenging, so I opened the door and slipped into the corridor.

"Now, bathroom. First, don't touch anything in the

medicine cupboard. There's enough drugs in there to fill a small shop. If you feel ill, ask me and I'll find the right stuff for you." Nan had always locked that cupboard when I visited as a child. Her hobby seemed to be collecting medicines, and as she used to work in a chemist she was able to get her hands on quite a lot. Now, though, she used the Web, and parcels of stuff were always arriving at the door. I had never got a straight answer out of her about why she needed so many, but I rarely had to go to the doctor. Nan always had something for me to take.

I shut the cupboard carefully. "Next – do you have flushing toilets?"

I pulled the chain and hoped that I wasn't going to have to explain that in too much detail. Aria peered over my shoulder into the minuscule bathroom.

"I understand this but it's very small," she said, pointing at the loo. "And there's only one. How do you talk?"

"Umm, we don't, not usually. This is a private room and you lock yourself in when you're in here, see?"

I shuffled round to face the door and showed her the small bolt.

"That's really funny!" she laughed. "I can't imagine having to—"

"OK, moving on," I interrupted quickly, not keen on finding out about the toilet habits of her home. "Next is the kitchen."

We worked our way through the other rooms in the house, and I explained the basics of the gas cooker, the

microwave and the TV, which mesmerised her.

Lily presses a button and one of the moving pictures appears, the colours glowing. There are people sitting at a table and talking, looking straight at me. I lean down towards the picture, trying to work out if they do see me, but close up it's a blur of colour. As I reach forward to touch it Lily takes my arm.

"Here, come back a bit, you'll be able to see it better," she says. "It's called a TV."

I step back. The colours are fantastic, and with a sudden burst of music the people sitting at the table change to a different person standing in front of a coloured wall full of shapes. The woman is talking about high pressure and rising temperatures. Then Lily clicks the little black box in her hand again and the woman is replaced by figures with big heads and wide eyes. They look like drawings come to life. The music is loud and jangling. I step back in surprise and feel the edge of something bang into the back of my knees. Glancing round I see the soft seat behind me. I sit down – sitting is safer, and it makes the pictures easier to see.

"What's this?" I ask. "What are those odd things?"

"That's Postman Pat," she laughs. "He's always odd. It's a kids' programme."

I still want to touch the surface to prove to myself that these figures aren't really there, but I can't reach. What other wonders do the Aboves have for me to discover?

Lily hands me the black box, which is covered in little buttons.

"Here, you can use this to change the channels, find something you like."

I take it carefully. The buttons feel soft. Lily reaches over and presses one with a tiny arrow on it.

"You use this one," she says, and the happy little people in the picture change to a glum-looking man dressed in grey with a very bright necktie. He's talking about a terrible accident where a family have been burned in a fire. I don't like it, so I press the button again and the picture changes to more moving drawings. I like those.

"OK, Aria, this is the plan," says Lily, perching on the edge of the squashy seat beside me. "I'm going to tell Nan that you are a friend from school, that you are very shy and don't like speaking much. That all right with you?"

I nod, not able to take my eyes off the moving pictures on the TV.

"I'll tell her that I've said you can stay the night because we have a deadline for a drama project and need to work late. If she asks about it, say that we have to produce a piece about … um…" Lily stares off into the distance for a moment. "Bullying – kids being mean to other kids. Say it's about bullying if she asks, but she probably won't."

* * *

When Nan came in she made a fuss about dinner being late, so the first time she had the chance to speak to Aria was when we were sitting down together to eat.

"So you're a friend of Lily's then, from school?" she asked, as she speared a pasta tube in her macaroni cheese.

Aria nodded. "Yes, that's right."

"And where do you live then?"

I tightened my grip on my cutlery hoping Aria would remember what I told her.

"Acton," she said, going pink and bending over her plate.

"That is a long way," said Nan. "It's such a shame that Lily has to live so far from school, but we didn't want to move her, not with her GCSEs coming up. I rarely meet any of her friends, do I, Lily?"

It was my turn to go pink. "No, Nan, hardly ever. But you can't expect them to come all the way over here. It's not exactly convenient."

After that I managed to steer the conversation on to safer topics, and Aria didn't have to say another word. As soon as we finished eating I said that we would clear up so that we could work on our project, so Nan disappeared into the sitting room to watch TV. I pulled out some school books and scattered them over the kitchen table, just in case she came back in, and then opened a notebook. I handed Aria a pen.

"Can you write anything at all? Just try."

Aria took the pen from me carefully, rolling it between her fingers and peering at the point. Then she sniffed it, wrinkling her nose slightly.

"I've never seen one of these before, not in real life anyway."

Her hand had already started out to pull over the notebook, but she waited for me to nod before she began, pressing the ballpoint on the paper, bottom lip clenched between her teeth. Very slowly she drew a line, and then, with a nervous glance towards me, she drew a very shaky "A".

"'A' for Aria," I said, smiling when I saw what it was.

She suddenly beamed.

"Is it? I was told ages ago that it was, but I wasn't sure if I could believe him."

"Who taught you?"

"It was Morris, one of the older boys. He was being very smug about how much more he knew than me. He said he had been taught to write, and I thought he was too stupid to learn. I said I didn't believe him, so he drew me the A on the eating table using some water and his finger. He would have been in big trouble if he had been caught." She paused, looking down at the letter. "I never forgot what it looked like."

"At least he taught you one letter. Perhaps he's not as bad as your leader."

"Maybe, but he'll never be our leader so it won't make any difference." Aria looked up at me from behind her long dark hair. "We need a new leader before anything can change."

She held my gaze for a fraction too long, making me feel that I was missing something.

"Well, there's not much you can do about that now, and you'll soon find out that things are very different here. Your friend was right about the 'A' though. Would you like to know how to write the rest of your name?"

She hesitated for just a second before nodding, and we were soon copying out the whole alphabet. We were so engrossed I didn't notice that Nan was in the doorway. She was watching Aria intently, frowning. I thought she was about to speak so I jumped up and pulled her back into the sitting room.

"Look, Nan, I hope you don't mind, but I'm giving Aria a few catch-up lessons. She's a bit behind at school so I'm trying to help. She feels pretty embarrassed about it so would you mind not mentioning it?"

I stumbled over the words as I was trying to say them all so quickly. Nan stared at me for a moment before smiling. She gave me a quick peck on the cheek.

"I think that's lovely, dear. It's nice that you're taking the time. She seems very nervous though. Is everything else OK?"

"She doesn't get out much, Nan. Her family are part of an odd religion so she spends a lot of time alone."

"Well, it's good to see that she has a friend then – that you both have a friend, actually." She smiled at me and gave me a quick hug. "I'm just going to turn in. Can you sort out a bed for your visitor?"

"Sure. See you in the morning."

Even Nan had noticed that I didn't have any friends. It was a relief to know that she was safely shut behind her bedroom door and there would be no more need for lies for a while.

"Nan's gone to bed," I announced as I went back into the kitchen, wondering just how much of our conversation Aria had heard. "Do you want to carry on with this or go to bed too?"

"Sleep sounds good," she said, stretching, "but I'd really like to learn some more of this tomorrow."

Her long fingers traced the outline of her latest attempt to copy her name.

"It's my mission!" I laughed, gathering up the books. "I'm going to teach you to read."

I made up a bed on the sofa for Aria but I could tell that she wasn't happy there. She picked nervously at the duvet cover as her eyes darted around the room.

"What's wrong?" I asked.

"I've … I've never actually slept alone before. Is it safe?"

"Of course it's safe! Who do you normally have in the room with you?"

She looked even more miserable.

"It used to be my sister, until she was Assigned. As soon as that happened I was moved into the dormitory.

No one ever sleeps on their own."

I sat down on the end of the makeshift bed, curling my feet up underneath me.

"Sounds a bit weird. Why do they do that?"

Aria pulled her knees up and rested her chin on them.

"I've no idea, it's just how it is."

"So do you have just the one sister?" I asked.

Aria nodded. "Yes, Carita."

"So when she left where were your parents? Why didn't they stay with you?"

She paused for a moment, biting her lower lip.

"We never live with our fathers, just our mothers, but mine is dead and has been for a while."

"I'm so sorry. I didn't mean to upset you."

"It's all right," she said, shrugging but holding her knees tighter. "Where is your mother? Is she dead too?"

For once I didn't mind the question. The kids at school tormented me with this every day, but Aria didn't already know the answer.

"My parents and my little brothers have moved away," I managed before my voice caught. I took a deep breath. "I stayed here because of school."

"Oh, I see," she said, without the curious raising of the eyebrows that people generally gave me when I told them. Before she could ask more I jumped in with a question of my own.

"What exactly is the Crop then, Aria? You must have some idea. And how did they get there?"

"I've never seen them," she said quietly. "Only the Farmer has anything to do with them. I can't believe that we got away from them earlier. The Farmer always says that no one ever gets away."

Her voice tailed off into a whisper.

"The Farmer? Who's that? You mentioned him before."

"The Farmer is our leader. He makes sure that everyone keeps to the rules. He says it's for our protection."

"Protection from what?" I asked.

She hesitated again.

"From the Aboves."

"I don't understand," I said, puzzled. "If we don't know that you're there, there's not much need for that."

"The Farmer says that we need the Crop as a defence in case you find us."

"Oh." I didn't really know how to respond to that – to think that I was one of the enemy was peculiar. "So what's this Farmer like?"

Aria looked at her feet.

"He's frightening. And dangerous. He needs to be stopped."

There was real passion in her voice.

"How did he get to be the leader – is he Assigned too?"

She paused for a second before replying.

"Actually, he's the only person who's not Assigned, because the Farmer has to have an Affinity with the Crop. The Affinity is passed on from Farmer to son, and each new Farmer takes on the responsibility to protect us."

"Are you saying that he has some sort of special power over them?" I asked, trying to keep a sarcastic tone from creeping into my voice.

"He is the only one who can do it. Something about his bloodline means that they won't attack him."

"But it's not possible. That sort of thing only happens in films."

"It doesn't matter if you don't believe me, but it's the truth. Things are different in the Community."

For a moment I could smell the Crop again, hear that strange slithering noise, and I shuddered. Whatever they were I was very glad that they couldn't get to me. I glanced at Aria and she was still hunched up on the duvet, biting her lip so hard I thought it might bleed. Talking about the Crop had obviously been another bad move on my part.

"So, um, tell me about the boys down there. Is there anyone special for you back in the Community?"

"What do you mean?"

"I mean, do you have a boyfriend – a partner? Or someone you'd like to be a partner."

"No, not yet. Our matches get made by the Farmer and the other Elders, so there's not really any choice in the matter."

Everything she was saying sounded worse and worse. "That's horrible! So you can't just choose someone you like?"

Aria shook her head. "No, it's all settled for us. Do you, then? Can you pick anyone as your partner?"

"Well, theoretically, I suppose, but you have to choose each other. I can't just go and pick someone. I have to hope that they like me too."

"That sounds much more difficult!"

"Well," I said, laughing, "it can be tricky, or so I've heard."

"And have you picked one yet?" she asked.

A picture of Will instantly flashed across my mind. Would he count? "There is someone I like, but I don't know yet if he likes me." I couldn't believe I was telling her that – I'd not said anything to anyone about him. In fact, I don't think I'd ever had much of a conversation with anyone about boys. Before my world fell apart – when I still had some friends – it wasn't really something we had talked about.

Aria gave me a shy smile.

The more Lily tells me about Above, the more surprised I am. The tales we are told about them being violent, aggressive and promiscuous seem very wrong. She is going pink talking about boys, just as I would if I mentioned Dane. Being Assigned to Dane would make the whole thing much more bearable, but it will never happen. He's far too young, and not important enough.

Up here we might have a chance, but I'll never persuade him to leave. He knows what it's like Above, and prefers to be safe underground. But it will never be safe for any of us in the Community while the Farmer is in charge.

I sigh, wishing that I could explain more to Lily, but until I know if I should continue with my mission I have to be careful what I say.

I reach for Lily's hand. "Whoever he is, I'm sure he likes you too."

It's her turn to smile, and her eyes glaze slightly. She must be thinking of him. As she does, her hand goes to the little necklace she is wearing. I've seen her do it several times so far.

"What's that?" I ask. "It's pretty."

I quickly let go of the necklace. Every time I was nervous or worried, my hand automatically strayed to the silver chain with the tiny yet perfect line of charms. I'd had it for years, a present from Nan when I was young, and it was supposed to ward off bad luck. It hadn't been doing me much good lately.

"Oh, it's nothing, just a bunch of little silver things."

"What are they supposed to be?"

I felt along the chain, although I knew each one perfectly. "There's a heart, a slipper, a whistle and a horseshoe."

"What funny things to be wearing round your neck!"

"I know," I laughed. "Nan is a bit superstitious. Anyway, do you want to hear my plan about how you can stay up here?" I had been mulling over my idea for the last hour or two, and the more I spoke to Aria, the more I knew that I had to keep her safe – from the Farmer, from her arranged marriage and from a community that wouldn't teach girls to read.

Aria gave me a grateful smile. "Yes, please."

"Underneath this flat is an empty one, and I have the keys. You can live there as long as you're quiet. No one will ever know."

Aria looked puzzled.

"Is that OK?" I continued, leaning towards her.

"I'm not sure that I understand."

"You can go and live downstairs! There's plenty of room, and the floors are so thick that Nan will never be able to hear you – as long as you keep the TV down."

"You mean I'll have a whole dwelling, just for me? Not sharing with you or Nan or anyone?"

"Yup, your own place."

Lily is offering me somewhere to live, somewhere I'll be safe from everything. I should be grateful – and I am – but I'm also confused. Why is she doing this for me? She doesn't know me and doesn't have any idea about why I really came up to the place with the trains.

I think of Dane and of all the time we hid together, making our plans to snatch Lily and take her back down with us. I wonder what he is doing. He'll know by now that everything has gone wrong, that the mission has failed,

but not how. Does he think that I fell to the Crop or that I chose to abandon him and start a new life Above? Will he try to find me?

I also know that by now everyone else will know I'm missing, and that means I can never go back. The Farmer will never allow it.

I have nowhere else to go.

The next morning was Saturday so there was no school, but we still got up early. It was a bright and sunny day, not overcast like the day before, and Aria gasped as I took her outside to get to the downstairs flat.

"Ow – that really hurts," she said loudly, clasping her hands to her eyes. We weren't even in the sunshine but rather on the shadowy side of the street.

"It's only a few steps. Here, I'll lead you. Keep your eyes tightly closed."

I manoeuvred her through the gate in the old iron railing and down the steep, narrow steps into the tiny courtyard. The place felt permanently damp, with green moss growing on the walls, and crumpled copies of *Metro* blown into the corners. I unlocked the door and ushered Aria inside.

The flat was owned by Nan's friend Marjorie, but she had broken her hip and was living in a care home while she recovered. Nan was supposed to be looking after the place but as she couldn't easily get down the stairs she had asked me to do it. I often used it to revise as it was nice and cool. The rooms I'd not been using were a bit dusty, but we opened the windows, which looked out on nothing but the mossy brick walls and a tiny patch of sky above, changed the sheets on the bed and soon it looked quite homely.

Settling down at the kitchen table we spent another hour looking at the alphabet, but it was clear that we were going to need some proper books to help us, as well as a good supply of paper and pencils.

"What we need is the library," I said, looking in vain through Marjorie's Mills & Boon books for something suitable for Aria to practise on. "Come on, we can be there in fifteen minutes."

"What's a library?" asked Aria, carefully putting all the papers into a tidy pile.

"Oh, you'll love the library! It's a whole building full of books that you can borrow."

"Will they have books that will help me learn to read then?"

"Loads. They have a big selection for little kids that have pictures and words so that you can see what is what."

"And they'll let us in?"

I couldn't help laughing at the question. "Of course, even us! Let's go."

The sun was still shining, so I rummaged in the kitchen drawers until I found an old pair of sunglasses for Aria to wear. She wasn't convinced they would help, and kept taking them off and putting them on again.

"Really, if you thought it was bright earlier, standing in full sunshine is going to be a bit shocking," I said, handing the glasses back to her. "Your eyes are going to take some time to adjust and you don't want to hurt them."

"But it feels so odd," she complained, fiddling with them again.

"Believe me, you'll want them when we get out there."

I kept close to Aria as we left the flat, holding her arm. Moving out from the shadow of the building she gasped and pushed the glasses more firmly on to her nose.

"You were right," she said in a small voice, shielding her face from the sun with her hair. "I'd never imagined anything like this. I can even feel it heating my skin."

She held her hand out in the sun for a moment before tugging her sleeve down over her knuckles.

We walked along the side streets to get to the library, avoiding as many of the busy roads as possible, but eventually we had to cross over.

"It's not much further," I cajoled, reaching for Aria's arm to reassure her when she stopped dead.

The guy behind us swore and stepped out in the road to get round us. Aria was staring down the road, her mouth hanging open.

"We have to go – now!" she hissed, before turning and running.

She was surprisingly swift, dodging people as she ran

along the street, long dark hair flying behind her. I finally caught up with her and dragged her into a shoe shop entrance. A woman who was leaving tutted at us for being in her way.

"Hang on, Aria," I gasped. "What exactly are we running from?"

"It's one of the Listeners," she replied, backing up against the door. "He saw me, I'm sure. We need to get away!"

"Why? Who are they? You never did tell me yesterday."

"They are the only ones allowed Above. They bring information and food, and make sure that no one knows about us. They listen. And they see *everything*." Her voice rose, quivering slightly.

From where we were in the shop entrance I could peer through the window display and back down the street towards the crowds of people.

"Is he still coming?"

"I think so. It's hard to be sure from here – I can't really see."

She craned her neck to try and see past the display of stilettos.

"Yes, there he is. We have to run, Lily. If he finds me I'm in real trouble. If only it were Dane then maybe I could talk to him, but this one will show me no mercy!"

"OK, don't panic. If we're calm we can get away." I had seen a way out – a few steps away was a bus stop, and the bus was just a little bit further down the High Street.

"Wait there," I told her as I nipped across the pavement to the ticket machine next to the stop. I rummaged in my jeans pocket for some change that I'd found earlier and shoved in the right amount for her ticket. The bus had stopped at some lights so we had another minute or two. I shot back to Aria.

She had shut her eyes tightly and I saw her clench her fists.

"I'm back. Are you OK?"

"All right," she said. "I'm calm. Can we go now?"

"Just a few seconds. We're getting on a bus, so do exactly as I say, all right?"

I saw fresh panic on her face as she realised what I meant.

"It won't hurt you," I added quickly. "Keep the glasses on; they help to disguise you."

I was watching the road as I was talking, and I could see the bus approaching. A young woman was standing at the stop just a few short steps from our hiding place.

"He's getting closer," she said, her nose pressed against the window.

"Which one is he?"

"There, that one in the grey top."

I glanced down the pavement but couldn't be sure which man she was talking about.

"Look, we only have to go over there," I said, grabbing her arm and pointing at the woman at the bus stop. "Where that woman in the stripy top is, OK? Just keep calm. You look really different in sunglasses. Here, put this on too."

I stripped off my favourite hoodie and shoved it on her waiting arms.

"Hair is the other thing. Quick, turn round."

I grabbed a band from my pocket and hastily scraped her hair back into a messy bun. With that, the hoodie and the sunglasses she was all but unrecognisable. I glanced down the pavement and still couldn't identify the Listener but the bus had arrived.

"OK, here's our ride. Walk calmly and let me do the talking, OK?"

Taking a deep breath I stepped out from the relative safety of the shop entrance. I kept a firm hand on Aria's arm, pulling her with me, and covered the short distance to the bus stop just as it opened its doors. The woman walked straight on board. I could feel Aria's arm stiffen as she readied herself to actually step inside one of the scary red vehicles. Holding on to her tightly we followed the woman. I showed the driver the ticket for Aria and swiped my Oyster card. Within about five seconds of leaving the shoe shop we were on the bus. Aria was shaking with fear.

"Come on," I said encouragingly. "Let's go up to the top deck. It'll be quieter up there."

I pushed her ahead of me up the short, narrow staircase, and as we rounded the corner the bus lurched away from the side of the road. Aria stopped dead, clutching the rail so tightly her knuckles went completely white.

"I can't do this," she whispered as I tried to persuade her to take the next few steps. Putting my hand over hers I attempted to prise her fingers off the handrail.

"You have to. People need the stairs. Come on, we're nearly at the top."

I could see that some of the other passengers were beginning to stare. Shoving her hard I finally got her up on to the top deck, manoeuvring round her so that I was leading. I glanced down into the street below and saw a guy in a grey jacket standing on the corner, straining to see above the heads of the crowds as he looked up and down the street. He was about thirty, pale and skinny with hair that was greying and thick, bushy eyebrows.

"Quick, let's sit down."

I tugged at Aria's sleeve and she dropped down into the seat next to me, grabbing the rail tightly. I could just see behind the glasses that her eyes were tightly closed and streaks of tears were shining on her face. The bus lurched again as the lights changed and it picked up speed. I sat back, breathing out heavily.

"We've lost him, Aria," I whispered, taking a quick glance out of the back window. "You can relax. I think that going to the library will have to wait. Now we're here I can give you a bit of a tour."

"Relax? In all this?"

She lifted one hand briefly but quickly thought better of the gesture.

"Look, he's gone. If he did see you he has no idea where you've disappeared to, so you're in no danger."

That didn't seem to have any effect on her and she continued to hold on so hard I could see every tendon in her hands. Finally the penny dropped.

"Are you worried about being on the bus?" I asked, trying to keep the relief out of my voice, at the same time glancing around to make sure that we weren't being overheard. "Really, it's quite safe."

"How can it do this? It feels so wrong!"

"They're probably not as fast as the Tube trains but you'll get a better view of the city." I gave her a quick hug. "Come on, open your eyes and take a look at London."

I saw her slowly open one eye and then the other. Sniffing loudly, she looked around, never relaxing her hold on the rail. The bus was coming up to St Pancras Station, the brickwork glowing red in the sunshine. A constant stream of people were coming and going.

"I knew there were lots of you up here," she said softly, "but I never thought it would be this big."

As we continued past King's Cross Station I saw her shake her head.

"There are more than eight million people in London," I said, remembering a recent geography lesson.

Aria grabbed me as the bus turned a corner, but she continued drinking in the view.

"I don't have any idea what you're saying," she said. "I've never heard of a million."

"No, really? Have I got to teach you maths as well?" I asked, smiling to show her that I didn't mean it. "A million is – well, lots. More than you could possibly ever count. If there are say, two hundred people in the Community, London has …" I tried to do a quick calculation in my head but failed, "… thousands of people for every single one of you. It's pretty huge."

Her eyes were glued to the window as we drove on into the City. Aria was enthralled by all the skyscrapers, even forgetting to hold on at one point as she leaned over me to look up at the top of a particularly tall one.

"They're so high," she breathed. "You can hardly see where they end."

"Wait until you see the Shard then," I laughed, enjoying watching her.

The bus finally lumbered down towards the river. I was really looking forward to seeing her reaction to all that water – the glistening reflections, the sunlight making the surface glitter and sparkle, the bow waves of the boats, the huge bridges. As we approached I got ready to point it out and watch her reaction.

"Look, Aria, what do you think of that?"

But she wasn't looking. She was staring open-mouthed at a building on the other side of the road.

"What … what is that place?" she whispered.

"That? It's the Tower of London. It's one of our oldest buildings. Why?"

"I know it. I've seen it before."

"How is that possible?"

She didn't answer for a moment but just sat there, staring. I could barely catch her whisper.

"If the building is real, perhaps the rest of it is real too…"

CHAPTER 5

"Do you want to get closer?" I asked as the "Bus Stopping" sign lit up. Her only reply was to nod slightly, never taking her eyes off the building. I hurried her off the bus and we stood outside the Tower on the long, wide slope down to the main entrance, being jostled by the weekend crowd of tourists.

"If we walk down there towards the river we can see the other side," I said.

Aria nodded. I took her by the arm to guide her through the people, but as we approached the gate she started to speed up. I pulled her back.

"Come on," she urged. "I need to see."

"I don't have enough money, not even for child tickets. We'll just have to look at it from outside. Sorry."

"What do you mean?" she asked.

"I mean money. It's expensive getting in there and I don't have enough for us both."

Nan had given me twenty pounds pocket money earlier, but it wasn't going to cover getting us both inside and then pay for the food that Aria would need for the weekend.

"No, I'm sorry, I've still no idea what you're talking about. What's money?"

"You don't have money? How do you get the things you need – the food, the clothes, that sort of stuff?"

"Someone brings it."

As soon as she said it, some of her earlier behaviour started to make a bit more sense. If the Community didn't use money I had some explaining to do.

"When we work, we get given money – like this." I opened my purse, lifting out the dog-eared notes that were the sum total of my cash. "Then when we want something – food in the café, new books, or to go into that building – we have to give some of the money to the person selling whatever it is. If we don't have enough money, we can't have it."

Aria caught her lip between her teeth and frowned as she listened to me.

"I don't have much money at all, so we can't go inside. I'm sorry," I continued.

"But I need to see! I need to know if it's real."

"If what's real?"

"I'm not supposed to say."

I took a deep breath. "OK, Aria. That's not very helpful. Why can't you tell me?"

I wish I knew how to answer her questions. The Tower is key to our history, to the creation of the Community, and I don't know how to explain all of that.

The Community was founded to get away from the Aboves and their evil ways. But Lily doesn't seem at all evil, and, looking about, none of them look or behave the way we were told that they do. Do I believe the stories I have always been fed, or do I believe my eyes? I want to think that the Farmer is wrong but now that I see the Tower is real ... he wasn't lying about that. What is the truth? And what do I tell her?

I realise that I have to tell her the truth as far as I knew it.

"I need to tell you some more about our history, but I can't do it here – I don't know who might be listening."

There are crowds of people pressing around me – so many strangers – and they all seem very excited. They are pointing little silver and black boxes at the Tower. I think they are using what Lily called a mobile, the same thing that she showed me yesterday. I don't like the closeness of the bodies. Some smell really bad, and I know that we have to leave. I want to leave now.

Lily reaches for my arm. "Are you worried about the crowd?"

I nod, trying to breathe steadily.

"Just our luck to arrive at the same time as all the coach parties," she said, guiding me through the people. One large group have eyes that are different to mine, and I stop to stare. Lily yanks my hand.

"Come on, you can't just stand there gawping. You'll get us into trouble."

She leads me back to the place where we got off the bus.

"Let's go back. You can explain everything when we are home again and no one can hear us."

It was a relief to get back on to the comparative peace of a bus. I was itching to ask her some more questions, but the middle-aged woman in front of us was obviously trying to hear our conversation so I kept quiet. Finally we inched our way down Oxford Street, and as we passed Selfridges Aria's eyes lit up.

"What's that over there?"

The window display was for the summer sale, and featured hundreds of bright-yellow carrier bags and boxes.

"It's a big department store, "I whispered as the grey head of the nosy woman tilted almost imperceptibly towards me. "You can buy almost anything there. Do you want to see?"

Aria nodded excitedly, no longer the frightened girl she had been earlier.

"There will be crowds," I warned, "so stay close." We

made our way down the staircase and waited to be let off the bus. It stopped almost immediately.

She grabbed my hand and led me back to the window with the display of bags. "I have one of those!"

"What, the carrier bag?"

"The yellow bag, yes. Dane got it for me ages ago. It's such a lovely colour. It's one of my favourite things."

"You mentioned Dane before. Is he a friend of yours?"

Aria nodded briefly, not taking her eyes off the window.

"Do you want to go inside?" I asked, holding open the door. She took a step forward, but the overwhelming smell of the perfume counters hit us and she stopped dead, sneezing loudly.

She stepped back, surprised, letting the steady stream of people through the door. "I can't go in there," she said, shaking her head. "How do people stand it?"

"Most people up here like it," I said, grinning. "Come on, let's go home."

I directed her up a side road and we made our way home via the back streets where there was minimal traffic and very few people.

Towards home we took a shortcut through the park. I loved the little park – it wasn't at all grand, just about a dozen London plane trees squished together around a scruffy lawn. Despite the sunshine there was a bit of a breeze, so the trees were moving gently above us. There were also some swings and a long line of wooden benches, most of which were dedicated to dead people.

As we walked through the gate I glanced over at Aria and saw that her lips were pressed together in a tight line and her hands were in tight fists. She seemed to be keeping her eyes fixed on the floor.

"I can't believe that those huge things can move so much," she said as a larger gust shook the branches. "I'm not sure I like being so close to them."

I was about to answer when I saw Will. He was circling one of the trees, obviously looking for something. Foggy was on the end of a long lead, sniffing around in a small patch of straggly flowers.

"Come on," I said. "Let's go and help him. And just ignore the dog," I added as she hesitated. "He's really not a problem."

I hurried Aria over to the trees, hoping that Will wouldn't find what he was looking for before we got there. He was peering into the long grass that had grown up around the trunk of one of the largest trees.

"Um, hi, Will," I called out as soon as I could. "Have you lost something?"

He straightened up and looked over towards us, a polite but distant look on his face. It wasn't until we stepped into the shadows that he smiled.

"Oh, hi, Lily, it's you."

He nodded quickly at Aria, having obviously not forgotten that she really didn't like dogs. Foggy's tail was the only sign of him as he rummaged deeper in the undergrowth.

"What are you looking for?"

"Foggy's ball. *Again*. Honestly, that stupid dog is supposed to be a retriever but he's completely hopeless. If it was one of the old tennis balls I'd leave it, but it's a new rubber one, so I'd quite like to take it home again."

"Do you want a hand?"

"Cheers, that would be great. I think it landed around here somewhere."

He swept his arm around, covering quite a wide area.

"Could you be a little more specific?" I laughed. "We'll be here all day!"

"I didn't really see," he said with a wry smile. "I don't have my contacts in."

I didn't realise he wore contact lenses, and was surprised at how pleased I was to learn that about him. It made him a fraction less perfect and, to me, a fraction more approachable. "Well, you need our help then. What colour is the ball?"

"Yellow, which isn't very useful in all this old grass." He dropped his voice and leaned in towards me. "Is she going to be OK today? I don't want her frightening Foggy again."

He was so close that I could catch the clean, shampooed smell of his hair.

"I'm sure she'll be fine," I muttered back, trying to keep my voice steady. "She just got a bit of a shock yesterday, that's all."

I turned to look at Aria, who was glancing between

the dog and the branches above us, biting her lip and clasping her hands together. She had taken a few steps back towards the gate.

"We're searching for a yellow ball," I called over to her.

She nodded briefly, but continued to stand there, tense and jumpy, her head jerking at every sound.

"So who is she then? A new girl at school or something?" Will asked.

"Yeah, something like that. I'm looking after her for a bit."

I knew that I should move away before he asked a question that I didn't want to answer, but I couldn't.

"She needs quite a lot of looking after, but she's all right really."

I glanced up at him and saw that he was watching Aria. She looked like a beautiful waif, thin as a willow and with skin so smooth and pale she seemed to be made of porcelain. Tendrils of her long dark hair had escaped from the hastily constructed bun and were wafting around her face in the gentle breeze. She was poised on the balls of her feet as if ready to run. For a second I could see the world from her point of view, the enormous trees moving above her head, the clouds scudding across the distant sky, the sheer *vastness* of it all, and I felt a wave of sympathy. It all must be so hard, and I wasn't sure that I would cope so well if our situations had been reversed.

I smiled at her, feeling suddenly ashamed for the

times I had been cross with her. She was actually doing amazingly well, considering all the things that she was having to learn about. She smiled back, a radiant smile that transformed her pretty face. She was stunningly, unbelievably beautiful. And then I realised that she wasn't smiling at me.

The boy with the dog is here, but it seems to be under control this time. I think she likes him – I see the way she glances at him when he's not looking. He has kind eyes, and seems strong. I don't really understand how they pick partners up here, but he must be a good choice. The idea of it makes me smile.

I looked from Will to Aria and back again. They seemed to be oblivious to everything. Aria obviously hadn't twigged that Will was the one I thought was special. With a sinking feeling in my stomach I realised that I should have told her about him when I had the chance.

"So have you searched over here yet?" I asked breezily, breaking their gaze. "It really shouldn't be that difficult to find. Aria, why don't you look over there, away from Foggy, and I'll take this patch. How big is this ball, Will?"

"Oh, it's, umm, a bit bigger than a tennis ball, I suppose." Will sounded distracted. "Yes, a rubber ball, yellow, about so big."

He made a fist to demonstrate the size.

"OK. All right, Aria?"

She nodded and turned to start looking in the grass. We worked silently for a few moments, Will and me kicking aside the long grass with our feet, Aria nervously picking her way through it, but disturbing it as little as possible. Foggy stayed obligingly out of the way. I watched them both out of the corner of my eye. Will seemed intent on finding the ball, but once or twice Aria glanced over in his direction. I was trying not to think about it when my foot landed on something hard. I lurched sideways, feeling the muscles in my ankle give as the small yellow ball shot off to the side.

"Owww!" I yelped. "I've found the ball."

Pain shot up my ankle and I hopped on the spot, trying to rub it better. Tears pricked my eyes.

Will was instantly by my side.

"What have you done?" he asked, putting out a hand to steady me.

The warm pressure of his hand on my arm momentarily distracted me from the red-hot pain, and I gulped back the tears.

"I've turned my ankle. I found the ball by standing on it."

I tried to laugh, but it turned into a sob as pain shot up my leg again. Foggy tried jumping up to help, almost knocking me sideways. Will batted him down.

"Stupid dog. Get out of the way!" he muttered. "Can you walk?"

His dark eyebrows were knitted together in a deep

frown. I took a tentative step and felt the pain as if a hot wire was being pressed deep inside my ankle.

"Not easily," I admitted, trying not to sob out loud again.

"Here, hang on to me."

He effortlessly hoisted me up and took my weight. I was pressed tightly against his side.

"This isn't going to work," he said, abruptly setting me back down.

"W … what? Why not?"

"Foggy! He's a positive menace, that dog."

I couldn't understand what he was on about.

"Sit down, Foggy! Keep still. Can you come and hold him for a moment? He's going to knock us both over." He was talking to Aria, not me. "Come on – can you hold Foggy's lead so that I can get Lily over to the bench?"

The pain was coming in waves. Had I broken it? I clenched my eyes tightly shut. "I'll help Lily to walk," said Aria.

Before I knew what was happening, she had her arm round my back, taking the weight of my bad leg, and was leading me towards the benches on the nearest footpath. Disappointment flooded through me – where was Will?

Aria was surprisingly strong, and she deftly manoeuvred me on to the bench before kneeling down by my foot and prodding and flexing my ankle.

"Owww!" I yelped again as she turned it too far to the

right. "What are you doing? What do you know about ankles?"

"We all know how to do this." I flash a quick smile at her. "Nothing broken," I add, loudly enough for him to hear. "Just a sprain. You'll need to get a bandage on it, but it should be perfectly fine in a day or two."

He ties up the big hairy dog a safe distance away and comes over.

"So it's OK, is it, Lily? Will you be able to get home all right? Do you want me to help?"

I am surprised at how pink Lily suddenly goes, and although she opens her mouth to speak nothing comes out.

"I can manage her," I answer quickly on her behalf.

I hope he won't think that she's frail. I'm pleased that for the first time since I came Above I can actually be useful.

"OK, well, if everything is going to be all right, I'll leave you girls to it. Thanks for finding the ball for me."

I smile at him as he puts the ball in his pocket and unties the dog.

The pain had fogged my brain, and I couldn't work out why Will was leaving and Aria was pressing her hands into my ankle. Had he really held me for a moment? I shook my head to try and clear it.

"Thank you for your help. I can manage, honestly,"

she said to him.

"No worries." He turned and walked away, dragging Foggy with him.

"We were lucky there," said Aria, hoisting me upright. "I'll finish treating this back at the house."

"Lucky?" I gasped as I tried to put my foot down. "Are you having a laugh?"

"You can't appear weak. We women must always be strong."

She wanted me to be strong. I wanted to be carried home by Will. Our cultures were proving to be very different after all. I sighed as Will turned through the park gate in the distance. He didn't look back.

CHAPTER 6

We didn't talk much as Aria helped me back to the flat. I still couldn't process how things had changed so quickly. As soon as we were in the kitchen she took control though, rummaging through Marjorie's first-aid kit until she found what she wanted. There was a lot of muttering as she dug things out of the big, green plastic box.

"I can't believe that you have so many of these – we hardly ever see them! And these too." She held up a pack of safety pins. "You're so lucky."

She knelt in front of me and took my ankle in her hands.

"Please be careful! It really hurts, you know. Are you sure I've not broken it?"

"No, you'll be fine. I just need to press right … here!"

A white-hot pain streaked up my lower leg and I bit my lip hard to stop from crying out. But before I could

74

snatch my foot out of her hands she changed her grip and pressed again. There was a distinct twanging noise and it suddenly felt much, much better.

"There," she said, winding a bandage tightly round it. "No lasting damage done. You should be perfectly all right now, and we can take off the bandage tomorrow."

I was so surprised that it no longer hurt I forgot I was annoyed with her.

"How did you learn to do that?" I asked, putting my weight gingerly on it and finding it was indeed perfectly OK.

Aria shrugged as she started to put all the bits and pieces back into the first-aid kit.

"One of the few things they teach us to do is heal," she said. "It's part of our function. No girl could ever expect to get a good Assignment if she wasn't a good healer." She paused for a moment. "And no girl would ever expect to get a good Assignment if she wasn't strong. I'm sorry if I upset you. I didn't mean to."

I felt really mean for my ungrateful thoughts earlier.

"I'm sorry that I was a bit snappy with you. It was all just a bit of a surprise." I did a circuit of the kitchen without feeling a single twinge from my ankle. "And I don't know about you, but I'm starving. Shall I make us some lunch?"

I resisted the urge to ask any questions until we were sitting at the table with our beans and cheese on toast. I didn't like to disturb her eating – everything I gave her seemed to be a feast, so I kept quiet until she was nearly done.

"Right, come on, it's time for a few answers. What was all that about today?"

"What do you mean?" she mumbled through her final mouthful.

"I mean, why all the sudden interest in the Tower of London?"

She carefully scraped up every crumb from her plate as she finished chewing. Finally she looked up at me.

"It's our most sacred legend," she said slowly, "and I'm pretty sure they wouldn't want me to share it with the Aboves. But I suppose that doesn't matter now."

She paused for a moment and ran her finger around the plate before continuing. "I didn't think that it was real – I assumed it was just a story. And now I find that it's true."

"So what's it all about?"

"This is our story of the 'Beginning' – how the Community came to be where we are." She paused for a second, looking towards the window, then slowly stood up. She carefully brushed all the crumbs from her lap and took the few short steps to the light. Holding gently on to the windowsill she stared up towards the sunshine. I was beginning to wonder if she had changed her mind about telling me the story, but then I saw her shoulders rise as she took a deep breath. Her head dipped for a moment. I could feel myself leaning forward in my chair, waiting.

When she started to speak her voice was low.

"The Beginning…" She paused again, and something about her tone sent a shiver down my spine.

"In the Beginning there was the Man. The Man was tried for crimes he did not commit and was imprisoned in the deepest dungeon of the oldest prison of the city – the Tower. His cell was an old cave, overrun with creatures whose eyes glittered like coal. The Man knew that he would die of the cold and the damp if the Executioner didn't come first. He argued to have his case tried again, but was refused. Realising that he must evade their unjust punishment he vowed to leave, but no one had ever escaped from the Tower. The doors were too thick, the walls too high, the moat too wide. But the Man would not be defeated.

"He planned and plotted and found a way out following the creatures who invaded his cell at high tide. Crawling on his belly through a long narrow tunnel, black as pitch, he found himself in a chamber above the high-water mark. The air was as sweet as honey, and nourished his candle when he lit it. From that meagre light he saw that the chamber continued.

"The creatures led him further and further from the Tower, into the depths of low caves, through impossibly tight crevices and sumps filled with water, and the Man began to doubt that there was an end. But finally the creatures emerged in a cavern so vast he could not see the far wall. It was dry and it was warm. The Man knew he could stay.

"If he was to return to the city he would be hanged. All his family and friends had either perished or betrayed him. It was time to start again.

"By watching and following the creatures the Man soon became familiar with the maze of caves, and under cover of darkness was able to creep back up to the surface. From the depths of an old, dark well he emerged to find air putrid with smog, and a cacophony of noise from the docks piercing his ears. The Man yearned for his quiet, clean cavern, but he needed companions.

"He searched out those abandoned by society and took them back below. The Man became the Farmer – a farmer of people – and over time the people grew and flourished, exploring further caves and eventually digging their own. They wanted for nothing. The Community had been formed."

As she had been speaking Aria had continued staring out of the window, but then her shoulders relaxed as she finally turned back towards me.

"And that is the legend of the Beginning. It's read to us every Sunday and we all get to learn it and repeat it if we're asked. No one must ever forget the injustice of the Aboves towards the First Farmer and those later."

"What happened later?"

Her eyes suddenly glistened. "There was a plague. Too many of us died."

"Oh, that's horrible. So how long has the Community

been down there? Do you even know?

Aria shrugged briefly. "Hundreds of years, that's all I know."

"Wow." I sat back, looking at her. "It's a lot to take in. So he set up the Community as a refuge, taking in people who felt like he did?"

She nodded. "A whole new community, a new way of life, with new rules and a new purpose."

"So has no one else left over the years? You can't be the first one to run away, surely?"

"People have disappeared before, but no one ever mentions them. There are stories though – does no one up Above suspect anything about us?"

"Absolutely nothing that I've heard. We could check on the Internet to see if there are any rumours out there, but I guess you've done a good job at keeping things secret." I hesitated for a moment, but there was one question I was dying to ask. "So what were the creatures he followed? What helped him?"

"It was the mice. He followed a stream of mice."

I shuddered.

"Oh, don't think that." Aria smiled at me. "The mice are very useful in lots of ways. The meat can be a little tough if they are too old, but in a stew they taste delicious."

"What! You can't be serious." I tried to keep my voice down. "That's gross."

"It's what they had to eat. If you have a choice of only mushrooms, bats and mice, mice is the best option. Bats taste horrible." She pulled a face as I tried not to gag.

"Do you still eat that now?"

Aria nodded. "Not just that though. The Listeners bring food down when they can – things that have been thrown away up here. Sometimes we get sacks of the sandwiches packed in little cardboard boxes. They're my favourite."

I wondered what the supermarkets and coffee shops would think if they knew that their donated sandwiches actually ended up underground. "The Listeners must get into trouble occasionally," I said. "That food is supposed to be for the homeless."

"I think they do sometimes." For a second or two she stared out of the window again, looking up towards the small patch of sky that was visible between the buildings. "Everyone respects the Listeners. They do a job that very few people want to do, but only the smartest get selected to do it."

There was something wistful in her tone.

"Is that what you wanted to do?" I asked.

"Ha!" she said, shaking her head. "As if I'd have the chance! Yes, I'd love to have been a Listener, and I know I'm smart enough. I wanted to come up here to check that everything was safe, to get the essentials for us all to live as we want. But the Farmer's rules say no."

I waited for a moment to see if she was going to continue, but she carried on staring out of the window. I gave her a quick nudge.

"Which rules, Aria? Tell me."

She shook her head again. "I never wanted to leave my world, but the Farmer has made it too dangerous a place to be. And now I'm up here and see all the things that women *can* do, but that we are never allowed to do, I wonder what would be better – him gone, or me?"

There was a real note of bitterness in her voice.

"Come on then, tell me," I said. "You mentioned yesterday that you had been given your Assignment. What had they Assigned you to do that made you run away?"

I can't tell her the whole truth, not yet.

"I was Assigned to be a Breeder," I whispered.

Lily's mouth drops open.

"You mean, having to have kids? At sixteen? No way!"

"I'm not lying, I promise."

"No," she says. "I mean, I couldn't. I wouldn't. That's terrible."

And then she asks me the question that makes me shudder to answer.

"Do you get to choose the father?" Her voice is hesitant, her hands still pressed against her cheeks. "Who do you have to have the kids with?"

"No, there's no choice. It's usually one of the Elders. I don't even want to think about it."

"The Elders?" she squeaks. "I'm so sorry, Aria, that's worse than terrible."

Lily rubs my arm in a way that is weirdly comforting. I try to reach my hand out towards hers, but it feels wrong, so I drop it back in my lap. She doesn't notice, but carries on talking.

"I never guessed that. That's a spectacularly good reason to want to run away. I can't begin to imagine…"

She breaks off, looking at the floor. We sit quietly for a moment, and I'm lost in my thoughts. How on earth have I managed to make such a mess of things?

"Women here don't usually have their kids until they are well into their twenties or thirties, sometimes even forties," Lily says.

"Forties! How is that even possible? How many kids do women up here have?"

"Most of them? Two, I guess. That's about average."

Two! For two maybe the Assignment would be bearable. I shake my head in disbelief.

"So how many do you have to have then?" asks Lily. "What's the average for the Community?"

I think of the dormitories, the rows and rows of little beds, with too many of them empty. I remember the women, exhausted and despairing, forever pregnant.

"Fifteen," I say quietly. "We're allowed to stop after fifteen."

CHAPTER 7

I went to bed still rocked by Aria's revelations. Fifteen children! And starting so young too. I couldn't imagine what my life would be like if I was expected to start having children instead of going on to do my A levels. I would have run away too, faced with the same prospect.

I found myself lying awake late into the night wondering about our different worlds. Aria had settled down in Marjorie's flat quite happily, and seemed OK about being alone. The Community clearly didn't set much store on individuality, so learning how to manage in this strange new world without support would have been almost impossible, and yet again it made me wonder about how she would have survived had she not met me. Despite her strangeness I enjoyed having her around, and I already thought of her as a friend. It made me realise how much I had been missing the girls I used to count as friends, before Jenny turned them all against me.

It had been such a gift for her. I'd gone from being the popular rich girl to being an outcast almost overnight when my dad was splashed all over the papers, in disgrace because of some banking scandal that I didn't understand. Our humiliation as a family didn't take long, and when Dad got offered a job in Shanghai everything left was sold off. I said that I wanted to stay and do my GCSEs, assuming that Mum would stay with me, but instead they moved me in with Nan and left anyway. Jenny loved it.

Thinking about the girls at school reminded me that the end of term was looming ever closer. It would be great to have Aria around to hang out with all day during the holidays, but with absolutely no money what were we going to do? Everything in London cost such a lot. I'd only really noticed that since my allowance had stopped. I couldn't even afford to take us both to the cinema, never mind feed her for a week. I spent a lot of the night awake.

I slept through my alarm, and even for a Sunday it was quite late by the time I finally woke up. I grabbed some breakfast, making a jam sandwich for Aria when Nan wasn't looking, and told her that I had loads of homework to do so I would be using the flat downstairs.

The door was unlocked so I let myself in, calling Aria's

name softly. There was no answer. Peeking into the bedroom I could see that the bed had been carefully made. In the kitchen all the cupboard doors were open and a selection of tins were lined up on the little table.

"Aria?" I called a little more loudly, beginning to panic that something might have happened to her. "Where are you?"

"In here," said a small voice from the sitting room.

I pushed open the door and saw Aria sitting on the floor surrounded by a huge pile of books. Marjorie's bookcase had been completely emptied. Along with the discarded paperback romances there was a large selection of coffee-table books full of glossy photos, and they were scattered around her, pages open at a random selection of things. There were also stacks of magazines – some thick monthly ones and loads of weekly gossip ones. I hadn't realised that Marjorie liked that sort of thing.

Aria had clearly been working her way through them all for hours, and my heart sank at the thought of trying to get them back into place and make it look as if we'd never been here.

"I brought you breakfast," I said, pulling the slightly fluffy jam sandwich out from my hoodie pocket and handing it to her. She almost pounced on it, looking inside quickly before smiling and biting into it. "Sorry it's a bit late," I added. "I overslept. You should keep that door locked, you know. It's not safe to leave it open."

"Oh, OK." She was quiet for a moment, eyes closed as she ate. "Thank you," she said finally, wiping the crumbs from her mouth with the back of her hand. The sandwich had pretty much already gone. "That was good. I've been up so long I've already had my nap."

"What have you been doing?"

She beamed at me, picking up a copy of *Hello!*

"I've been busy looking at all these. I have so many questions!"

I laughed. "You have pictures here of all the wonders of the world but you want to ask me questions about celebrities. I like your priorities!"

We giggled over the magazines for the next hour or so, and Aria learned to recognise some of the names. It was a much easier way to learn to read than with the kids' books. She was particularly fascinated by the celebrities who were splitting up.

"I don't understand how it works. You say that no one tells you who to choose, but they're still miserable. Why aren't they happy?"

"Who knows?" I said. "Some partnerships – marriages – work, and others fall apart. Everyone hopes that theirs will be one of the happy ones, but loads of them fail."

"There's a lot of hurt in this world too," said Aria, looking at a picture of a young woman carrying a baby and trying to avoid the cameras.

I thought of my parents and the fights that they had, and I could only nod in agreement, blinking hard. To

distract us both I turned the pages of the magazine to find some pictures of boys.

"OK – of these two, which do you think is better looking?"

She blushed scarlet. "I couldn't say that! It's not proper."

"Who's going to tell? Go on – this one or the other one?"

"Do you mean the one with the yellow hair? We don't have anyone with that. He looks a little like your friend Will." She paused, holding up the picture. "I like him."

"Oh. I guess. Maybe he looks like him a little bit." Something in me really didn't appreciate the thought of Aria liking Will, not the way I thought she meant, anyway.

"Does everyone in the Community have dark hair then?" I asked.

"Yes, everyone. Some go grey, of course, but the rest of us have brown or black hair. The people here with yellow hair are just … beautiful. Don't you think so too?"

"We call it blonde," I said, dodging her question.

"Blonde. I like that word." She rested her chin in her hand and stared off into the distance, a small smile on her face. I wished I knew what she was thinking.

If he was my breeding partner I wonder what our children would look like. Would they have yellow hair too? I try and imagine a little girl with my face and Will's thick yellow hair. It's a lovely thought, but hopelessly impractical. No,

I mustn't think about it – I must concentrate on what I'm going to do next.

My mission is finished. I can't do what I was supposed to do, to take Lily back below, so I must decide – risk going home or start a new life up here. And as I think it, I know that there is no choice.

I take a deep breath and look up. "I have to stay here now. I don't know how I'm going to manage but I'm going to have to try."

"Forever?" Lily's voice sounds squeaky.

"Yes, forever. I have to leave everything. Everyone. All of my old life." I pause and think into the future. "Maybe there is someone I can share a life with here."

I glance over at Lily's shocked face. She has been so kind, and the guilt threatens to overwhelm me again. Am I being a coward for not warning her about the Farmer's plans?

I could see the guilty look in Aria's eyes before she quickly turned and started tidying a pile of magazines, and my heart sank. She fancied Will, it was pretty obvious, but did she really think that she could start a new life with him? I couldn't see how that was ever going to work, even if he wanted to.

And I wasn't sure how I could help either, not in any practical way. It was all such a mess.

"I don't know what we're going to do if you stay," I said.

"What do you mean?" she asked.

"I mean, you won't be able to stay here – in this flat – forever. And somehow we have to be able to feed you. I can't do that alone. We need help."

"But why can't I live here?"

"Because it's not our flat. It won't work." I wished that it had been a year ago, when my life was so different. I'd have had no problem finding the money to look after her then. I tried to imagine how I would have managed if I'd been left here all alone without Nan, and shuddered. However brave she seemed, Aria must be terribly homesick. I felt the familiar prickling in my eyes as I thought about my mum.

I reached out to take Aria's hand, probably more for my comfort than hers.

"It'll be OK, I promise you. We'll think of something. I will find a way to help. That's what friends are for, right?"

I almost smiled as I thought back to Jenny's nasty text comment, which had pushed me into inviting Aria home, and realised that I had barely looked at my phone since I'd met her. Jenny was right – I'd needed a friend, and now I had one.

There was obviously still plenty of stuff that Aria wasn't telling me, but I decided not to push it. I didn't understand her world or her rules. I just wished that I hadn't introduced her to Will, because there was absolutely no way I could compete with her looks.

I decided there was no point worrying immediately,

and we continued poring over the magazines for what remained of the morning. After a tiny lunch I had to do my homework. Aria sat quietly on the sofa leafing through more books, and every time I glanced up she seemed completely absorbed. She was following the text with her finger and mouthing letters, occasionally raising her eyebrows as she turned a page. She kept quiet though, and finally my end-of-term English essay was done. I threw my pen down on the table and shut my books. It was time to show Aria a bit more of the city.

"We're going window shopping," I announced, standing up and stretching. "Come on, leave that. We'll clear up later."

Aria looked confused. "Shopping for windows?" she asked.

"Not literally. We're just going to have a look at stuff. Let's go back to Selfridges – the place where it smelled of perfume, remember? We can go in the back door where the smell won't be so strong."

"All right," she said slowly. "But if it makes me sneeze again I'll have to leave."

Within twenty minutes we were at the back entrance to the store. Aria followed me in, sniffing the air.

"It's not too bad back here," she agreed. "What did you want to do?"

We rode up and down the escalators for a while, Aria's eyes getting wider and wider, "It's all so beautiful," she said, stroking a silk dress in the Prada concession. "This is so soft, but it would be hopeless to wear."

I could see the assistant eyeing us up and getting ready to come over to shoo us out of the way.

"Come on, you'll enjoy this – the easy way to travel!" I took her hand and pulled her towards the back of the store to the bank of lifts.

We stood waiting for the lift to come but as soon as the metal doors slid open Aria jumped backwards, her mouth open in horror, in the process nearly knocking over a woman with a toddler. I mumbled an apology to the angry mother and helped to pick up her bags while Aria was pressed up against the far wall, just staring at the lift. Finally the doors closed and we were alone on the landing.

"What's the matter? You can't possibly be claustrophobic. What is it about lifts that you don't like?"

"Can I tell you about it outside, please?" she asked. "I don't want to be near these things." She shuddered as another of the lifts arrived with a loud ding, its doors gaping open.

"OK, if you insist. Come on, I know what will cheer you up."

We left the store and started to make our way down past Oxford Circus to Regent Street, and Aria started to relax a little, despite the crowds of tourists. "Lifts then," I said. "Why are they such a problem? They can't do you any harm."

"Are you sure? We have one, and unless you have the

right protection, if you go up in the lift you'll never come back. No one in the Community would risk using one."

"Really? Let me guess – the Farmer is the one who gives you the protection?" I tried hard to keep the sarcastic tone out of my voice.

"That's right! How did you know? It's certain death to use the lift in secret."

"Oh, lucky guess. Your Farmer seems to control most things. Do you have many lifts?"

"No, just the one that is used to get the food down to us. The Listeners organise that, and they have to go up and down in it. The Farmer makes sure they are safe, but Dane says it's very scary. I don't know how he does it." There was a touch of awe in her voice.

"It's a good job you're not going to get to be a Listener then," I laughed, trying to get her to join in, but the best she managed was a watery smile.

Lily is trying to get me to understand the way that the Aboves live, but it's so hard. There are so many times when I think things are under control but then something horrible appears. How can she joke about lifts? She's right though; it's one of the few things that would put me off being a Listener.

Lily is dragging me along a wide road that has lots of the big red buses on it. There are huge windows too, showing lots of strange things. Some of them seem pretty straightforward, with jumpers or plates in the windows, useful stuff like that, but others I can make no sense of. One building just has a picture of an apple outside. Inside dozens of people seem to be crammed around white tables, looking at small flat things.

Finally we dive off the busy road and go under an archway to a much quieter one. Ahead are lots of the fat grey birds that seem to be everywhere. They don't like us coming round the corner and leap into the air, wings flapping. I can feel the wind they make on my face as they suddenly all change direction at once, skimming over the tops of our heads. I don't like their pink feet, and duck to make sure none of them touch me. They are a bit like the bats at home, but noisier and more stupid. There are only a few bats loose in our tunnels, ones that have escaped from the caves where the Farmer keeps them all. Sometimes the women chase them with brooms. I always help them get away if I can.

Lily slows and turns to me, a big smile on her face.

"You're going to just love this. I should have brought you here before!"

She turns me round and walks up the road. The sky has got darker with clouds, and in the shop windows all the lights seem brighter, and other lights on tall poles flicker on, casting a yellow light.

We reach a place where lots of roads meet.

"Look up there!" she laughs.

High up the buildings are covered in lights making huge moving pictures. Some are of words, some are *of people, others are of things I've never seen before. I watch, mesmerised, as the lights glitter and dance. Around me there are hundreds of people, and hundreds of cars and the big red buses. The noise is all around and I can smell burned sugar. A man has cones of something sticky he is giving people from a cart. Everyone seems happy. Usually they look miserable and rushed, but here there is laughing and smiling. I can't help laughing and smiling too.*

This world can be a lot of fun. Nothing at home is fun.

I fell into bed exhausted. The trip to Piccadilly Circus had been followed by Soho and then Covent Garden, and by that time we were almost too shattered to walk home. Aria went to bed as soon as we got back to the flat, even more wiped out than me. Nan hadn't asked me any questions about what I'd been doing all weekend. I was relieved about that as I didn't want to lie, but it made me feel even guiltier about what I was keeping from her.

It was really hard to get out of bed in the morning. It was the last Monday of term, and the tedium of teachers trying to fill lessons that no one cared about was almost unbearable.

I left Aria with a pile of magazines and an exercise book, and told her to practise her writing while I was out. As I walked down the road I worried about how on earth I was going to feed her. I'd no idea that the fresh stuff Nan and I ate was quite so expensive, and the twenty pounds

I had got at the weekend was barely going to cover another loaf. Luckily Marjorie's flat had lots of tins – she obviously thought there might be a siege or a nuclear winter at any moment, so she had lots of supplies – but I was still going to have to replace them eventually.

I was deep in thought as I worked my way down the escalators at the Tube station, and wasn't really paying any attention to the announcements. I'd long since got used to the inconvenience of having to get the Tube to school. Some days it seemed to take forever, and as I reached the platform I realised that it was one of those days – the platform was packed and the signs showing how long it would be until the next train seemed to be out of order.

Sighing and heaving my school bag further up on to my shoulder I forced my way along the platform to my preferred spot near the back of the train. The usual silence was punctuated by the grumbling of the passengers as they actually spoke to each other to complain but I tuned it all out as I worried about the money. As a result I didn't realise that the person standing just to the side was actually talking to me, and it took me a moment to recognise him – he was often on my morning train but he'd never spoken to me before. Tall and dark with very pale skin, he was probably in his late teens. He looked very athletic.

"It's a bit of a nightmare today, isn't it?"

He had leaned in close to make sure he was heard. He

was gorgeous, his dark eyes twinkling in the harsh neon light.

"Yes," I squeaked in surprise, feeling myself turning pink. I cleared my throat to try to sound more normal. "You'd think this close to summer it would have started to quieten down a bit."

"I know. It's rubbish, isn't it?" He smiled at me, then nodded at my bag. "College not finished yet?"

He was unbelievably good-looking and so far out of my league that it wasn't even funny. I couldn't work out why he was talking to me after all these months. He was also expecting me to answer him.

"Umm…" I started, but the squeak was back. I tried again. "Only a few more days."

"Yeah, me too. I seem to live either here or in the coffee bar next to the station during term time. Be nice to get a break."

I was saved from having to think up something else to say as a train roared unannounced into the station. In the crush and jostling of the crowd we got pushed into adjoining carriages. I glanced through the windows of the emergency doors, and he was looking at me, smiling. The windows at the end of each carriage were fully open, but the roar of the wind rushing in made it impossible to talk. I kept glancing at him, his dark, slightly spiky hair easy to spot among the balding heads of the commuters, but I lost sight of him as another crowd of passengers squeezed on. I craned my head round to try to see, but

when a load of passengers left at the next stop I realised that he had already gone.

Lily has gone out today to school, where they teach the children to read and write. I wish I could go with her. I can't think of anything better than being in a place where all they want you to do is learn. I've looked through the magazines and the books, and practised copying out the words that she left for me, but it's hard when she's not here to show me where I'm going wrong. And I want to go outside – there is so much to see and try to understand.

I need some time to walk and think, to see if I can find some answers. The conversation with Lily has made me think – which life do I really want, and, realistically, which options are still open to me? Will Dane have the strength to challenge the Farmer alone? I wish I could talk with him, but if one of the other Listeners saw us it would mean certain death for him.

Picking up the purse of money Lily has left for me, I gently open the door and step out of the flat. Turning, I lock it carefully behind me as Lily has shown me, feeling the key rotate and click. For the first time I am alone outside – I have no destination, not the shops, or the library. My heart flutters and I realise I am holding my breath. Part of me wants to run back inside and hide from the strange, moving sky, but I know it can't hurt me and so I set off. I have to keep breathing – gentle breaths that slow the panic creeping up my back.

Walking gives me time to think. I've only ever wanted to be part of the Community, but a safe, happy Community as it was years before, as the stories tell us. But now I see Above for myself, I'm no longer sure what I want. The people I've met are so kind, and I've seen things that I couldn't even have imagined. Why didn't Dane tell me it was like this?

I realise I've made up my mind to stay Above, but if I could, would I go back? Should I?

As I think, I walk. My ability to navigate the tunnels at home seems to help me find my way here. I can build a picture in my head and work out where things are and how to get back. There are so many streets, and many of them look identical. I walk down one road and see lots of big windows at the front of each building, some with big glass doors too. They must be little shops. Inside one there are racks of clothes, all white, and a headless figure in the window wearing an enormous white dress. I can't imagine what it's for, it seems so impractical, but I can see from the detail on the material that it must be something special. Almost every house on the road has a similar display.

I turn away from the window and start to walk again. I wish I knew what to do. By now, everyone at home will think that I'm dead. Does Dane think that too? Or did Neville really see me the other day and tell everyone? With so many people here what were the chances of that happening? Frustrated, I stuff my hands in my pockets and walk on, looking at the pavement. A horn blares – I have arrived at a busier road, so concentrate on getting to the other side safely.

I have to decide – try to make contact, or do I move on?

Then I glance down a side road and see his face. Instinctively I dodge into a doorway, and I realise that what I do next will change my life again. Shall I stay hidden or betray Lily and all she's done by stepping out into the sunshine?

CHAPTER 8

I couldn't resist the temptation to peep into the coffee bar as I came out of the station later, and he was there, lounging on the sofa reading the paper. He glanced up and saw me looking, but before I could turn away he smiled and waved for me to come in.

I pushed open the heavy door and stepped in, enjoying the cool air and smell of freshly roasted coffee. He looked even more gorgeous than earlier, but maybe slightly younger in the daylight than he had seemed on the Tube. He had to be older than me though. What on earth did he want with me? The girl sitting at the next table looked at us with undisguised surprise.

"Hello," he said, making room on the sofa for me to join him. "I was hoping that I'd see you this afternoon. There was something I wanted to ask you. Nightmare this morning, wasn't it?"

I nodded mutely, not really knowing what to say as I hovered next to the sofa. I shouldn't really be talking to him anyway. He was practically a stranger.

"Oh, come on, I'm not going to bite. Sit down for a minute, will you? What harm can it do?"

The coffee shop wasn't busy, but there were enough people in there for it to be safe. I perched on the edge of the sofa and couldn't help smiling back a little when he gave me a broad grin.

"Did the delay make you really late for college?" he asked.

"Umm, no, it wasn't too bad in the end," I mumbled, not wanting to admit that I went to school and not college.

"Good." He smiled again, then picked up his cup and peered into it. "Can I get you a coffee? I could do with a refill."

There didn't seem to be any point in refusing. "Coffee, please. Cappuccino if that's OK."

"Two minutes then. Don't go away!"

He jumped up out of the deep sofa easily, reaching in his back pocket for his money as he walked away from me towards the counter. He was incredibly fit, and I couldn't quite believe that I was sitting there with him. The girl at the next table couldn't either, and, having admired him as he walked off, looked me up and down again before shaking her head. Sitting back, I tried to look as if I had coffee with gorgeous boys every day.

He reappeared with the drinks and folded his long frame back down on to the sofa. Taking a small sip of his coffee he nodded as if it were good and then set it back down. Finally he sat back and turned towards me, one arm resting casually along the back of the seat.

"So, Lily, what *are* you planning to do with Aria?"

I had just lifted my cup and almost dropped it back on to the saucer in surprise. The coffee sloshed over the edge.

"How … how do you know my name? And how do you know about Aria? Are you from Social Services or something?"

I pushed myself to the edge of the seat again, ready to jump up and run for it.

"Calm down. You're not in any trouble. Sit back – we need to talk."

He took hold of my arm and firmly pulled me back. As I eased back into the sofa I could still feel the press of his fingers on my skin. He was very strong, and I doubted that I would get far if I decided to run.

"Who are you?" I demanded, folding my arms and sticking out my chin as he sat back in a relaxed pose.

"My name is Dane and I'm a friend, that's all you need to know. I'm not from Social Services, that's for sure."

He smiled again, but I refused to smile back. He leaned forward, resting his elbows on his knees. Aria had mentioned a Dane, so this had to be him, but was he a

friend or not?

"The thing is, Lily, I have a bit of a problem and I need your help."

"Hang on a sec, I need some answers. What makes you think that I know anyone called Aria?"

"Don't be difficult. You were spotted with her at the weekend."

"I'm not being *difficult*! And how do you know me? Have you been stalking me?" My voice was getting higher, and I could see some of the other customers turning to see what was going on.

"Keep your voice down," he said, hands out as if to calm me. "It's nothing like that, I promise. Aria ran away, and one of my friends saw her at the weekend just around the corner from here. So I was watching out for her myself yesterday when I saw her with you." He smiled a little, looking away briefly. "I couldn't believe that of all the people in London she could befriend, she found you. What are the chances of that? I knew that I would see you on the train this morning, so I waited."

"Why the subterfuge? Why didn't you just come and say something – you're a friend of hers, aren't you?" I asked, hoping that I was remembering correctly.

"I didn't want to frighten her off. She knows that she's broken all the rules, and if she had seen me she might have run again. I didn't want to risk it."

"Presumably she'll take off because she doesn't want

to talk with you. Why would I – should I – help? She's my friend."

"Exactly – you're her friend, so she'll listen to you. You must have noticed that she's a bit – how shall I put it – different. What has she told you about her home?"

"Some," I said, shrugging, not wanting to give away what I knew. "She's not said a huge amount, to be fair. She doesn't seem to want to talk about it. Just that it's a closed community with pretty strict rules. I'm assuming it's something to do with your religion."

The guy nodded. "It's a good guess, and about right. Our community is very sheltered and Aria knows very little about the outside world. Our leaders are worried – I'm worried – about her ability to cope."

"She seems to be doing OK."

"I'm sure you're looking after her really well but it must be hard. She's a little backward in her understanding of the world and she has been known to rather exaggerate things. Has she been telling you some outrageous tales?"

He smiled at me and picked up his coffee. What should I say? Was Aria telling me the truth, or was the whole thing an elaborate hoax? If I agreed with him and told him what she'd said I could put her in more danger. I didn't know what to do, and the longer I hesitated, the more he was going to suspect me. I leaned forward and lifted my coffee cup too, buying a few precious seconds of thinking time. I stirred the froth slowly before taking a sip, and the answer was suddenly clear. Aria couldn't have been lying to me. Somehow she'd known how to get through that wall, and *something* had been on that disused platform. So if she was telling the truth, what was he up to?

"No, not really," I said. "She's doing OK. She doesn't seem to read particularly well, but that's all."

The guy's shoulders relaxed – was that what he wanted to hear?

"Cool, cool," he said, nodding. "So, is she staying with you then?"

"Umm, actually no, she's staying at a friend's house. There's no room in our flat."

He nodded again, apparently satisfied with my answer. I sat back with my coffee, taking another sip and trying to look relaxed.

"So," I asked. "You didn't answer *my* question – how do you know my name? Secret Service if not Social Service?"

"Ha! Good one. Nothing so dramatic. I just read your name on the files sticking out of your bag this morning."

"Oh." That really was possible. I had taken in all my homework so not all of it fitted properly in my rucksack. "OK then, why have you come to look for her? Why not send someone she would trust immediately?"

He looked at his hands for a moment before answering.

"I volunteered. I'm really, really keen to talk with her."

He finally looked up at me through his long dark lashes, his gaze steady.

"Why?" I asked again.

There was a moment's hesitation while he seemed to be weighing me up.

"Because I love her," he said.

I sat back in surprise, lost for words for a moment.

"You didn't expect that, did you?" he asked, leaning forward with his elbows on his knees. "She doesn't know, does she?"

"No," I said. "I really don't think she does."

He looked at me for a moment longer, then dropped his head into his hands.

"I thought she knew, I really did. I wish I'd been clearer – if I had, then none of this mess would have happened."

"I think it's time to be straight with me, Dane. What's going on, and why do you need my help?"

He was hunched over, all his previous poise gone. For a moment I even wondered if he was about to cry, but he washed his hands across his face and sat back up, exhaling loudly.

"The truth is, Aria came here as a favour to me, to help me do something, but it's all gone wrong. She shouldn't be out here as it makes it really hard for her to go back. I need to talk with her. Can you bring her to me? I think she trusts you."

"But why would she be nervous about seeing you? It doesn't make sense."

"She may think that I'm going to be angry about the mistake she made, but I'm not. I just want for both of us to be safe."

"I thought it was just Aria who was in trouble?"

"It is, but I won't be happy until I know that she's OK. I need to see her, to find out what she wants to do. We have to talk about the future." His dark eyes seemed full of pain. "Our future – hers and mine."

He didn't seem to be lying any more. He wanted to help her too.

"What do you need me to do?"

My head was whirling as I made my way back towards home. My simple, dull life had evaporated so fast that I could barely remember it. Smiling, I walked down the old iron staircase to the basement flats and turned the handle on the door of Marjorie's flat. I was relieved to find that it was locked, as I had suggested, so I knocked gently.

Nothing happened, so I knocked slightly more loudly. There was still no response. I leaned round to look through the window to the front room, but found the view blocked by the net curtains. Cupping my hand over my eyes I tried again, and could just see the basic outline of the furniture. There was no sign of Aria.

"Where on earth have you gone?" I said out loud to myself as I leaned on the door.

Where could I start looking? She had no mobile so I

couldn't call her; she couldn't read a note if I left one for her; and she couldn't use a phone to call me. Maybe she had gone to see Nan. It was the only other thing I could think of, and I was just about to go up to the flat when I heard footsteps on the metal stairs behind me. It was Aria, looking relaxed and happy.

"Hi, how are you? I was wondering where you'd got to."

"I had to get out. I hope you don't mind."

"No, not at all. So where did you end up?"

"I just walked around the streets a bit," she said, unlocking the door as if she had been using keys her entire life.

The inside of the flat was cool and welcoming, and I instinctively moved towards the kitchen and the fridge. I dropped my heavy school bag down and picked out a can of Coke.

"Do you want one?" I asked, but Aria just shook her head.

"I saw lots of shops with white dresses in the window. What are they for?"

"Umm, white dresses, that will be … oh – wedding dresses, of course! There's a whole street of little shops that seem to sell nothing but wedding stuff. Did you end up there?"

Aria nodded. "Ah yes, weddings – you were showing me the wedding stories in one of the magazines. I should have guessed."

"The dresses are beautiful, aren't they? Expensive though."

"Very beautiful, but not very practical!" She smiled at me.

"You're not wrong," I laughed.

I took a glass from the cupboard and flicked open the can before sitting down at the table.

"Do you guys have any sort of partnership ceremony like getting married? You said something about being matched up by the Elders," I asked.

"We are, so we never pair up out of choice. They put us into breeding pairs and there's no ceremony for that."

I couldn't help shaking my head, relieved that my world was different to hers. I took a quick swig of the Coke then poured the rest into a glass.

"What if you actually do love someone? That must happen sometimes."

"It's not encouraged, because the breeding pairs get regularly rearranged."

"So they set you up with one bloke and then move you on to another?"

"Yes, it would be pointless having fifteen children with the same partner. It's our duty to breed stronger members of the Community."

"And you get no choice at all in the men?"

She gave a bitter laugh.

"None. Usually we get paired up with the Elders as they are the first in line to have descendents. Later we might get one of the younger ones, but that's quite rare. We accept what we're given. Well, the others do anyway."

"But not you."

Aria looked down at the table, tracing a knot in the wood with her finger.

"Everything there is wrong," she said quietly, not lifting her head. "Especially the way they treat us women. I knew rebelling against the Farmer was right, but the fight is so much bigger than that. It's only since I've come up here and seen how you live that it has become so clear."

"Don't any of the women protest?"

This time the laugh was more of a snort.

"No! Never. Everyone knows their place. I would never even have thought about trying to change anything until Dane talked me into it."

Dane. Should I tell her that I saw him, even though he had begged me not to?

"So what was his plan?" I asked.

Aria looked up at me, then her eyes slid back down to the table. She looked as if she was about to start talking then stopped. Finally she took a deep breath. "I was supposed to find someone – someone special – down on the Tube platform. The idea was to take them back to the Community. Dane had a plan, but I didn't really know the rest of it. I knew he had a map of the old Crop tunnels, and we used them to find a secret way up. I waited until I knew that the Crop was busy and I took the risk, but then of course I got lost, and you found me."

Was now the time to tell her? If I mentioned Dane wouldn't that make things easier for her? I was about to say something when Aria continued, almost talking to herself.

"I'm beginning to wonder if Dane didn't have a rather different plan in mind. Maybe I was supposed to fail. He lies so well – how can I be sure that he wasn't lying to me?"

I shut my mouth. Had he lied to me too? I couldn't know. I reached over and took one of her hands.

"Don't get upset. You can't change that now. What's important is that you got away, and you found me too, which was a bonus. We've been doing OK, haven't we?"

She nodded and looked up, and I could see that her eyes were moist.

"Come on then," I said. "Tell me a bit more about today, not about things that are going to worry you. What else did you get up to?"

"I walked around a bit, trying to make sense of the area in my head. It's how we learn the tunnels when we're little."

Lily laughs. "How did you get on with that then?"

"Not bad, I think."

"You're better than me then. I'm rubbish at knowing which way I'm going."

"We have to be good at it," I tell her. "There's a test when we reach six. We need to be able to find our way from one end of the Community to the other."

"Sounds tough for a six-year-old." Lily laughs again, clearly trying to cheer me up. "I hope you didn't fail."

"No one fails. The Breeders make sure of it. If they raised kids with no sense of direction it's not good news."

Lily raises her eyebrows but asks no more questions.

"Your school – was that good today?" I ask.

"You know, for a change it was OK. I managed to get the better of Jenny in an argument, which was awesome."

I remember Lily mentioning a Jenny, but not why.

"Is she one of your friends?"

"Ha, no! She's the one who's constantly making things miserable for me, sending me the mean text messages. I got one just after we met, remember?"

"Oh yes, I remember the one. She's horrible to you."

"But not today!" Lily beams, holding up her mobile. "Not a peep out of her."

"And that is good," I say, smiling back.

"So come on," Lily continues, finishing the last of her sickly-smelling brown drink. "Is that all you did today? What else happened?"

I remember the best bit of my day, and smile.

"I met Will. We went for a coffee."

I nearly spat Coke across the kitchen table.

"I'm sorry, did I hear that right? You met Will?"

"Yes, he was lovely. He took me for a coffee. Well, obviously I didn't actually have one of those, just a glass of water, but he said that's what he was having."

I couldn't believe it. I'd left her for just a few hours and she'd already had more of a date with Will than I'd ever managed – or ever would manage by the sound of it. Aria was sitting in the kitchen I'd sorted out for her, eating food I'd provided and was sleeping in a bed I'd made. The very least she could do was keep her hands off the guy I fancied.

"How was he?" I asked through gritted teeth, but she was oblivious to my discomfort.

"He was really great, really helpful in explaining where things are. We had a nice time."

She gave me one of her sunniest smiles.

"Likely to see him again?" I said as casually as I could manage.

"Yes, I think so. He seemed very happy to help me understand the area."

The late afternoon sun appeared from behind a cloud, bouncing off a window opposite and shining through the only gap in the net curtains, briefly throwing her face into shadow. I was glad I couldn't see her expression as I jumped up to rinse out my glass, hoping that the activity would calm me down. It didn't work.

"Look, Aria." The words burst out before I could stop them. "Up here you don't go picking up the boys your friends fancy, do you understand?" I gave her a pointed look. "You know I like Will."

"You didn't tell me he was a special friend," she said in a very even voice.

I still couldn't see her face.

"OK, let's make it clear now. I'd rather you didn't make a move on him."

"What do you mean?"

"Making a move – it means getting him to like you," I said.

"I'm not 'making a move on him' then. He's just explaining the area to me – where everything is." She paused for a moment. "And he's already promised to do some more of it tomorrow when you are out."

"Doesn't he have to go to school?"

She shrugged her shoulders.

"It seems to be finished, or that's what he said. Honestly, we had a lovely time. He thinks I'm funny, you know."

There was a smile in her voice.

"He thinks you're funny." I repeated her statement slowly, trying to keep my emotions under control.

"Uh-huh, and he's really happy to help me again. He said so."

The damage was done then. There was no way that he was going to look at me now, not if he thought he was getting somewhere with Aria. After all this time, all the plans I had for Will, she had snatched him from under my nose. And added to that, she seemed to have no idea of the pain she was causing me.

"Why couldn't you just leave him alone?" I asked, knowing how whiney I sounded but unable to stop. "Why did you have to arrange a date with Will? I'll have no chance now."

"I don't understand why you're so upset. I'm not doing any harm. It's not as if I'm about to breed with him!"

For a moment I was speechless.

"Do you have any idea of the effect you'll be having on him?" I finally managed to whisper.

"What do you mean? What effect?"

"You're stunning, Aria. Every boy we pass has his tongue hanging out, including Will. You're just leading him on and he'll be disappointed in everyone else, especially me!"

"Why? What are you talking about?"

I knew I was being unreasonable, but I couldn't stop.

"It might suit you to come swanning up here and steal other girls' boyfriends, but it's just too unfair, especially when you have a gorgeous boy of your own begging you to come back!"

There was a stunned silence as I realised I wasn't supposed to tell her I knew that.

"What do you mean?" Aria's voice was low and expressionless.

There was no way to avoid telling her.

"I met Dane. He wants to see you." I paused for a moment. "He says he loves you."

"What?" Her voice was suddenly icy.

"He found me earlier and we had a long chat. He wants you – he says he loves you and he wants to meet."

"He wouldn't say that. He just wouldn't," she said slowly.

"Well, he did!" I exploded. "So go and get him and leave Will alone. Having both is just unfair!"

Aria sat there, saying nothing. I could feel my frustration boiling over.

"I've had enough. This is all too weird – you're too weird. I'm going home and so should you!"

I didn't want to cry in front of her so I turned my back as my eyes filled up. I could hear her start to protest but the words were lost as I slammed the kitchen door behind me.

DON'T LOOK BELOW the SURFACE

CHAPTER 9

I woke up the next morning to a gaping feeling of loss, as if someone had crept into my room during the night and stolen all my possessions. Life was going to be easier without Aria, that was obvious – I wouldn't have to sneak about avoiding Nan, I wouldn't have to find her food or worry about what I would do if she was discovered by the authorities. But still something left an empty hole in me, a hole that was rapidly being filled with guilt. I wondered where she would go and who she would be with – Dane or Will. Deep in my heart I knew the answer.

Cross with myself for not even being able to get through breakfast without feeling guilty, I grabbed a hoodie and my school bag and was about to leave the house when I saw the little purse I had given Aria sitting on the doormat. She must have posted it through the letterbox earlier.

I picked up the purse and could feel a small amount of change and the front door key to the flat safe inside. She had gone, and it didn't look as if she was planning on coming back. The blanket of guilt got much stronger. I was suddenly appalled at just how unprotected she was against all the horrors of London. What was I thinking, letting her go off into the night? What if she had gone back to the Tube but been picked up by one of those men they kept warning us about in school? She wouldn't know any better and would end up in a drug dealer's bed before she realised what was happening.

Putting the purse in my back pocket, I glanced at myself in the hall mirror. A messy, tired and spotty figure looked back at me.

"Some friend you are," I said to my reflection before swallowing hard. The unease I'd been feeling about where she would end up circled around me.

No, it couldn't be too late – I had to do *something*, to go and check at the places we had been, see if I could find her, come up with a proper plan about where she could go. Maybe she was still sitting in the park or on the Tube platform, wondering what to do next. I had to check.

Slamming the door behind me, I ran down the steps and turned towards the station. As I started up the road I saw Dane coming round the corner and froze in my tracks. Our plan had been for me to bring Aria to the coffee shop where she would feel safe and he could talk with her. He wasn't supposed to be on my road.

When he saw me, he stopped dead for a second, then took his hands out of his pockets and marched towards me. An ugly scowl was etched on his face and he gave me an icy stare. I stepped back as he reached me.

"Dane? Is everything OK?"

"What have you done? I thought we had an agreement?"

"I don't know what to say," I protested quickly as he opened his mouth to speak again. "She's not here any more. I'm so sorry. I sort of mentioned meeting you and we had a bit of a row and now she's gone, and I don't know where."

"I know she's not here. She went home."

"Really?" Relief washed over me. "So she's safe – that's good news."

I gave him a nervous smile. He seemed nothing like the friendly, vulnerable boy I'd spoken with yesterday.

"Safe? That's not how I'd describe it. She's made her way back and he's going to punish her for her disobedience. What were you thinking? Why didn't you do as I asked?"

A gaping, sick feeling opened in my stomach and I grabbed at his sleeve.

"Why? Why would they do that?"

"Didn't you ask her anything about the Community? I wanted to talk to her here, to make sure she stayed safe!

Didn't you *listen*?"

He shook me off as he turned away.

"Wait, Dane, don't go! How did she find her way back down?"

"So she did tell you then? About where we live?"

I nodded miserably, biting my lip.

"She went to the warehouse. I've no idea how she found it but she did, and one of the other Listeners caught her. He took her back down immediately."

"What warehouse? What are you talking about?"

"It's how we get up Above and back with the food," he said dismissively. "Only the Listeners use it." He paused and raised his head to look at me. "And now the Farmer has her."

Something about his tone suddenly made me very afraid.

"What is he going to do to her?"

"You really don't want to know that," he said, dropping his gaze.

I grabbed both his arms then, and shook him as hard as I dared.

"What's happening to Aria? TELL ME!"

A woman approaching with a pushchair heard the raised voices and stopped, wondering if I needed help. Dane shushed me with a look.

"OK, OK, keep it down. I'll tell you," he said, shaking off my grip effortlessly.

"Are you all right, love?" asked the woman, glancing

between us.

I stood back and faced him, arms crossed, pausing briefly to nod at her.

"Thank you, I'm fine."

She raised her eyebrows at me but then nodded back.

"If you say so. Don't let him give you any grief, all right?"

She took a tighter grip of the pushchair and gave Dane a wide berth as she passed. He waited until she was well out of earshot before he spoke again.

"She was caught last night and taken to the Farmer. Did she tell you about him?"

"A little," I said cautiously.

"He's trying to find out how she got up here, and as soon as he breaks her, he'll…" He stopped abruptly. "I've said enough. It's too late now anyway."

"What do you mean?" I asked, instantly worried about the Crop.

He was as white as a sheet, his hands shaking, and as he looked over my shoulder into the distance I could see the pain in his eyes.

"She'll be going for trial tomorrow."

"And…?" I prompted as he continued staring into space.

"She's got no chance. He'll get what he wants from her and then make a spectacle out of her. It'll be a good way of keeping everyone else in line."

I felt as if I had turned to ice. "I – I don't understand.

What does that mean?"

"He won't let the rest of the Community think it's OK to try and come here. He has to show his authority. People are sent to the Crop for less – much less."

What had I done? My mouth worked silently for a moment before I was able to continue.

"Why don't they just send her back up here? Back to me?"

In that second I knew that I'd been a complete cow in turning her out, that a proper friend would have let her stay however difficult it was. I wanted her back to prove that we could make it work, to say sorry.

Dane gave a short, humourless laugh.

"Don't be ridiculous. She's been re-Assigned to Feeder. It's our ultimate punishment."

"Feeder? Does that mean she'll be in the kitchens or something? Like a cook?"

"She didn't give away all of our secrets then. No, the Feeders have an entirely different role, one that is vital to the Crop."

He paused for a moment as if weighing up whether to tell me, then he took a deep breath before pressing his lips together in a thin line, choosing to remain silent.

I felt my world shift as his words sank in. "Do you mean…"

I couldn't speak; my mouth was suddenly too dry.

"Everyone gets to be a Feeder eventually," he said, his eyes glazing as he looked down the road. "It's the last Assignment for us all, and we accept that. And we all know that people who are too ill, or who break the rules, get re-Assigned. It's the best way of maintaining control." He gave a weird smile. "Of the people *and* the Crop."

"That can't be right," I whispered. "It can't possibly be right."

As I spoke I was screaming inside – *she's going to be fed to the Crop! Sacrificed!* How could this possibly be happening? My hands were clammy and I took several shallow breaths to stop myself from retching.

Dane just stood there looking over my shoulder, his expression unreadable. I wanted to jump up and down and shout, thump his chest and pummel him into helping me, into helping Aria, but something told me I'd be wasting my time. He'd given up.

"Send her back to me, now, forever. I'll make sure she's OK," I said.

"It's too late. There's nothing you can do, even if you could get down there. It'll all be over soon, so just forget about her."

My heart felt as if it was being squeezed in a vice. What had I done?

"Please, Dane, there must be something? This is all my fault and I have to put it right!"

He finally turned to look at me.

"You're right. You have ruined everything. All the plans we had in place to change things are now in tatters, every route closed, and he'll be even more paranoid than before. There's nothing you can do. Nothing. I only came here to tell you to forget that the last few days ever happened. Get on with your life."

As he finished he gave me a look I couldn't fathom, but before I could say anything else he turned on his heel and disappeared around the corner, leaving me shaking so hard I had to lean against the wall.

Aria was about to die.

It's very dark and I don't know where I am or how long I've been here. My head feels as if it's been stuffed with wads of material, pressing down and pinning me to the ground. I don't remember anything at all. Under my fingers I can feel the damp rock, and then the smell comes to me. It's a smell I didn't realise that I had been missing: the smell of home.

I ran without thinking, away from the house, from Dane, from everything I knew, desperate to do something but utterly lost as to what. How could the Community do that to her? Why hadn't I kept her safe? What sort of people live like that? The questions kept building, unanswered, as I stumbled into the park, not knowing what to do next. I slumped down on one of the benches and put my head in my hands, but that just made things worse. I had to keep moving, to keep thinking. Pacing helped a bit, but not much, as I tried to think of what I could have done differently. The whole thing was just a nightmare.

"Maybe I should go to the police?" I muttered to myself.

Would they believe me? I had no proof of any of it. The army? Surely the Crop were a danger to the population? What if they got out? Someone *had* to be interested in that. But I didn't even know what sort of animals we were talking about. Ones that smelled bad and made a strange slithering noise? They would laugh me out of the room. But I had to try. I had no idea where the nearest police station was so I pulled my phone out of my pocket and dialled 999. A woman's voice quickly answered, asking which service I wanted.

"Police, please," I said, trying to keep my breathing steady.

There was a long moment when all I could hear was an empty clicking noise, and then there was another brisk female voice, asking for my name and mobile number. I gave her both, still trying to breathe.

"OK, Lily, tell me what's happening."

"It's my friend. I think she's about to be killed."

"Where is your friend?"

"This is the difficult bit. She's a member of a strange cult and she's disobeyed their rules."

The voice was still calm but persistent. "And where is your friend?" she repeated. "What's the address?"

"Her cult lives in a community below the Tube network in old tunnels."

"I see." A hint of disbelief was creeping into her voice. "And how do they get in and out of these tunnels? Where is the entrance?"

"I don't know!" I wailed, realising that I should have made Dane tell me.

"Keep calm, Lily. How about you tell me your friend's name?"

"It's Aria. I never asked her if she had a surname."

"And what makes you think that they are going to harm her?"

"She's going to be punished, and it's all my fault. They're going to feed her alive to … to … *something*. I just don't know what."

The woman's voice was turning icy. "Wasting police time is a criminal offence, Lily. I'm sure you know that."

"I'm telling the truth! There are hundreds of them and they've lived there for years, protected by some sort of wild animals…" My voice faltered as I realised that I was making things worse. "Please, I'm telling the truth!"

"If you can't tell me where your friend is and how we get to her, we can't help, can we?"

No, I mouthed silently as I pressed the button on my phone, cutting her off. You can't.

I felt horribly sick but had no idea what to do. The only person who could help me was Dane, and he'd gone. I slumped back on the seat and pressed my hands against the old wood of the park bench, not knowing what else to do with them. My friend was in desperate trouble and it was all my fault. I had to find a way to help her, I just had to.

"Lily? Are you OK?"

The voice behind me made me jump. I'd been so caught up in my thoughts that I hadn't seen Will approaching. He was carrying a long red lead, and a ball on a bright-yellow string, and looked worried.

"You were pacing up and down like a mad thing. What's up?"

"It's Aria," I said, trying not to sob. "She's gone."

He frowned as he sat down next to me on the bench. Foggy continued rummaging around in the bushes nearby.

"Gone already? That's a shame – for you, of course. But she was always going to go home sometime. What's the big deal?"

"She's in terrible danger. I think they might kill her."

"Whoa – what? What are you talking about?" he said, pulling me round to face him. "Tell me!"

"Her people say she has broken the rules."

"You've got to be kidding me! What sort of weird cult is she involved with?"

I looked up at his concerned face. At least I wasn't completely alone.

"It's a very long story, and I'm not sure I have the time. I have to try and do *something*!"

"I think you have time to tell me first. Here," he took a small bottle of water out of his back pocket, "have a swig of that, take a deep breath and tell me everything. What's she caught up in?"

"Well…"

I hesitated, wondering where on earth to start and how to get him to believe me.

"How much did she tell you? What do you know already?"

For all I knew she had told him all about her life when the two of them had been chatting alone.

"Almost nothing, really. The only time we spoke about it was when I saw her briefly yesterday. She said that she came from a very sheltered society where everyone has pre-assigned roles, and that she had run away because she didn't like hers. When I asked her more about it she clammed up."

"She didn't tell you where this place is then?"

"I've only really had one conversation with her, and it didn't come up."

I glanced at him quickly, wanting to believe that his coffee with Aria had been swift and functional and not the lengthy wandering around that she had implied.

"Are you sure? She didn't say anything?"

"No. To be honest, she didn't say much at all. So where is it? Don't you know?"

"I know exactly where they are," I sighed, pushing the dog down as he tried to jump up on my lap, "and you're partially right. She comes from a group called the Community, which has very strict rules and very little

technology. And they're right here."

I stamped my foot to emphasise the point. Will looked around.

"Here? What do you mean?"

"Right here, under our feet. Underground."

He shook his head. "Nah, you've got to be mistaken. No one lives *underground*!"

"They do. I've met another one of them too. They live very deep to avoid detection, and have been there for a long time."

"Oh, come on, Lily, this is getting ridiculous. Next you'll be telling me that they breed dragons or something! How did you get taken in by all this?"

I leapt up, pushing the dog aside again.

"It's not rubbish. I'm telling you what I heard from Aria! It's a very strange place with very strange ideas, and I don't know everything. But I do know that she is in danger and sitting here isn't actually going to help her. I'm sorry, Will, but I'm off." I turned and marched off down the path, tears of frustration stinging my eyes. Within seconds I could hear footsteps running towards me.

"Hold on," he called, catching me by the arm. "I didn't mean to offend you. You have to agree that it does sound a bit odd though."

"I know, and it took me long enough to get my head round it, but I believe her. When I first saw her she was running down the tracks of the Bakerloo line, about to get squashed by a Tube train. She wasn't faking that."

"She told me that," admitted Will, falling into step next to me. "I assumed she'd just fallen on the track or something." He paused for a second to call the dog. "So where are we going? How on earth do we find her?"

I stopped dead, turning towards him.

"We? You don't have to come!"

"No, I want to. If she's in trouble then we have to go and sort it out. That's what friends are for, right? Anyway, I like Aria, and if she needs us I want to help." He gave a swift cheeky grin. "But we could do with a plan."

Relief washed over me – he believed me enough to want to help. But I also knew why he wanted to join me, and that was to get Aria back. There was nothing I could do about that, so I had to concentrate on finding her before it was too late. Two would be better than one.

"OK – plan. Good point," I said, resisting the urge to start pacing again. "We have to get underground, as deep as possible, and we could probably do with some sort of weapon."

"You don't seriously think that they are going to hurt her, do you?" Before I could answer he carried on. "How about Foggy? Would he do?"

I wasn't entirely sure if he was joking. Following his gaze I turned round and saw Foggy's rear end. His front end was still rummaging in a bush. He was pretty strong, so might well be useful.

"I don't know. Can he keep quiet?"

"As long as I have enough bribery material about me.
Watch."

Will pulled a small pouch from his pocket and shook it.
The dog froze. Then with almost a single bound he was
over by Will's leg, looking up expectantly.

"Settle…" said Will in a long, drawn-out tone.

Foggy lay down at his feet, eyes watching his every
move. Will placed a small biscuit from the pouch just in
front of the dog's nose. Foggy was almost quivering with
anticipation but he didn't budge until Will whispered,
"Take it!" and then he leapt up and scoffed the biscuit
in a single swallow.

I smiled weakly.

"It's tempting, Will, but I can't let him come. I don't
want to be responsible for any harm coming to your dog.
Or to you, for that matter. It's going to be dangerous –
very dangerous. They don't have dragons, but they do
have something protecting them – they chased me in
the dark – and I don't know exactly what it is. They call it
the Crop."

"The Crop? Sounds really scary." He laughed. "It'll be
the Attack of the Killer Vegetables! I'm sure Foggy will
be able to sort them out."

I couldn't join his laughter.

"Really, Will, no. Foggy can't come. And there's one
other thing you need to know before you agree to help
me."

I looked up into Will's curious eyes, wondering if he

would mark me down as a mad person in the next thirty seconds. It seemed pretty likely, but I couldn't let him volunteer without being completely aware of what he was getting into.

"I told you that Aria is about to be killed. Her people are going to feed her to the Crop because she left the Community for a few days. Whatever the Crop really is, it's deadly."

Will's face struggled for a moment and I could tell he was trying to work out if I was taking the mickey. I knew I hadn't convinced him.

"It's all true, I promise you!" I burst out before he could say anything. "I just have no way of proving it. Look, I'm sorry for mentioning it. I don't want to get you involved. But now that you know, if I don't come back will you please tell Nan where I went? It would be horrible for her to be forever wondering where I've gone."

My voice quavered a bit towards the end, but I turned on my heel and marched away from him. He wasn't going to see me cry. I was going to have to rescue Aria alone.

DON'T LOOK BELOW the SURFACE

CHAPTER 10

I walked quickly out of the park and down the road, not wanting Will to see how upset I was. For a moment I had thought we might be able to do something, to be able to work together, and whatever his motivation that would have been good. I blinked back the tears that threatened to come, wondering exactly how I was going to do what I said I was going to do. How on earth could I get into the tunnels and past the Crop? I had no idea where the warehouse was. The only thing I could think of was the disused platform where Aria had taken me in the first few minutes after we met. Perhaps from there I could find the way down. And what about a weapon? What could I use for that?

I was going to have to get my hands on something. Nan had an old walking stick – would that be enough?

I could get in and out of the flat without her noticing to collect that and a torch. Glancing at my watch I sighed in relief – Nan would be out at her regular coffee morning, so I could go home.

I was turning into our road when I heard a voice calling behind me.

"Wait, Lily. I'm sorry, I've been an idiot."

I swung round to see Will running towards me, dragging a reluctant Foggy, who was trying to go in the other direction.

"What? Do you mean you believe me?"

He and Foggy eventually caught up with me. "I do. I'm not entirely sure why, but I do. Let me help."

His ruffled hair and crumpled shirt gave him an even scruffier appearance than normal, but his brown eyes held mine steadily. I wished that his earnest expression was because he wanted me, not my friend. But I wasn't going to complain.

"OK then, thanks," I muttered, not really sure what to do next.

"You mentioned a plan?" he said, smiling.

"The best plan I have is to go down into the disused Tube tunnels, and from there find the way into the lower level. I'm going to get one of Nan's old sticks and a torch now."

"Isn't there an easier way? Didn't you say that there are others up here? They can't all go racing down Tube tracks."

"Apparently they have a warehouse, but I have no idea where it is. There might be an entrance there, I suppose."

Will looked quizzically at me. "Go on, fill me in."

"Aria said that they get most of their food from up here. They have a warehouse where they collect the stuff together and then they take it down. Aria went there last night and got caught. They took her back down."

"So where is it then? You must know."

"I don't," I admitted in a small voice. "I've not got a clue."

"Do you know," Will started slowly, staring at the ground, "where Aria was going when I met her yesterday?"

"I've no idea. I didn't even know that she had gone out."

"I was on my way back from the dentist," he said, still looking intently at the pavement, "and I saw her on the corner of the street, just standing and staring at something over the road."

"What? What was it?"

"She was staring down a side road, but there was nothing much down there as far as I can remember. I didn't really take much notice; I was more concerned about whether she was OK. She looked upset. I stopped to ask her if she was lost, and she seemed so miserable I took her for a coffee."

"Do you remember where she was?" I asked.

I tried not to give in to the new feeling of dread that was creeping up on me. Aria hadn't gone out looking for Will, he had found her – stumbled over her, even – and asked her to join him. I had been accusing her of something she hadn't done. I felt cold sweat prickle the back of my neck as I realised that I was doubly responsible for this whole mess. I had to try to fix it, and there was no time to lose.

"Come on, Will, where was it?" I urged.

Then I realised that he wasn't really staring at the ground, but thinking hard. He put up his hand to keep me quiet.

"I came out of the dentist's, turned down past the church, then ... where? Where was I going?"

He was muttering to himself. I kept still, hardly daring to breathe.

"I had to get a loaf for Mum, so I was heading to the supermarket on the High Street!" he exclaimed suddenly. "I can't remember exactly where she was, but if we retrace my steps I should recognise it."

"That's great, Will! Come on then!"

We hurried down the road, stopping at Will's house to drop off Foggy first. He wasn't happy about it, but at last Will had agreed that he didn't want to be responsible for any harm coming to the dog. We shut him in the back garden and then dodged into my place to pick up Nan's old stick and a couple of torches. Nan loved a torch, and there were usually plenty of them round, but this time they proved tricky to find. As I searched, the realisation that I had driven Aria into running away kept me in a constant state of feeling sick. What if we didn't get to her in time? Her death would be my fault. Every time I had that thought I had to take a deep breath and focus on getting everything that we needed for our plan.

One thing I absolutely had to do was ring the school and pretend to be sick. I dialled the number from the phone in the hall and held my nose as the school's absence line answerphone picked up.

"Hello," I said croakily. "This is Lizzie Wakefield, Lily Blackthorne's guardian. She's very under the weather today, terrible cold – we both have. She may be out for a day or two. Thank you."

"That was terrible acting," said Will. "And two days? Do you really think it'll take that long?"

"I was just trying to sound convincing," I admitted. "But who knows?"

I grabbed the hall notepad and scribbled a note:

Hi Nan

I forgot to remind you about the choir trip to Coventry. Back tomorrow.

Love Lily xxx

I looked at it as I put it down on the table. Hopefully I would be back before Nan even saw it. I couldn't let myself think of any other outcome.

"Will that be enough to convince her?" asked Will. "My mum always worries way too much about my sister, but she's more relaxed about what I do. I've just sent her a text though, so she should be OK for a bit. You're lucky that you don't have to worry about your mum..." His voice tailed off. I glanced over at him. His face was stricken.

"It's OK, Will, honestly. I'm used to it."

"I know, but that was thoughtless. Sorry." He gave me an apologetic smile.

He was right though. Mum would never have believed that note, so I was lucky that she was on the other side of the world.

"OK," I said as positively as I could manage. "That's the torches and the stick. Let's go and find this warehouse."

We jogged through the streets until we were at the far end of Marylebone High Street. Will stopped and looked around, a deep frown on his forehead.

"So where now then?" I asked impatiently.

"Shhh." He motioned me to be quiet with his hand. "I'm thinking."

"OK, sorry," I whispered, backing away and looking around.

This part of London was pretty old, with some tiny streets and lots of mews houses all jumbled together behind the big white mansions on the main roads. It was also stuffed full of restaurants, pubs and little boutiques selling hopelessly expensive things. There seemed to be plenty of deliveries in progress – white vans and lorries littered the roads, blocking some of the smaller ones as the surly drivers hefted large boxes into the service entrances.

Will suddenly looked up.

"Down here, I think," he announced, before diving across the street.

The street was narrow and bent around to the right, the tall buildings on either side blocking out all the sunshine. We dodged around the few pedestrians on the thin pavement and Will stopped dead.

"Yup, here. She was looking over there."

As we turned, a delivery truck pulled away and I could see a small road – barely more than a gap between the buildings with a cul-de-sac sign. An Italian restaurant was at the end, and to the left of it I glimpsed a grubby shutter.

"Look, there!" I hissed. "That looks like a warehouse!"

"It *could* be," he agreed, "and that was broadly where she was looking."

"You run over and see if you can see anything useful. They – or at least one of them – know what I look like, so I'd better not get too close until we're sure they've gone."

"OK, sounds sensible. Wish me luck."

As he turned to run over the road he gave me a quick smile, and I felt my heart melt. This was so ironic, the two of us working together to save Aria when it was going to help them be together, but I knew that I had to do it.

I stood in the doorway of a small bakery opposite the cul-de-sac, trying to look inconspicuous as Will checked out the building. In a few minutes he was back.

"So? What can you see?"

"There's nothing to see, only that shutter and a door with no window. I'm pretty sure that it doesn't belong to the restaurant though. There's a name on the door."

"And? What did it say?"

"Community Recycling," he said triumphantly. "Didn't you say that they called themselves the Community?"

I nearly hugged him in excitement, but stopped myself just in time.

"That has to be it. It's too much of a coincidence otherwise. Come on, let's see if we can get in there."

We tried not to run down the little lane but even so I felt really conspicuous. I couldn't help looking over my shoulder as we went, but Will was more confident, approaching the door as if he had every right to be there. The shuttered entrance was set back slightly into a corner, at right angles to the restaurant, and looked as if it might have once been a garage. The building was very old, just one storey high, and seemed to be squeezed into the gap left between the restaurant and the back of a shop. Next to the shutter was a painted wooden door.

I sauntered over to it as casually as I could. Will was right – it was really solid-looking. I tried the handle gently but it wouldn't budge. Pressing my ear as close to the wood as I could, I listened to what was going on inside. For a moment there was the distant hum of machinery, and then it went quiet. I froze, waiting to see if the machinery started again, but there was nothing. Grasping the door handle more firmly, I tried it again, but it still didn't give. Using both hands I gave it a hard wrench. Nothing happened. I hadn't really thought that we might actually have to break in. I turned to look at Will, hoping that he had some bright ideas. He was examining the shutter.

"Can you get this door open?" I hissed out of the side of my mouth.

He tried to look casual as he sauntered the few steps towards me, but it was blindingly obvious we were up to no good. Luckily the little street was deserted and no one on the main road was looking in our direction. He grasped the handle and tried to twist it sharply, the tendons on the inside of his wrist suddenly taut as it refused to turn.

"Er, no, I can't," he admitted. "Well, that blows that plan, doesn't it?"

He pressed his hand against the door but there was no give in it at all.

My sense of helplessness reared up again. She was going to die and it was all my fault. We *had* to get inside. The lock on the door seemed pretty old, and I wondered if we could slide something in like they do in the films. I started patting my pockets, hoping to come across something useful, and found my Oyster card.

"How about this?" I asked, trying unsuccessfully to force the piece of plastic in between the door and the frame.

"This might be easier," said Will, his back to me.

"What?"

"Look, down there. Something is caught under the shutter."

The grey metal security shutter was all the way down, but on the far side a discarded Coke can was wedged under it. The fire escape from the building next door provided some cover from the road, and no one could see Will kneel down next to it.

"I can get my fingers under here," he grunted, trying to pull the shutter up. "Come and help."

The metal was cold and felt utterly immovable, but I got a good grip.

"OK, when I say three, heave!" Will instructed.

This was our only chance. I had to make it work! On his count I pulled with every bit of strength I could find. I could feel him straining next to me, but nothing was happening.

"Come ON!" I muttered to myself.

Suddenly the shutter started to move, just fractionally at first, but as we heaved again it gained some momentum, creaking upwards to about knee height.

"We're in!" Will leaned in, bracing himself to take the weight. "Quick, get inside. I'm not sure how long I can hold this for."

I rolled under the shutter as quickly as I could, shoving the stick and the torch ahead of me, then took the strain from the inside, tensing my back and knees so that I didn't drop it and crush Will.

"I've got it. Come on under," I hissed, conscious of the darkness in the room.

In a moment he was through, and we lowered the shutter back into place before turning round to see what was behind us.

DON'T LOOK BELOW the SURFACE

CHAPTER 11

It was completely dark in the room apart from the tiny sliver of light coming from under the shutter.

"I'm glad we brought torches," whispered Will. "Ready to turn them on and see what's there?"

I nodded, then realised he couldn't see that.

"Uh-huh," I agreed, reaching for the torch in my pocket.

I knew from the smell that the Crop wasn't around, but who knew what else might be lurking in the shadows? Taking a deep breath, I flicked the switch.

The beam of light sliced through the dark, revealing a huge room with racks of shelving. The place was much colder than outside, with a slightly damp feel. It made me shiver. Carrier bags lined the shelves, but the place was hardly packed. Nearest to us was a large pile of bags that hadn't been put away.

"It must be the stuff they collected last night," I guessed.

I lifted myself up off the floor and swung the torch around. No one else was there. Will was already peering into the top bag of the pile.

"Sandwiches," he announced. "Hundreds of packets of out-of-date sandwiches. They look like the sort of stuff donated by the supermarkets to the homeless. I wonder…"

He paused for a moment but in the gloom I couldn't read the expression on his face.

"What?"

"How many of Aria's people can there possibly be? This would feed an army." His voice faded.

"Look, it's not too late to turn back, I promise you. I don't mind doing the rest of this alone now you've helped me get in."

"Don't be stupid, I'm not backing out now. It's just, I guess I wasn't expecting the Community to be so well organised."

"I suppose they've have had plenty of time," I said, using my torch to explore the rest of the long room.

At the back there was a door, and next to it was a really old-fashioned lift. The doors to the lift were just metal grilles that could concertina up, and in the thin beam of light I could see the gaping void going down into the darkness. That must have been the machinery that we heard, I realised. I gently tried the handle of the door, and for a moment I thought that was locked too, but as I applied a bit more pressure it suddenly gave. It squeaked horribly as I opened it enough to shine the torch inside.

"Stairs," I called over my shoulder.

I leaned over the banister and shone the torch beam downwards. The stairs spiralled down, disappearing into the dark.

"So that's our choice, is it?" asked Will, still peering into the bags. "Take the lift or go down the stairs?"

"The lift will be far too noisy," I replied. "Have you seen those gates? We'll never be able to slide them open silently. Everyone down there will know someone is coming. I think we'll have to walk."

He was about to reply when above us the lift machinery suddenly groaned, then slowly laboured into action, squeaking and protesting. Far away I could hear a chain rattle.

"Quick!" I hissed. "We have to go down the stairs. If they find us here we'll be in real trouble and we'll never save Aria!"

We were opening the stairs door when there was another sound, much closer. It was definitely scratching. My heart almost stopped beating. Was the Crop already here, hiding in a dark corner somewhere, or coming through a small, unnoticed entrance? I swung the torch around and saw a shadow shift out of the corner of my

THE
BENEATH

eye. Whatever was moving was by the shutter. Suddenly there was a long, drawn-out howl, making me jump.

"What the hell is that?" I whispered, feeling the hair on the back of my neck rise.

"Foggy!" exclaimed Will, racing over to the small space by the bottom edge of the shutter. "Did you follow me?"

I ran over with my torch and saw that the dog had got his leg through the gap and was scratching, trying to get inside. He didn't let up with the howling. Behind us, the lift machinery continued to groan.

"What are you going to do?" I asked, looking between the trapped dog and the lift. "You have to decide quickly!"

"He's going to carry on howling until we go back out there," shouted Will over the din. "I'll have to take him home again and come back."

"I'm sorry, Will, I can't wait. Aria's life is in danger and it's my fault. I have to go down those stairs now. I'll see you later."

"No, you can't go down there alone. Foggy will just have to come with us."

Will was hauling on the bottom of the shutter and suddenly Foggy burst through the gap, tail wagging furiously. The noise from the lift was much, much louder. Will let the shutter drop, and this time the can was crushed completely. There was no way we were going to get back out that way.

"Come on then, quickly! Get to the stairs."

I shone my torch towards the door and Will grabbed the dog by the collar, dragging him with us. As we eased the door shut behind us I could see the light of the lift coming up to the top of the shaft, and we were barely one turn down the stairs when I heard the clunk as it juddered to a halt. Light flooded the warehouse, outlining the door we had come through so brightly that we could see each other perfectly.

I motioned to Will to stay still, and he gave Foggy one of his stern looks. We were in full view of the doorway – if anyone opened it and looked down we would be utterly exposed. I realised that I was holding my breath, and released it as quietly as possible. Will looked equally tense as we listened to the lift doors being dragged open. Were they coming for us? The blood was pounding in my ears so loudly it was hard to hear what was happening. There were some scraping and thumping noises and the lift rattled.

"I think they're loading the sandwiches," Will mouthed at me. "Just stay still."

He kept his hand on the dog's head, and Foggy sat there, happy by his master, waiting for the next stage in this exciting game. He kept eyeing the stick, as if hoping I might throw it for him.

The loading seemed to take forever, and Foggy was just beginning to get restless when we heard the noise of the lift doors again and suddenly the lights went out.

It was pitch black, and Foggy whined slightly. I could hear Will comforting him, and then the lift rattled past us and was gone. We listened as it whirred for what seemed like an age, and finally it was silent. The lift had reached the bottom.

"That is a *long* way down," whispered Will. "Walking back up isn't going to be a lot of fun."

"And it's going to take us quite a while to get all the way down there," I replied, switching on my torch briefly. "Come on, we need to get going."

I tried to keep count of the number of turns in the staircase, but it was impossible, and the uneven steps didn't make it any easier. We tried to move silently, not knowing exactly who or what was at the bottom listening to us, but every so often I stumbled. A couple of times I heard Will swear under his breath as he missed his footing too. I tried not to think about what would happen if either of us tripped. There would be nothing to stop us tumbling all the way down.

I hadn't realised that walking downstairs so far would hurt quite so much. My legs were just about ready to give up when Will, who was ahead, gave a muffled grunt and the noise of metal clanging filled the stairwell, echoing around me.

"What's that?" I whispered, stopping immediately.

"Something across the stairs. I walked right into it – smacked into it with my leg. Hang on while I check it out. I think it might be a door."

The torch light was shockingly bright, but it showed us that Will was right – there was a heavy-looking chain-link gate barring our way, leading to a small landing.

"Do you think we're at the bottom?" he asked, rubbing his knee.

"I'm not sure. It seemed a long enough way."

He pointed his torch across the landing, but all I could see was a corridor snaking off round a corner.

"We have to go through the gate, but it doesn't look as if it's locked. Are you ready?"

I didn't know what I was supposed to be ready for, but I was about to agree when Foggy charged past me, nearly knocking me over. He had followed us obediently down the stairs but was now bouncing around, clearly enthusiastic about this change in scenery.

"Hang on a sec," I said, grabbing the dog by the collar. "We have no idea what's down there and we don't want Foggy running off. Have you got something that you can use as a lead? How about your belt?"

"I could use that, but … umm … the thing is, I'm not sure how well my jeans will stay up without it."

I was pleased that he couldn't see my expression in the dark. "We can use mine then. It just won't be as long as yours."

I quickly unthreaded mine from the belt loops of my jeans and strung it through Foggy's collar. He sat for a moment while I did it, then scratched his ear so enthusiastically that he rolled off the step, nearly knocking me over.

"Lucky that the gate is there," said Will, "or you'd have been off down the stairs."

He paused for a second as I gathered up the end of the makeshift lead, his hand resting on the latch for the gate. I flicked on my torch and directed the beam so that we could see what we were stepping into, but all that I could see was more stone floor.

"Here, let me have the stick," he said as I juggled the torch and the lead. I handed it over. "Ready?"

He waited until I nodded before undoing the gate. It squeaked horribly as he pushed it, and Foggy lurched forward, growling.

"OK," I whispered, following the dog through the gate into the space beyond. "What have we got here?"

The smooth stone floor of the landing turned a corner into a corridor that led to a vast, echoing cavern. The rough ceiling was supported by stone pillars, which made seeing any distance with the torches quite impossible. It was warmer than up in the warehouse, and there was a distinctly musty smell. The stone floor was covered in a sprinkling of what looked like dark gravel. There was no obvious sign of either the lift shaft or any more stairs down.

"Is this the bottom?" asked Will, keeping close behind me and checking our backs as we walked further into the cavern.

"I've got no idea. We need to find the lift."

"We can't have got too far from it. That has to be completely vertical, and the stairs seemed to be reasonably straight, at least for most of the way."

"Well, we don't want to go too far in here. We'll get hopelessly lost. Let's go back to where we came in and see if we can work it out."

All the time we were talking I could feel Foggy straining on the lead. I shone my torch on him briefly; he was poised to attack, his hackles up and his teeth bared. A low grumble came from his chest.

"Will, look at Foggy!" I hissed.

Will swung round.

"Wow, there's something here he really doesn't like. Come on, let's back up. Let me take the dog."

I gratefully handed over the belt, which had been digging into my palm, and looked at the corner we had come round.

"Where is that lift?" I asked, mainly to myself.

I tried to visualise where we might be, but there was no clue. It was difficult enough to see where we had come in; the place was a complete warren.

"What's that noise?" asked Will, swinging his torch around wildly.

I listened hard, and for a moment could only hear our own breathing and the continued low growl of the dog.

"Shh, Foggy, that's a good dog."

Foggy stopped to breathe for a moment and then I could hear it – the distant hum of machinery.

"It's the lift! It must be going up again! Quick, if we can find the sound we might be able to find the stairs down."

The noise got louder and both Will and I ran to where we thought it was, but the strange chamber made the acoustics difficult. Any minute and it was going to be past us. Suddenly there was a loud metallic scraping sound from somewhere directly behind us.

"There! Quick, that must be it! The stairs just came out facing away from it, that's all."

We ran to where we thought we had heard the noise, dodging round columns and dragging a reluctant Foggy behind us. He seemed to want to stay and investigate.

"Here," said Will triumphantly. "Look, a lift door."

As I shone my torch beam towards him I could see that he was nearly right. It was the entrance to the lift, but there was no concertina gate like the one upstairs, just a gaping space. In the thin beam of light I could see the greasy cable, quivering as it pulled the lift up to street level. I didn't dare get too close, but the shaft down disappeared into darkness.

There was a distant clunking noise and the cable stopped suddenly. In the unexpected silence I could hear something else, a scraping sound that was getting very distinct over the growling of the dog. At almost exactly the same time I became aware of a musty, dead smell. It was a smell I knew, and a shiver of fear ran through me. It took me a few long seconds to find my voice.

"Will! The Crop is coming. We need to find that way down now!"

"Wh – what? Where?"

"Out there – look!"

The scraping noise was getting closer, and the darkness was playing tricks with my eyes. I knew they were there in the gloom – I could somehow sense them even if they were still invisible.

"I can't see anything," said Will, but there was a hint of panic in his voice and I knew that he could smell them too. "Where are they? *What* are they?"

"I don't know but we have to go. NOW."

"Where the hell are those stairs?" he shouted. "They have to be here somewhere. Think. Come on, stupid! THINK!"

I realised then that he was talking to himself. He paced up and down in front of the lift shaft a few times, torch beam sweeping backwards and forward as he struggled to control Foggy. I turned to face the chamber, holding the stick up in front of me, not wanting to be attacked by something I hadn't seen. Foggy was straining to get past me. Whatever it was, he thought that he could give it a good fight.

From the corner of my eye I was conscious of the shadows starting to move, but every time I tried to shine my torch towards them, they were gone. The noise was all around, and I knew that we were surrounded. I stepped

backwards to be closer to Will. If this was going to be it,
I could at least go holding his hand. The slithering noise
I remembered from before was getting closer, and the
smell made me want to gag.

"Get away from us!" I screamed, as Foggy erupted
into a frenzy of barking.

I took another step back and heard a gasp, followed
by a sudden draught of air behind me.

"Will?" I called. "Where are you?"

I spun round, waving my torch to and fro, but all I
could see was the empty shaft. Foggy shot past me, his
lead dragging on the floor, before coming to a sudden
halt. He growled menacingly but started edging his way
back to me.

"Will?" I whispered into the darkness. "Will? Where
are you?"

The blood drained from my face and I felt instantly
cold. As Foggy reached me I automatically stooped to
pick up his lead, not wanting to believe what I suspected.
But I could see with my torch that Will was gone. He must
have stepped back over the edge in the dark.

I had killed him.

My heart contracted in a vice-like grip. In the distance
I could hear a low moaning, and it took a few more
seconds to realise that it was me. I'd fallen to my
knees and was rocking, hanging on tightly to Foggy's
comforting neck.

What had I done? He'd only been trying to help me,

to rescue the girl he fancied. He didn't deserve to die. If the Crop came to kill me now, then I truly deserved it.

"But you don't deserve it, Foggy," I gulped through my tears, holding on to the dog. "I'm so, so sorry."

The route back to the landing was now a seething mass of shadows, and there was no way back. Nan would never know what had happened to me.

I was suddenly very, very angry. I stood up straight and pulled Foggy close to me.

"Leave us alone!" I hissed into the darkness, just as Foggy let out an ear-splitting howl and something grasped my arm. Spinning round I saw Will, grinning in my torch beam. My heart leapt in relief.

"Where did you go?" I spluttered, outrage instantly overtaking the relief.

"No time. Quick, come with me, but stay very close."

He dragged me towards the side of the lift shaft, and, standing on the edge, reached around *inside* the shaft and pulled himself out of sight. Stifling a gasp of horror, I peered around with my torch. The shaft wasn't just a straight column up and down – from about a metre below me the side wall had been dug away to make a small ledge that ran the width of the shaft from front to back. Will was standing on a ladder built into the wall, his torch in his mouth. I lit up the ground below him with my beam, and could just see that at the far end there was a metal door. It was very well hidden – it would be utterly invisible when the lift was stopped, and when the lift was gone the vast drop down the shaft would stop the Crop – whatever it was – trying to leap across to the ledge.

"Quick," called Will. "Pass Foggy to me."

"Are you mad? He's far too heavy – I'll drop him!"

He hesitated for a moment, frowning.

"OK, you get down there and I'll let him down to you."

Will scrambled off the ladder and grabbed hold of Foggy and the stick while I reached round to find the stone steps. Although Will was shining his torch in my general direction I was very glad that I couldn't see the drop. The stone was warm and slippery, and as I tried to hold it I could feel my hands start to slide. The musty-smelling air coming from the depths of the shaft swirled around me, and for a second I had a vision of letting go and tumbling head first into the blackness.

"Don't think about it," I told myself. "Just hold on…"

I looked over at Will, who was holding on to Foggy's lead tightly.

"No rush here, Lily," he said, glancing over his shoulder. "You take your time."

"Sorry," I mumbled.

I took a deep breath and forced myself down the steps on to the ledge at the bottom. It was wider than I thought, running towards to the back of the lift shaft, where I could just see the door. I put my torch on the floor so that I could see without having to hold it.

"Here, take Foggy," Will urged, a hint of panic in his voice.

He was leaning over, the dog in his arms. Standing underneath I could just get my fingertips to him, but Will was going to have to drop him. Foggy didn't like it at all and started to wriggle and whimper.

"Foggy!" shouted Will.

He let go and Foggy dropped into my arms. My knees nearly buckled, but I held on the thrashing mass of fur and claws for long enough to lower him on to the ledge, holding tightly to his makeshift lead.

As soon as he was safely down I looked back up at Will. He was no longer looking down at me, but over his shoulder, his torch beam swinging wildly.

"Don't look, Will, just jump!"

I grabbed the dog and backed carefully up the ledge towards the door so that there was room for Will to land.

"Jump! Come on!"

The old, rotting smell of the Crop was almost overwhelming.

"What the hell are these things? Get back!"

I heard a scuffling noise and he jumped. Foggy leapt towards him, blocking most of the light from the torch. Will thumped down next to me and swore loudly. As I hauled Foggy back I could see Will hadn't jumped far enough and was teetering on the edge of the drop. I lunged forward, grabbing his hand and wrenching him towards me. We fell backwards, a jumble of arms, legs

and dog, then he leapt up.

"Quick, Lily, we've got to get out of here!"

He threw open the door and the three of us tumbled through, slamming it shut behind us.

CHAPTER 12

The sudden silence was disconcerting. The old metal door was really solid, studded with rivets, and nothing like the flimsy chain-link one that led upwards. I sank to the floor in relief, and Will sat down beside me, leaning back against the rough stone wall. Foggy was bouncing around with the excitement of it all, leaping between us and trying to lick our faces. I felt as if my heart was about to burst through my chest, and tried to breathe steadily to calm it down.

"Whatever that is, they don't want it coming down here," said Will, examining the door with his torch before turning the beam on to his own feet. "I must have caught my ankle on something. It really hurts."

He leaned forward and pulled up the leg of his jeans.

"You're bleeding," I said. "Let me see properly."

I put my torch on the floor so that I could use both my hands and see what I was doing. On his ankle was a deep scratch, and as I tried to look at it he winced and flinched away.

"It looks really painful. How on earth did you do that?"

"When I was jumping I felt it catch on something. I didn't stop to see what it was."

"I don't know what I have to put on it," I said, patting my pockets. "Ah no, hang on, I've got a tissue."

I pulled the slightly fluffy tissue from my back pocket and folded it open before pressing it on the scratch.

"There," I said, leaning back. "You should be able to pull your sock up over that to keep it in place."

"Thanks," he said, smiling. "All better now."

"Don't be so sarcastic," I said, laughing in relief and playfully thumping him on the arm.

We sat in silence for a moment, catching our breath.

"What are they?" I asked. "Did you actually get to see one of them?"

He shook his head.

"No, nothing, but they were very close as I jumped down. I thought I was done for, but Foggy must have scared them off."

I glanced around.

"Where's the stick?" I asked.

"Ah, sorry. It's still up there. I think I threw it at one of them."

We were now completely defenceless with only Foggy

to help us. Would he be enough? I pulled the dog closer to me and he gave a little woof in response.

"How on earth did you spot this door?" I asked.

"To be honest, I was panicking," Will said. "With the Crop getting closer I knew we had to escape, and the lift shaft was the only guaranteed way down. I looked over the edge to see if maybe there was a ladder down the shaft when I saw the ledge and the door. I had to check it wasn't locked, so I jumped over. It practically blew open with the rush of air from down there."

"I felt the air," I said in a small voice. "I thought you'd fallen … or jumped."

"Don't be daft! You're not that scary."

He nudged me hard with his elbow as he laughed.

"Ha ha." I was still too traumatised to be able to laugh about it. "I just can't believe how close that was. I mean, if you hadn't found the way out we'd be dead by now."

"I'm sure they're not that dangerous, not really. I mean, they can't possibly have that many, whatever they are. And how would they breed them to live in the dark?"

I could tell that he was trying to make me feel better about the whole thing.

"Maybe," I said, not believing a word of it. "But neither of us is going to risk going back out there in a hurry, are we?"

That thought hung between us for a few moments as we caught our breath, and neither of us mentioned the problem that we were going to face going home.

We started down the corridor, which turned sharply to the right and led to a very narrow spiral staircase. This one was a much tighter spiral than the one above the Crop level, and walking down it I very quickly felt light-headed and dizzy. At one point I had to stop Will and Foggy and sit for a moment with my head in my hands, waiting for the world to stop spinning. Will looked equally grateful for the pause, but clearly hadn't been going to ask, and Foggy seemed blissfully unaffected. All too soon we were on our way again.

After what seemed like an age Foggy started to strain at the lead.

"I can smell something," I whispered, putting my hand out in the dark to stop Will.

I expected to tap his arm, but I realised too late that it was his waist. Snatching my hand back, I was pleased that he couldn't see the colour of my cheeks.

As we stood in the dark on the stairs we became aware of other noises – clattering and the murmur of voices. It all sounded spookily familiar.

"It's the canteen!" I whispered to Will. "It sounds just like the one at school. That's what we can smell."

"I guess it makes sense to have the lift with the supplies going somewhere close to where they eat."

"If it's just the canteen, maybe there's not too much security," I suggested.

"They seem quite keen on security, if you think about it." He sounded doubtful.

"I know, but perhaps they don't think that anyone will make it past the Crop. Maybe, anyway," I finished lamely. My heart was sinking fast as I faced the enormity of what we were trying to do. We were about to launch ourselves into the middle of a hostile community, with no idea of where we were going or what sort of technology they had, armed only with couple of rubber-handled torches and a hairy dog.

"Will…" I started, but he spoke at the same time.

"Well, at least we are at the bottom now. That's one step closer to Aria."

He sounded remarkably cheerful.

"Right, yes," I blustered quickly before he could realise I was getting cold feet. "I guess we need a plan. How are we actually going to find her?"

We listened to the noises of the people below us. There seemed to be quite a crowd.

"If we just march in there we'll have no chance," said Will. "Perhaps we can find a back route, or maybe we could mingle with them inconspicuously – what do you think?"

"It's a tiny community – they'll spot strangers in an instant," I snapped. "Sorry," I added quickly. "It's just … I'm just getting really worried about how we're going to do this."

"I know, and we have to find her soon, or…"

The two of us stood silently for a moment on the stairs, listening to Foggy pulling at his lead to get to the food.

I was just about to suggest that we see if we could bribe someone to take us to Aria when Will breathed in sharply.

"Yes! Why didn't I think of that earlier?"

"What? What have you come up with?"

"Foggy!"

At his name the dog jumped back up the steps to stand next to his master.

"How can he help?"

"He can sniff her out!"

"You're kidding me," I said, remembering all the times I'd seen Foggy searching for lost balls. "He can never find anything."

"He's not good at finding toys, that's true, but he's not bad at people. At home we hide and get him to find us. He really enjoys it."

He paused for a second and I could almost sense him thinking through his plan.

"Do you have anything of Aria's with you?" he asked.

"No, not with me, but she borrowed this hoodie from me yesterday. She wore it for most of the day – would that do?"

"Well, it's worth a go, don't you think?"

As I peeled off the hoodie I braced myself against the cold, but it was warmer than I expected. I just wished that the T-shirt I was wearing wasn't quite so tight. I handed the top over to Will and he scrunched it up before pressing it to the dog's nose.

"Here, Foggy, smell this. Find her!"

There was a moment's confusion as Foggy tried to leap up and lick me, but Will pulled him back down again and gave him another sniff of the top.

"No, Foggy, the other one. Find her!"

There was no way that the dog could possibly understand what he was saying, but he hesitated for a moment before making off down the stairs, dragging Will behind him.

"We still have to keep out of sight," I reminded him as with each turn the dark of the stairs gave way to a stronger light.

But the two of them were on a mission and had raced ahead. As I turned the last corner I saw them both silhouetted in a small stone archway, and then they were gone.

CHAPTER 13

I peered cautiously out of the archway and into the narrow corridor beyond. It was made of stone, rubbed smooth with years of wear. A wire was tacked along the centre of the rounded ceiling connecting a string of light bulbs that were giving off a gentle glow.

The corridor was completely empty except for Will, who was being dragged along by Foggy. If anyone were to come out of any of the many other archways I could see we would be spotted in an instant. It was also eerily silent – the canteen noises we had heard earlier had stopped. All I could hear were Will and Foggy's footsteps.

"Will!" I hissed. "You can't just go marching off! You need to be able to hide." I glanced into a room that we were passing. "This is empty; get in here for a moment."

"Look, I know you're worried about getting caught," he

said as he followed me into the gloomy, cave-like space, which was little more than an alcove in the corridor, "but honestly, we don't have a lot of choice, do we?"

I was about to object when he put his hand on my shoulder.

"I'll keep you as safe as I can, Lily, I promise you, but if we want to save Aria we have to get on with it."

Swallowing hard I looked up and wished for a second that we were somewhere – anywhere – else. And then I heard a distant bell. It sounded like an old-style handbell, and it was being rung really slowly as if by someone who was really bored by the task. Will leapt towards Foggy, clamping his jaws together and cutting off the bark that was about to erupt from him.

"Shhh, Foggy. Here, have a biscuit."

The dog instantly changed from an animal that was alert and ready to fight to one begging enthusiastically. Will whipped out the little pouch in his pocket and dug around inside it. He produced a tiny ball of dried food.

"Is that really going to do it?" I whispered, still listening to the bell, which was definitely getting louder.

"Every time. He's easily pleased, aren't you, boy?"

Foggy sat there, tongue lolling, as Will patted his head. I held my breath, waiting to be discovered, straining for any change in the noise.

After a few long minutes I heard Will exhale noisily. "I think the bell is getting further away now," he said. "I wonder what all that was about?"

As he spoke the lights in the corridor silently blinked out, leaving us in total darkness.

I come round as the nap bell rings and the room is suddenly plunged into darkness. I will have an hour's peace before he starts on me again. So many questions! I keep telling him it was all a mistake, but I can tell he thinks that I'm lying, and I know that his patience is wearing thin.

What would the Farmer say if he actually knew about our plan? Would he be surprised that some of us had had the courage to try and mount our own revolution to depose him? Some of the Elders must know that the Farmer's ideas are madness, that there is no way he can attack. Some of them may even think like us, but I'll never know. Right now I'm safer saying nothing. I know that he wants to send me to the Crop – that was clear as soon as he started to question me, but he is desperate to find out how I got past it and up Above.

I would really like to see Carita again before … I can't even think the words. I wish I'd gone to see her before I went Above and started this mess. Maybe she would have talked me out of it. Maybe I'd have accepted my Assignment and would now be snoozing gently in my bed instead of lying on this cold floor, waiting.

An image of Dane flashes through my mind and I feel a stab of real pain in my chest. I know that I failed in the mission, that I should never have gone beyond the tunnels – and stayed Above – that he must feel I betrayed him. If it had only been him on the street the other day and not Neville, if I hadn't felt so bad about staying, if only he had spoken with me, maybe things would be different. And worst of all, I can't believe that he told Lily he loved me. Not now it's all too late.

I saw him briefly when I was brought back down – he was part of the group of Listeners who escorted me through the Community to the cells. I tried not to look at him too much, but I was able to stand close to him as they led me through a small doorway. I didn't dare say much, but I did mumble "I'm sorry" to him as I pretended to bump into him. He wouldn't even glance in my direction.

He must be terrified that I'm going to reveal his part in our plan, because that would earn him a place next to me with the Crop.

When I think about the Crop, I find it hard to breathe and I start to shake. I curl up in a small ball and try to shut out the nightmares by telling myself one of the stories that Lily read to me, but my thoughts quickly turn to the wonders I have seen Above. I can't – and I won't – forget. At least I won't die having spent my entire life below ground; I won't die never having seen anything important or never having tasted the air. Proper, fresh air. But I will still die. Nothing can change that now.

"Maybe it was a bell for lights-out. Aria mentioned something the other day about having a nap."

There was a chuckle in the darkness. "Of course! They've all gone to bed."

"I didn't realise that they all do it at once though," I said. "This will make it much, much easier to investigate the place. They'll all be tucked up in bed!"

"Even if it does make finding Aria much, much harder," agreed Will with a smile in his voice. "OK, torches at the ready."

We slipped back out of the door, and, keeping our torches low so that they would attract less attention, started making our way down the corridor. The yellow pools of light lit up the dusty floor, which looked like polished rock.

"I think this must be a service tunnel," whispered Will as we went past a series of dark openings, which seemed to be rough doorways without actual doors. "Look in there."

He pointed with his torch. The doorway opened on to a chamber that was packed full of crates. We couldn't resist seeing what was in the top one.

"Tins of corned beef," he said, putting one back in the crate. "Yuk. All the labels are damaged, as if they've been under water. This one's rusty. Even Foggy won't eat that. It's a wonder they've not all died of food poisoning."

"So if this is a service tunnel connecting the lift and the supplies with the canteen, there must be some sort of main street, I guess."

I was trying to imagine a map of the tunnels.

"That was probably where the person with the bell was walking," said Will. "It wasn't too far away from here."

His logic seemed sensible.

"OK, let's keep on this one for now, if we can. I guess it will all depend on where Fóggy leads us."

The dog looked up at the mention of his name, and Will gave him the top to sniff again.

"Right then, Foggy, find her!"

Foggy jumped up and started off out of the little room without hesitation. I flicked my torch left and right – luckily the corridor was clear in both directions so the two of us jogged along behind him. All the time I was watching over my shoulder for light or movement, trying not to think about what might happen if someone turned into the corridor and saw us. But no one appeared.

As we ran we kept the torches on. The darkness without them was so utterly black we would have run straight into the first bend in the wall, but even with the comforting little puddles of light I hoped that Foggy wasn't going to suddenly nip to the side and cause a pile-up.

He led us unerringly through what must have been a maze of tunnels, with turn after turn. I tried to keep a picture of where we were going in my head, but it was impossible. With the limited light we had there was no way of spotting any landmarks, and I tried not to think about how we would get back out again if we didn't find Aria. There was no way we could instruct the dog to retrace our steps. At one point we crossed a very much wider corridor. I could feel a breeze of warm air on the side of my face, and the floor was so polished and worn it was no longer flat. Countless feet had worn grooves in the rock, and when I lifted the torch the thin beam of light disappeared into the distance. Still Foggy carried on, taking us further and further from any escape route. As we rounded one corner I stumbled on a ridge in the ancient floor, putting out a hand to steady myself in the dark. Will grasped it to stop me falling but didn't let go.

"Are you OK?" he whispered.

Will was holding my hand.

"I think so," I mumbled, distracted.

We negotiated another bend in the corridor and I was suddenly conscious of a change in the air. There was an unexpected feeling of space and distance all around us. I stopped dead, and I felt Will freeze too. We both clicked off our torches. Some strange sense told me that we were no longer alone.

Gripping tightly on Will's fingers, I tried to pull him back to the tunnel. There was an unmistakable noise of people – lots and lots of them moving, breathing and snoring – and I knew we were in trouble.

"Hey, you, what are you doing out of bed?" hissed a man's voice. "It's nap time."

We froze.

Will was the first to gain his voice.

"Toilet. Not well," he hissed back as I quickly groped for Foggy. If the dog growled, we were finished. I clamped my hands round his muzzle and we backed carefully into the tunnel without anyone raising the alarm. Feeling my way along the wall I led Will back round the corners we had turned before he risked flicking on his torch for a moment, shielding most of the light with his hand.

"That was close," he whispered. "What are we going to do now?"

"It was *too* close. They might follow us at any minute. We need somewhere to hide, and quickly."

Will turned the torch on the walls, but there were no doorways into rooms where we could hide.

"Quick, back down here. I think we passed some doorways down this one," Will said, catching my hand again to pull me along.

"Here, look down here," I gasped as we passed a small corridor with lots of archways off it. "Another service route."

"Good call," agreed Will, turning to following my torch beam.

We moved silently down the corridor and stopped by the first doorway. Will flicked his torch around it briefly. It looked pretty empty, so we slipped inside, safe again in the dark. I felt my way along the rough wall and then stopped, leaning my back against it. I could hear my heart thumping in my chest.

"That was too close," I said to Will as I felt his warmth close beside me. "What on earth are we going to do now?"

"I don't know. Give me Foggy's lead, will you? I'll give him a treat."

"I don't have it – I thought you did."

"What! Where's he gone then?"

We heard a brief scraping noise. Will snapped on his torch, lighting up the face of a young woman who was hunched in the corner of the room. She let out an ear-splitting shriek that echoed around the empty corridors.

"Run!" I cried, grabbing Will's hand again and dragging him back out of the room.

"Strangers!" screamed the woman's voice behind us. "Strangers among us! Get them!"

As we ran the noise increased, more and more voices taking up the call. We ran almost blindly, torch beams waving madly around as we turned corner after corner, trying to get away. I thought we were pulling away, that the voices were getting fainter when yet again I was aware of a much bigger space around us. The torch couldn't find the wall so I shut it off quickly.

"Will," I hissed, stopping abruptly. "This isn't right. We must have gone in a circle."

"I know." His voice was wary. "Stay close to me."

Back to back we peered into the dark, only too aware of the commotion approaching from behind us. There was no way back that way.

"Have you got your torch ready?" he whispered over his shoulder to me.

"Yes."

"On the count of three, let's see what we've got here."

I felt my mouth go dry and could feel my heart pounding in my chest.

"One," he started, his voice wavering a little.

"Two…" I joined in, holding my finger ready over the switch.

We never got to three. The room was suddenly starkly bright as all the lights came on. Blinking, I squinted around, pressing myself closer into Will's back. We were in a huge chamber, and all around the edges men were sitting up in low, uncomfortable-looking beds. As each one saw us they gasped, and the noise ran round the room like a wave. Then slowly – and almost as if they were being pulled by the same string – they got up and started advancing towards us.

Will's hand found mine and squeezed tightly. "Not exactly part of the plan then," he said, obviously trying to sound calmer then he felt. "Can you see Foggy anywhere?"

"N … no," I stammered as the crowd began to tighten in a ring around us.

This was all my fault – I had to try to do something about it. For a second I closed my eyes and took a deep breath, trying to calm myself so that I wouldn't squeak.

"I'm sorry that we disturbed you," I said as clearly as possible, trying to catch the eye of any of the men who were now circling us. "I'm afraid we got lost. We're—"

"You, strangers! What is the meaning of this?" I spun

round to see a thickset, bearded man advancing towards us from the line. He was wearing a badly fitting suede jacket and pinstripe trousers, all hugely creased, and he looked furious. He stopped a few metres away and folded his arms. "Who are you? How did you get here?"

"We're from Above," said Will, standing up straight and tightening his hold on my hand before leaning back towards me and muttering under his breath, "We're just going to have to brazen this out."

We stood back to back in the middle of the circle of angry men.

"And what are you doing here, eh?" said the man menacingly.

"We're looking for a friend of ours."

There was a murmur from the crowd and I sneaked a glimpse at them. They were watching us closely, pointing and frowning, and commenting to each other. Will's blond hair particularly seemed to fascinate them. All of them were wearing a strange mix of clothes that looked as if they had all come from a raid on an Oxfam shop. Nothing matched and, like the clothes of the man who had spoken, everything was really crumpled. The men themselves were very lean and some looked very grubby, which seemed out of place in the otherwise clean environment.

"What makes you think he'll be all the way down here with us?" asked the bearded man.

"It's a girl, actually," started Will. "Her name's Aria."

The muttering of the crowd stopped abruptly. You could have heard a pin drop.

The bearded man took the last step and thrust his face close to Will's.

"Aria? You come here looking for Aria?"

Will didn't flinch.

"Yes, sir. She's our friend and we believe she needs our help. Can you take us to her, please?"

There was a gasp from the crowd.

"Oh, we'll take you to her, don't you worry," said the man with a nasty smile.

I felt a distinct chill ripple through me. "What do you mean?"

"I mean that you can join her in fulfilling a useful function. We're a bit short of Feeders at the moment, you see, so the Farmer will be delighted to have some visitors."

Everything stopped. Without looking I could feel Will close beside me.

"I don't understand," he said to the man.

"It's very simple. You're not welcome down here, and yet you came, so you must be punished. You'll get a trial, but as you're clearly guilty the Farmer will have no choice – you will both become Feeders." He looked slowly from Will to me, and back again. "No one leaves the Community. Ever."

CHAPTER 14

Will and I were grabbed from behind and our captors wrenched our arms up behind our backs. The pain was excruciating.

"Hey," I called after a few minutes. "There's no need to be so rough. Where am I going to run to?" The man holding me ignored me completely.

"Can you give her a break, please?" asked Will, calling over his shoulder. "She's right – where are we going to go?" The next thing I heard was a grunt as his guard practically doubled him over. Neither of us said another word.

We were bundled along the twisting corridors, unable to make any sense of the direction in which we were travelling, before stopping abruptly. I lifted my head to see a wide door, which was thick and studded with huge strengthening bars. Whatever was on the other side clearly wasn't getting out – or in. I shivered, hoping that it wasn't another entrance to the Crop. I really didn't want to face it again, not before I'd had the chance to make some sort of a deal, and there was no point in making a deal with guards, if that's what they were.

"I need to talk to the Farmer," I announced as we waited outside the door.

There was a moment of stunned silence before one man gave a hollow laugh. Will was doing his best to stand upright with his wrist rammed up between his shoulder blades, but he caught my eye and nodded.

"We both need to see him," Will said in a strained voice. "We've got important information for him."

The man holding him relaxed his grip momentarily, allowing Will to straighten up. He was taller than most of the men and I could see them take an almost imperceptible step backwards. The guy with the beard pushed his way through the crowd.

"What's this? What's going on?" he boomed in his deep voice.

"We need to see the Farmer. Both of us."

"What business do you have with him?"

"I really don't think that's any of your concern, do you?" retorted Will, staring at him unblinkingly.

The two of them eyeballed each other for a moment before the bearded guy looked away.

"Maybe they've come to let us know about an

invasion," called one guy from the back.

"Silence!" roared the man with the beard towards the small crowd. "Not another word in front of them. Lock 'em up," he said gruffly, handing over a large key to the man holding Will. "I'll get the Farmer."

There was a great wrenching noise as the key turned in the enormous lock and slowly the door swung open. We were bundled into another dimly lit corridor, but the men seemed to be treating us with slightly more respect. The Farmer was clearly not someone you called on lightly.

All the other corridors had been clean and smooth, but beyond the door the air was damp and the floor was roughly dug stone, which was awkward to walk on. A couple of times I stumbled when I caught my toe, and the man holding me hauled me back upright again. Above us, the lights on the string were dim and really far apart, creating long stretches of gloom in the low, winding tunnel. The man holding my arm suddenly stopped. He yanked my wrist up and gave a smile I didn't like.

"You'll not be needing this now," he said, laughing, and ripped my watch off. He threw me to the side. I crashed down on to the rough floor, sharp stones digging into my knees and arms.

"Give me that back!" I yelled, jumping up, but it was too late. He slammed a metal gate shut behind me. Then there was a scuffing and a clanging noise some way off to my left and I guessed that they were throwing Will into another cell.

"What's happening? Where are you going?" I grabbed the bars, shouting as I heard their retreating footsteps. "I want to see the Farmer!"

There was no answer, just the dull thud of a distant door slamming shut.

Everything went quiet.

I looked around. I was in a small cell with stone walls, locked in by the metal gate made of rusty bars. They had used a huge key which must have been centuries old. Was the rest of the gate that old? I shook it gently, seeing the red dust fall from the extensive rust patches.

"This is ancient," I said to myself as I shook it harder. More rust fell on to the uneven floor. I stood back and faced the lock, and summoned all my anger at being caught. Then I took a deep breath and kicked out, remembering a long-ago judo lesson. There was a satisfying crack.

Without thinking about how much it had hurt, I kicked again. The old lock fell to pieces and tumbled to the floor. I was free.

Something strange is going on. There has been shouting in the distance, and the sound of the door slamming, and although the lights have come back on the Farmer hasn't returned yet to question me again. I take the chance to look round my little cell properly. I always wondered where they kept the Feeders before the end. I had hoped it was somewhere nice, perhaps with a few little luxuries, but clearly not. The stone floor is damp, and the mattress of old rags I'm sitting on smells horribly mouldy. I'm trying to decide whether to risk eating some of the food they left me earlier when there are a couple of short, sharp bangs, and then moments later the sound of an unexpected voice getting closer.

"Where are you? Please say something!"

I'm so surprised that I freeze. Surely that can't be Lily? The voice gets louder.

"Are you OK? Please – where have they taken you?"

Footsteps are coming. I can't believe that this is happening. How has Lily got in here?

I hear her mutter, "This is hopeless. It's a complete rabbit warren." Then she takes a deep breath. "WHERE ARE YOU?"

The noise reverberates around the walls, making me jump.

"Lily?" I ask. "Is that you?"

My voice seems tiny and insignificant after that monumental bellow. There is a moment of silence before I hear feet running towards me.

"Aria?" The voice is quieter now, more tentative. "Are you really here?"

"I'm this way," I call. "Follow the sound of my voice. You're not far away now."

As I utter the last word, a figure appears in the open doorway of my small cell.

"Aria? Is that really you? Thank goodness you're OK!"

Relief and fear wash over me in waves. Relief that I haven't lost my friend after all, that she's risked everything to come and find me, but utter fear that she is here. Fear that I've actually completed my mission and what that means for her. I move out of the shadows.

"Lily – what are you doing here? How on earth did you manage to get past the Crop?"

Lily looks over at me and takes a small step, her hand reaching out before she drops it back to her side. She looks uncertain and I can't run over and hug her like I want to, to show her everything is OK.

"I'm so sorry, Aria. I made a terrible mistake and I had to try and put it right."

"What do you mean?"

"I mean that I thought that you—"

"Shhh! Wait a minute." *I put my finger to my lips.* "There's someone else here."

I listened hard, then caught the sound – a rhythmic thumping, and then, more distantly, a shout.

"Let me out of here! Lily! Where are you?"

I can't believe that Lily has taken such a terrible risk.

"Did you bring someone here with you?" *I ask.*

"It's Will. He wanted to help find you, obviously."

I sit back on the rag mattress, appalled.

"Will? You brought him down here? You have to get him out of here, and now!"

"It's OK for the minute. We've asked to see the Farmer."

This time I'm so surprised I can't actually speak. Lily can see my face.

"It's the only choice we have. He's the one in charge, isn't he? We were hoping to sneak down here and fetch you without being spotted, but it was harder than we thought, and calling on the Farmer seemed the only other choice. I'll just have to try and persuade him."

"The Farmer won't care what you want, believe me, and he absolutely won't tolerate Will," I say. "He'll be killed. You have to get him out of here, and quickly."

I can't keep the note of desperation out of my voice. I can't be responsible for Will's death.

"They're not really going to kill anyone, I'm sure. That would be barbaric."

Her voice is beginning to quiver and I can tell by the way she is biting her lip that she is trying to convince herself as she speaks. Before I can answer she takes a deep breath and steps back towards the door.

"Come on, you can fill me in on the important details as we release Will and find the way out. We need to escape."

She turns to leave and I lift my leg to show her my ankle.

"I'm not going anywhere. You're going to have to sort this out alone."

The heavy manacle has cut into my skin, leaving it red and raw.

"Oh my God!" Lily is on her knees, trying to prise the

metal ring off my leg. "It's inhuman! They can't do that to you."

"You have as much to learn about life down here as I did up there, you know. This isn't important; Will is important. You must go and rescue him. Men are not the ones needed down here."

"But—"

"Listen to me, I'm stuck here." I grab the chain and yank it hard to prove my point. "That's why there is no door on this cell. You have to get Will, please, before it's too late! Hide by the door and run for it as soon as it's open. Find your way back out again and leave immediately. And don't ever come back in here…"

I'm willing her to leave while I'm still being brave. I don't want to break down and sob like a child. I can't believe that they've come to rescue me, and for a moment I am overwhelmed. I feel the tears threatening to come. I don't deserve their help, so I turn away quickly.

Lily's hand is gentle on my shoulder.

"I'm so sorry, Aria. I had no right to expect you to forgive me. I didn't mean for any of this to happen."

She leans over and rests her cheek on my head. I reach for her hand to squeeze it, to show her that there was nothing to forgive, but she's gone, finally taking me at my word.

I lie back on the mouldy mattress, tears blurring my vision, and at last I feel at peace. I'm glad that she doesn't know the truth, and now there is no need to share it. I

know that she is my friend and will always be there for me. She's just proved that.

I can die more easily now I know I have a friend.

I ran blinded by tears down the dark, winding corridor away from Aria's cell, unable to believe what I'd done to her. She was chained to the wall! And from the way she had reacted to me, the way she had turned away, she still blamed me. She had every right to as well. If only I hadn't jumped to the wrong conclusions she'd never have come back down. And knowing that Will liked her too made the whole thing worse. My selfishness had created this mess. I had to find Will and get him to help me get her out.

After turning down a few corridors I stopped and leaned against one of the dank walls, groping for the tissue in my pocket. I blew my nose as quietly as possible, trying to keep from sobbing out loud.

"Lily? Is that you?" a voice hissed in the darkness.

Pale hands were clutching a set of bars that reached across the width of the corridor, and almost hidden in the gloom behind was Will. I wiped my eyes and ran towards him.

"Lily, thank goodness you're all right. When they took you off I thought..." He stopped as he saw my tear-streaked face. "You *are* all right, aren't you? They didn't hurt you, did they?"

"No, no. I'm fine. I've just seen Aria. She's—"

"Alive? Is she OK?" he interrupted before I could finish.

I nodded. "Alive, but trapped. She wants us to leave her and go. She says that there's no time to waste and that you are in terrible danger – and you specifically, but I'm not sure why."

"What? I'm not leaving her. Rescuing her is what this is all about, right?" He rattled the bars again. "Come on, help me get out of here. And how come you're not in a cell too?"

"I don't think they have very much regard for us girls. They put me a cell so flimsy that a quick kick sorted it out. I broke the lock on the second attempt."

I stepped back, sniffing loudly and wiping my face again. The bars spanned the full width of the tunnel, with a small door in the middle, like an old-fashioned prison cell. The door had a solid iron lock, and I shook it hard but the gate didn't budge.

"It looks as if you've been rather more securely locked up. Did you see what they did with the key?"

"No, they threw me in here and slammed it shut before I could turn round."

"I can't believe this is all going so horribly wrong," I whispered. "We're all locked up in here and waiting to die."

"I'm not waiting around for that, thank you," said Will. "Stand back!"

He took a flying kick at the lock before landing in a

heap on the floor with a loud groan. The lock hadn't budged.

"Damn it. That always works in the movies," he said, getting up and rubbing his foot. "Shouldn't have used my bad ankle either, really."

But I was watching the little trail of stone dust that was still tumbling from the ceiling where the bars were fixed in.

"The lock didn't move, but the whole line of bars did. I wonder…"

I took a firm hold of two of the bars near the wall and began to push them backwards and forwards. At first the give was almost unnoticeable, but quickly the metalwork began to move.

"Come on, you've weakened it. You get the other side."

With Will pulling as I pushed, we soon had the whole section of bars moving by a couple of centimetres, and eventually the old, rusty iron could take it no more. One of the main crossbars broke and a section of the bars fell in, showering us with stone dust and rust. Will eased through the gap, then stood up and gave me a quick hug.

"Thanks, Lily, it feels good to be out of there. Now, let's see if we can persuade Aria to come with us."

"She's chained to the wall, so we'll need to fix that first."

I was talking over my shoulder as I led the way back

towards Aria's cell.

"Chained? Nice people. Which way now?"

I stopped dead. I had no idea, and two corridors twisted and turned away from us.

"It's not too far. I was only running for a minute or two, and we could hear you banging on the bars. We have to be quick though."

"OK, there's only one quick way to do this," he said. "ARIA! ARIA, where are you?"

There was nothing but silence as a faint echo died away.

"She wants us to leave, to save ourselves and not waste time," I guessed. "ARIA! We're not leaving until we speak to you, so hurry up and tell us where you are!"

I paused for a moment, listening hard.

"I mean it, you know I do!"

"Over here."

Her voice was flat and resigned, and it came from a doorway not far from us. Will was off like a shot so I hung back slightly, not wanting to see their reunion. I couldn't help but hear though.

"My God, look at you!" Will's voice was shocked. "Are you OK apart from that? Have they hurt you?"

"Never mind that, you must go, now, both of you. You're in terrible danger!"

"Not without you, Aria. You're why we're here so it would be pretty pointless leaving without you."

There was a moment of silence and I jumped when I

heard my name being called.

"Lily, where are you? We need your help!"

I looked back down the dark, twisting tunnel. There was no sign of anyone coming. Inside the small cell, Will was sitting on the mattress next to Aria, pulling at the chain fixed into the wall.

"Come on, we need another one of your smart ideas. How are we going to get this free?"

A thought was nagging at my mind.

"The cell you were in wasn't exactly secure, was it?" I said. "I mean, they clearly don't expect people to choose to escape. It's very odd. Here, let me look at the manacle."

Aria held out her slim ankle, which was now bloodied and bruised. I sat down, resting her foot gently on my knee so that she didn't have to hold her leg up. The metal ring had a rough hinge and a rusty-looking keyhole. I wiggled the locked side but all I succeeded in doing was making Aria gasp as I accidently jarred it against her raw skin.

"Watch it, Lily. Be careful," muttered Will.

I guessed that he would rather be the one helping her. I sneaked a quick glance at Aria but she was looking down, bottom lip caught between her teeth.

"It's not as easy as I hoped," I sighed, bending over to try and see better in the dim light.

"They know there's nowhere to go!" exclaimed Will. "That's why security here is so rubbish."

"Of course!" I said. "That's exactly right. Why make it hard to escape when you're a prisoner in the first place?"

I straightened up for a moment, holding the manacle so that it wouldn't rest on the damaged skin. As I changed my grip I felt something in it move.

"Hang on a second," I whispered to myself as I turned it round her ankle, hinge side uppermost. "All we need to do is take out the pin!"

"What's that?"

Will jumped up from where he had been trying to dig the bolt out of the wall and bent down to see.

"The hinge – look, it's held together with just one small pin. All I need is a bit of metal to push it with. What have we got?"

I looked around the dimly lit, damp room, which was completely bare apart from the mouldy-looking pile of rags that Aria was sitting on. There was absolutely nothing that might do the job.

"I can go back to the other cell; there might be something there," said Will, standing up again and walking directly in front of me.

"No. Look, we can use this." I grabbed his hand and hauled him back. "Your watch strap has a metal bit on the buckle. Let's try that."

He tore the watch off and thrust it into my hands, then leaned down towards Aria's foot, considering our best angle of attack. I could feel the heat of him radiating towards me.

"Please, I know that you're trying to help, but this is taking far too long," Aria pleaded. "The Farmer will be here any minute, and then he'll have you both killed. Why don't you understand? I'm a lost cause, and I took that risk, but you two don't have to die."

"Why does he want to kill us?" asked Will. "There are only the two of us, after all, so we're not much of a threat. All we want is a conversation."

Aria sighed. "He's been getting worse and worse for years. He really hates the Aboves and has been breeding larger and larger numbers of the Crop, ready to attack. Or at least that's what Dane told me. And more of the Crop means more Feeders are needed to feed them, so he's been getting really harsh with his punishments. I think he's gone mad. Dane thinks he's just plain evil, but almost everyone else just blindly obeys him, regardless of how bad their situation is becoming. We had to do *something*."

"So what were you hoping to achieve Above? Dane mentioned that you were helping him with something. Was that to do with it?"

While we had been talking I had been jabbing at the hinge with the buckle, desperate to find that small bit of movement I'd felt before. And suddenly it slipped home, the pin dropping noiselessly into my lap. I grabbed either side of the manacle and pulled hard, expecting resistance, but the whole thing just fell apart in my hands.

"Oh, you did it!" said Aria, reaching down to rub her

ankle carefully. "Thank you."

She looked up at me and smiled before turning to Will.

"Thank you too. I don't deserve it, but it's good to see you."

She hadn't answered my question, but I didn't push it. Instead I handed the watch back to Will and stood up, pulling Aria upright with me.

"Can you walk?" he asked as she gingerly put her weight on the injured ankle.

"Yes," she hissed through gritted teeth, carefully stepping with just the toes of her left foot on the ground and leaning on me for support.

"This is no time for bravery," I said. "Will, get on the other side. If we both help it'll be quicker."

Will scooped up Aria's other arm and slung it round his shoulders, and between us we lifted her towards the door.

"OK, Aria," said Will as we got to the entrance. "A bit of local knowledge would be good at this point. Where do we go now?"

The pain in my ankle is pulsing, and I wonder if I broke something when they threw me in here. My friends are carrying my weight as I direct them out. My heart feels so free because they are here, risking everything to save me, and yet I can't stand being responsible for their deaths. I have to find a way to get them out of here, away from the Crop and the Farmer. I lead them back the way we were all bought in, and we soon arrive at the heavy studded door.

"That door means business," says Will, touching the old iron studs. "I'm not sure how we're going to get that open."

"Can we take it off its hinges?" asks Lily, running her fingers around the edge.

"They're not that daft," says Will, shaking his head.

"How about we pretend that one of us is sick, and when the guard comes in we overpower him?"

"Oh, come on, really? Which cheesy films have you been watching?" he asks.

I feel helpless as they discuss how they might escape – I know it's impossible. Finally Will starts banging on the door.

"Quick, come quickly, please! She's dying!" he shouts over and over, before turning back to Lily with a crooked smile. "I can't believe you persuaded me to do this."

Lily is about to answer when we hear the great bolts being drawn back on the other side.

"Ready?" hisses Will, poised to jump.

Lily nods and the door slams open. Will presses his back to the wall in the gloom, waiting, while Lily and I stand in the light. I see a figure step through the door and I recognise the silhouette. Dane. I can't warn him.

Will leaps from the darkness and grabs him by the neck. They fight, and fall to the ground, but the shadows *make it hard to see. Then I hear Lily gasp, "No, don't!"*

The door is pushed wide and light floods the corridor. Will has been completely overwhelmed, his arms pinned behind him by two other men. Dane is holding a knife so tightly against his throat that I can see a trickle of blood. Lily leaps forward, but the knife glints as Dane slices it across Will's neck.

CHAPTER 15

I froze, horrified at what I was seeing. Dane lowered the knife and shoved Will away from him, letting him slump to the floor. Aria reached forward to stop me but I shook her off and dived across the corridor to where Will was lying.

"What have you done?" I shouted at Dane. He ignored me.

I turned Will over, hardly daring to look. He was gasping for breath, and I pressed my hand over his to stop the blood seeping through his fingers.

"Let me look, Will," I said, trying to get him to focus on me. The gasping continued, but his eyes met mine. "Let me see," I whispered, my hand over his.

Will's shoulders heaved. "Give me a minute," he coughed. "He winded me."

"I just need to see your neck – how badly are you cut?"

Out of the corner of my eye I could see the men were advancing towards Aria, and I realised that there was no way I was going to be able to help both of them. But Will was in the most immediate danger, so I focused on him, lifting his fingers. A vivid red line ran across his neck, but it wasn't the gaping wound I had feared. Most of the blood seemed to be coming from a small cut where the point of the knife had been originally pressing into his skin, and it was dripping, not pumping. Had Dane spared him deliberately?

"He missed the artery." I gave Will a brief smile. "You're not dying right now."

"Probably not long though," he whispered back, still trying to catch his breath. "They don't look friendly."

The men had surrounded Aria. She looked very small and defenceless, her slight frame dwarfed by the crowd, most of whom looked extremely menacing as they hunched over her, fists clenched. As I watched, one of the men called to the others.

"He's here!"

Everyone in the corridor turned to watch as a tall, dark-haired man swept through the entrance. Wearing a white shirt and waistcoat, he looked better coordinated than all the others, as if his clothes had been actively selected rather than thrown on from a charity shop bargain bucket. A stick or cane of some sort was under his arm. With a look of utter contempt at Will and me, he turned to the crowd and raised his hand. The men fell silent and shuffled apart to reveal Aria. She was standing as tall as possible, showing no sign of the pain in her ankle, with her hands clenched into tight fists. But her face was white with fear. Behind her, two of the crowd held her arms securely.

The dark-haired man walked slowly towards her, looking her up and down as she stared at the wall behind him. Finally he stepped back and, using his cane, moved her chin until she was looking at him.

"Really, Aria, what have you been doing now?"

His voice was low and surprisingly calm. Aria ignored him, but I could see that she was shaking.

"I said, what have you been doing *now*?" An edge of steel crept into the last word.

Aria's jaw was clenched tight. "Nothing," she hissed.

The Farmer leaned towards her, waving back her guards with a flick of his cane. He shook his head slowly.

"I expected better of you. Revealing the Community to strangers is treason. You know that. What would your mother have said?"

Aria swallowed hard, but the look in her eyes had turned to pure hatred. She said nothing.

He lifted the cane back under her chin, making her flinch. She was shaking so hard I could almost hear it.

"You have forgotten your place," he said in a low but clear voice. "I expect an apology."

Still she said nothing.

There was a sharp intake of breath from someone in the crowd, and he stared at her for a couple of seconds before looking away, sighing loudly.

"Beyond hope, as we feared. Take them all to the Assembly Chamber. We need to get this trial out of the way as quickly as possible."

We were bundled out of the cell-block corridor through the heavy door. There was no chance to talk with Aria as we were whisked along endless low, stone tunnels. Thankfully Will and I were kept together, and we tried hard to reassure each other that everything was going to be OK.

"I mean," said Will at one point as we were walking a little more slowly along a winding section, "what good would it do to harm us? We're only here to rescue Aria, not to run off with the silver or something."

"Exactly! I'm sure they'll be letting us go once we've had a chance to explain ourselves."

I tried to sound convincing as I couldn't bring myself to say out loud what I feared. "How is your neck? Has it stopped bleeding?"

Will looked very pasty under the artificial lights.

"It seems fine. I feel pretty rubbish though. Really cold."

"It's probably shock. It's not every day that someone tries to cut your throat."

"Maybe," he said, pulling his sleeves down over his hands. "I'd really like to know where Foggy has gone," he added, peering down another tunnel as we passed. "He's always running off, and he's pretty good at finding his way home, but it would be a relief to know that he was safe."

"Foggy will be fine, I'm sure – didn't you say he has a knack of being in the right place at the right time? Perhaps he'll come and rescue us!"

I didn't believe that any more than Will did, but we gave each other strained little smiles as the guards pulled us apart again.

News of our capture had obviously spread among the Community, and faces were appearing at the doorways and tunnel mouths as we approached. They must have been falling into place behind us though, as I could tell by the footsteps and murmuring that there was a huge crowd following us. We were dragged on, moving between pools of light from the dim bulbs strung just above our heads. I couldn't believe how far we had walked – the place was a vast warren of small, intersecting tunnels. For a fraction of a second I could feel the weight of all the mud and stone above me, and a wave of claustrophobia gripped me. But then the low ceiling was gone.

It was replaced by an immense vaulted chamber that was lit at head height all around the edge by a string of bright white bulbs. The space was about the size of my school assembly hall, and empty apart from a carved chair with a plush-looking cushion on a stage at the far end. Some odd, abstract art was painted on the walls.

To the right was a tall, raised platform about twice my height – the sort of stone plinth you would put a statue on – and Aria was being pushed up a ladder to the top. Several other similar platforms were arranged around the edges of the chamber, and I could see a man pointing to Will and me.

"This doesn't look good," said Will, looking over at Aria's frightened face as she stood alone on the top.

"I'm so sorry that I got you into all this," I said quickly as the men holding our arms started to separate us. "So very sorry."

Will was pulled backwards, and he looked as if he was about to say something but the crowd poured in between us. I was dragged along to the nearest platform, and the man finally let go of my arms when we reached a ladder made of a mismatched selection of wood lashed together with strips of rag.

"Up!" he ordered, poking me in the back with a stick.

The ladder was pretty rickety, and I wasn't sure that some of the rungs would take my weight, but I didn't have much choice but to continue. As soon as I reached the smooth stone surface at the top, the ladder was taken away. It seemed much higher than it looked from the floor, and the square of stone wasn't huge either. I knelt down, keen to keep a sudden wave of giddiness under control, and took several deep breaths.

"Don't look down, don't look down," I repeated to myself.

The attack passed, and when I finally opened my eyes I looked straight out, trying to ignore all the hustle and bustle below me. I was trying really hard not to give in to the panic that was threatening to overwhelm me. On this stone platform, with a top that was barely larger than Nan's kitchen table, panicking wasn't going to be a good thing.

I glanced around the circular vaulted chamber. It was about a quarter full of people, but others were arriving all the time. From my vantage point I could see everything. Aria and Will were on similar plinths, looking nervously at the drop below. As the people filed in they lined up in rows facing the single chair, before sitting down on the floor. The men were at the front, and the women and a few children were nearer the back. Each member of the Community looked eerily similar – dark-haired and pale, just like Aria, and very few of them were particularly tall. They were dressed in a weird concoction of clothes, all in drab colours and showing very little skin. I had never got back the hoodie from Will after he had been using it to give the dog the scent, and I had no idea where it had gone. My skimpy vest top was making me feel almost naked among this crowd. Every single one of them was staring up at Will and me, open-mouthed. Some pointed and laughed, and being so closely observed when I had absolutely nowhere to hide was making me even more uncomfortable.

Will was crouching down, brushing his hair out of his

eyes and looking around in amazement. I raised my eyebrows at him and I could see him mouth something at me – "OK?" I nodded back, determined to be brave, and turned to look at Aria. She was standing upright with her shoulders back, hands clasped behind her, staring at the wall above the chair. I looked over to see what she was staring at and started in surprise. What had seemed at first glance to be a random jumble of shapes painted on the wall, I could now see was a representation of the Tower of London.

I glanced around to see if I could make sense of any of the other pictures around the room but before I could, the crowd suddenly got to its feet. The Farmer walked on to the stage and stood in front of the chair. He sat down and raised his hand to the silent crowd before nodding. Almost in a single movement everyone in the room sat back down. The Farmer then turned to look at the three of us.

"Stand up," someone below me hissed.

I scrambled to my feet and saw that Will was doing the same. Aria continued standing motionless, looking at the wall.

"People of the Community," said the Farmer, "thank you for coming to this special trial. I am sorry that we have had to take you away from your daily tasks but, as you know, by our laws, everyone needs to witness the passing of judgement on transgressors. I do not, however, expect that this will take very long.

"As you may have heard, two of the accused here before us are from Above. They have tricked their way down here with the express intent of stealing one of our own and taking her back Above."

At this there was a general gasp around the room, and a wave of faces turned to get a better look at us.

"And the reason that these Aboves even knew we were here?" He paused, making eye contact with as many people as he could before pointing at Aria. "Because she told them! She revealed our secrets to these strangers and told them how to find us. Why? She refuses to tell us, but there can be no excuse.

"Aria insists that she hasn't told anyone how to reach us, or what our defences are, but these two clearly made it down with ease. How can we be sure she didn't tell more people?" He stood up, his fist waving in the air. "At this very moment, whole legions of Aboves may be preparing to do battle with the Crop, to force their way in here and take you all away to their world of lies, pain and hatred. It's my job to protect you from that terrible fate!"

The gasps of amazement had turned into mutterings of agreement, and all round the room I could see heads shaking. But when I turned to look at Aria she was standing as still as before.

I stand on the column of shame, determined not to show my fear. I've seen many people beg and cry and plead for mercy from these columns, but no one has ever been forgiven. I try to keep my attention fixed on the picture on the wall, knowing now that it is a poor impression of a majestic building. I try to remember every detail of the real thing, keeping my mind off what is going on below me.

A man at the back of the crowd shouts out. "Feeders, the lot of 'em! Get 'em to the Crop now!"

Everyone joins in, shouting and shaking their fists at us.

"Feeders, Feeders, Feeders, FEEDERS!"

There is always shouting at trials, because everyone is desperate to be seen to be supporting the Farmer. I feel ashamed of the times I stood at the back shouting too.

The Farmer holds his hand up and the chanting stops. It is always the same, and there is never any response, but the law says that we must ask before the vote is taken.

"You each have a vote," he starts, "and every vote will count, but as custom dictates I will give you my advice. I must first ask if there is anyone in the room who will stand in defence of either of these invaders, or the traitor. If anyone here would say a few words for the prisoners, to present alternative evidence or to claim leniency, you are now to declare it."

As usual there is an expectant hush, and everyone peers around to make sure that no one is actually going to say anything.

"Good people, this is a crime unlike any other we have

ever seen, and I believe that it should reap the harshest penalty. My advice is to Assign these people to—"

"Farmer, I would say a few words."

There is a gasp from the crowd, and all of them are straining to see who is standing up. I can hear the whispers.

"It's Dane!"

"Dane?"

Dane. My heart almost misses a beat. Just what is he going to say? Part of me wants him to confess, to admit that he and I were working together to kidnap Lily. I want them to know that the whole thing was part of a plan to bring down the Farmer. Lily has no idea that she is one of us, and as the Farmer's daughter the only one who can take on the Farmer's role. Without her to control it, the Crop will kill us all.

I try to speak, to stop him from revealing his part in our conspiracy, but my mouth is so dry that nothing comes out, and then it is too late.

"Farmer, I would stand for one of the prisoners."

"I will hear you, Dane. Which of the prisoners do you defend?"

"I stand for her."

I gasp. Dane is pointing at Lily.

CHAPTER 16

There was utter silence after the gasp, which echoed round the chamber. Dane continued to stand there, pointing in my direction. I could see Will looking confused, and then I looked at Aria. She had been utterly composed up until then, staring impassively at the wall above the Farmer's head, but as Dane had spoken she'd turned to look at me. It was as if someone had put the light out inside her.

The Farmer was still on his feet. His tone was icy.

"As is the custom, any of us has the right to stand for any accused. What would you say to the Community in her defence?"

Dane lowered his arm. His voice carried clearly around the chamber.

"She is a female of a certain age. Our women can't

carry our children any more, so I think we should try an Above. I want her as a Breeder."

As he said the word, Aria's head snapped up and she shot him a look I couldn't decipher.

How can Dane possibly want her to be his Breeder? Did he want this all along, or is he adapting the plan to suit the events?

I see his face and I know. She is what he wants, and I'm to be the sacrifice. I feel my heart breaking.

The Farmer spoke up.

"This is unacceptable. The girl is an Above, and therefore completely contaminated. She can't possibly join the Community. The rules are very clear."

"Farmer, I understand that, and I wouldn't want her unclean ways infecting our world or our people, but I believe that she can be kept in isolation and used for breeding. Wouldn't it be good to have some healthy babies in the cots for a change?"

At this he looked around as if inviting responses from the rest of the audience. There was an indistinct mutter and a few heads nodded, but most people seemed to be waiting for the Farmer's verdict.

My head was swimming. Dane said he wanted to save my life, but only so that I could join his breeding programme. Death, or a life locked up and pregnant? I didn't want either. Was he serious, or was this some elaborate double-bluff to help us all?

"What proof do we have that she'll breed true?" challenged the Farmer, crossing his arms as he stood facing the crowd.

"We have no proof, Farmer. Just the knowledge that the women Above seem to have very few problems in delivering healthy children." Dane hesitated for a moment. "It's a chance we would have to take, but really, what do we have to lose?"

"How do we know that she isn't already carrying a child from Above?" This time it was one of the men in the crowd who spoke.

Dane laughed. "I know that you think she looks otherwise, Farmer, but for an Above, she is a mere child. No one will have touched her, I guarantee it."

"What about him then? Wasn't she with him? How do we know he hasn't touched her?"

The shout from the crowd caused all heads to turn towards Will, who blushed scarlet and shook his head.

"Really, I mean, of course not! I wouldn't – I couldn't!"

The people in the chamber roared with laughter, and I felt sick. The Farmer held out his arms to quieten the crowd and started to speak.

"People…"

"I will speak!" I called out.

The people nearest to me heard, and turned to look at me in surprise, nudging their neighbours. The silence radiated away from me like a ripple in a pond. I was almost paralysed with fear, and I could feel the sweat breaking out on the palms of my hands. Wiping them quickly on my jeans I tried to stand up as tall as possible, facing the Farmer.

"I will speak," I repeated more quietly, glancing at Aria, who was watching with her hands over her mouth.

"I don't believe we have invited you to do so," said the Farmer.

"And I don't believe that you can volunteer me for a breeding programme either! I'm only a child. Why would you possibly want me to breed? You have dozens of women here. They can have your children – pure, Community children."

"You are unaware of our customs so I will be lenient. But remember, girl, here people on trial only speak when they are spoken to."

"From what I'm hearing, I don't have a great future here anyway, so you might as well tell me what's going on. Why do you need me?"

It was Dane who spoke up.

"Farmer, may I explain to her?"

The Farmer nodded almost imperceptibly, so Dane turned to face me.

"The women here are no longer able to breed as they used to. Only one out of every five or six babies is born alive, with many others dying in infancy. We are now not producing anything like enough children to sustain the Community."

He turned back to the older men.

"If this experiment works, if she can produce three, four or five healthy children in the next few years, then we can try getting some more Aboves. Within ten years we could be back up to pre-crisis levels." He opened his arms to the crowd immediately around him, palms up. "Don't you men want children who'll live? Children who will take your name and secure the future of the Community? She can do that for us!"

There was a murmur of agreement from the front of the room. The women at the back all looked appalled, and a few of them shouted out.

"She's contaminated!"

"Send her back!"

"I have another question!" I shouted over the rising clamouring. "Why don't you just ask up Above for help? Aria can tell you that we are not evil. If people knew you were here and needed medicines, they would bring them."

The chamber fell silent as I spoke, and as I finished the people all started turning back towards the Farmer. I could have heard a pin drop as I held my breath, waiting to hear what he had to say.

He shook his head.

"How little you know about your own people," he said, sitting back in his chair. "The Community was set up because the Aboves didn't want our ancestors in their society, and when we have asked for help in the past, none has been provided. So we will never ask for help again, but we will take revenge and take back what is rightfully ours."

His conversational tone made the words all the more chilling. Tenting his fingers he looked at me with a slight smile.

"We will take it back," he repeated. "And soon."

The cry from the crowd made me jump.

"That's right, take it back!"

"They don't deserve it!"

"It's ours!"

The call continued around the chamber.

"Take what back? What is it that you want?" I shouted.

The Farmer fixed me with an unblinking gaze as the room fell silent again.

"London. We will take back London."

Lily has asked the question that proves my point – the Farmer is utterly deluded. However big the Crop is – whatever it is – it can't take out all of London. I wonder for a moment if he has ever been Above and seen the scale of it for himself. Will some of the others join us now and rise up against him? I look around the room but all I can see are people congratulating each other. Howard is even slapping Dane on the back. The Elders have approached the Farmer and they are having some sort of discussion. While they are busy I steal a glance at Will. He is looking towards Lily and as I watch he mouths

213

a word to her. I can't be sure but I think that it is "Sorry".

I felt so alone standing high above the crowd, watching my fate being discussed. I couldn't quite believe that those really were the only choices available to me. There had to be some alternative that would allow me to go home.

For a second the thought of Nan made my eyes prick with tears, and my hand automatically went to the necklace she gave me. What would she think if we never returned? When they realised Will had gone too, would she believe that we had run away together? Would she think that I would do that without leaving a note?

Whatever she thought it was better than her knowing the truth. Somewhere up above us she would begin to get worried. When would she realise the note about the choir trip was a lie and start to call the girls in my class, the hospital, the police? And when would she actually pick up the phone to tell my parents?

Thoughts were crowding around my head and I was finding it hard to breathe. I really needed to sit down, but I didn't want to seem weak. Soon, though, I was going to keel over. The crowd were still looking up at me and whispering to each other, and the general level of noise in the room was rising. And it was getting hot, I realised, as I felt a drip of sweat run down my back. If I fainted and fell off the column I would be horribly injured. Sitting down with my feet over the edge might work. I didn't

want to kneel in front of Dane and the Farmer.

I sat down on the column and swung my legs over the edge, trying to appear nonchalant. The whispering increased but the roaring in my ears started to ease. I really wanted to put my head between my knees, but that was out of the question. I glanced over at Will and saw him copy my lead. Even from a distance I could see that he looked pale and was shaking.

The group of men talking to the Farmer turned away, several of them nodding at each other then glancing up at me as they went back to their places in the crowd.

Whatever the Farmer had decided about my future I was about to find out.

I have to be strong. The Farmer is about to announce his decision and if I am to have any influence, I have to speak out. The thought of interrupting him is terrifying, almost more terrifying than what is bound to come, but if Lily can do it, then so can I. I must stay calm and remember what she has taught me about everyone being equal.

The Farmer stood motionless, his hands spread wide towards the crowd, and I could almost feel their reverence. I gripped the stone edge tightly, trying hard to appear calm, but I was scared stiff. I shut my eyes for a moment, trying to get my breathing under control, desperate not to miss something vital.

"People of the Community," the Farmer started. "This has been an extraordinary gathering and I know that emotions are running high. There are three people on trial. The charges are clear, the punishment less so. A petition has been made to keep this female from Above and use her to breed from. I have spoken with the Elders and made my decision. But first we must have the vote."

There was a murmur around the chamber before everyone fell silent again, watching the Farmer.

"Please stand if you believe the prisoners to be guilty of the charges."

A sea of people got to their feet.

"Be seated. And those who say not guilty?"

Not one person stood up.

"Dane, please rise."

Heads turned to look at Dane, and for the first time I saw him look nervous, flexing his fingers as he stood up before wiping his hands down his trousers.

"You asked to stand for this woman accused of violating our home. Do you confirm this request?"

"Yes, Farmer. Yes, I do."

"In that case I grant your request, with certain conditions. The woman will be Assigned to be your Breeder. You will take full responsibility for her security in the cells. There is to be no contact between her and the people – none whatsoever. If she fails to produce a healthy child in the first year, she will be re-Assigned to Feeder."

I couldn't believe it. I felt breathless, my heart racing as I thought of the implications. This couldn't be happening. Maybe it was part of another one of Dane's plans. There had to be some way of making it stop.

The Farmer was still speaking. "As for the other prisoners, the punishment is much clearer. You are a trespasser," he said, pointing at Will before turning his stare to Aria. "And you, you have flouted some of our most sacred rules. You are well aware of the consequences. The Crop will enjoy your nourishment before I send them Above. You are both re-Assigned to Feeders. Take them away."

There was a low murmuring from the crowd, rhythmic and chilling.

"Feeders, Feeders, Feeders, Feeders…"

Will leapt up to stand on his column as people started to reach up for his legs. I could see him shaking his head and trying to back away. But there was nowhere to go.

"As a member of the Community I have the right to speak."

Aria's voice cut across the mantra, and the chanting faltered. The Farmer turned towards her looking slightly surprised.

"Lily and Will are not about to let an army of people down from Above. No one knows that they are here and so it's not time to release the Crop." I saw her take a deep breath. "And while I'm here, I'd like to tell you all the truth. Having seen Above, the Crop would never be able to take over the city. London is huge, with more people than we can begin to count, none of whom have done us any harm at all. *It will not work!*"

I glanced over at the Farmer, and could see his colour rising. Some of the men near him looked very nervous, glancing between him and Aria. She was getting more confident as she talked, her voice getting stronger and clearer.

"People of the Community, please listen to me. He is wrong, so wrong. The Crop cannot do what he says, but the people up there can help us. They have medicines that can make you well when you are sick, and can help you to live to be a hundred!"

The crowd, which had been transfixed, suddenly laughed. The Farmer spoke up in the brief pause.

"See the delusion, people? Her mind has gone. Who would ever live to be a hundred?"

The jeering started then, and Aria looked around as if unsure how she had gone from having them hang on her every word to being ridiculed. She spun round, arms out in an imploring gesture.

"No, listen, it's true, I tell you!" But the crowd drowned her out. Her shoulders slumped, defeated.

The Farmer shook his head, then tented his fingers. For a long minute he said nothing, but then he turned to face me, an evil smile on his face.

"You will be a Breeder. I was going to let Aria stay with you for a few days – an act of kindness if you will – but

THE BENEATH

I see now that she is quite mad. Nevertheless, the Crop don't need to be fed twice, so you get to decide. Aria or the boy? Which will die today?"

CHAPTER 17

My jaw dropped. Had I misunderstood? Aria and Will were looking stricken, and Will's hand was stretched out towards me. Aria had buried her face in her hands, and I could only see her eyes over the tips of her fingers.

"I'm sorry?" I asked, stalling for time. "I don't understand."

"Are you sure you want to breed from this one? She seems a bit slow!"

The mocking voice echoed around and was followed by a brief wave of laughter. But no one wanted to miss my decision.

"It's very simple. One of them has a stay of execution for a few days. Pick one." He smiled again, enjoying the torture he was inflicting with his words.

How do you make a choice like that? For whoever

220

was alive there was some hope, however slight. Aria was my friend. She had tried so hard to help us escape, and had never asked us to come here in the first place. I was responsible for her being in danger. It should be Aria.

But Will – how could I not pick Will? He was the love of my life, even though he didn't know it. And although he'd come down here for Aria, it was because of my mistake. I'd already made him lose his dog. There was no way that Will deserved to lose his only chance at a future too.

I looked between my two friends, people who had come to help me out when I had got them into trouble, and shook my head hopelessly.

"Lily!" called Will.

The crowd turned towards him. His face looked unusually pale and had a sheen of sweat.

"Save Aria. Keep yourself safe and you may get a chance to get home one day. Please? For me? And if you do get back, tell my mum so she knows there's no hope. And, Lily, I—"

"Enough!" said the Farmer, raising his voice for the first time. "Another word from you and I'll have all of you sent to the Crop now!"

I looked at Aria, tears streaming down my face. She shook her head and pointed towards Will.

"Take him," she mouthed.

I didn't dare look at Will again. The thought of his family forever wondering what had become of him tore my heart to pieces. The thought of actually telling them that he was dead, that I hadn't saved him, was infinitely worse.

I opened my mouth to speak, but nothing came out.

"A decision, *now*."

My heart was pounding; my palms were slick with fear. But I had something that they wanted, and that gave me room to negotiate. I held his gaze.

"If you want me to have your children," I nearly stumbled over the unlikely words, "then both of them have to live."

There was a hush, and I waited with growing dread to hear what the Farmer was going to say. In the quiet I heard a strange gargling sound. Will, still white as a sheet, was clawing at his own throat. He teetered on the edge of the column.

"Will!" I cried, reaching out towards him.

He looked at me briefly as he fell, crashing down on to the very edge of the platform. His head made a sickening crunch as it hit the stone, and he lay motionless.

The silence fell like a blanket across the crowded chamber, every eye turned towards Will, every mouth hanging open.

"Will!" I gasped again, trying in vain to reach him. "Help him, please!"

No one responded. Aria's strangled voice reached me from the far side of the room.

"Did he get bitten, Lily?"

My mind flashed back to the nightmare journey down, and Will examining his ankle where he had been scratched by something. Could he have been bitten by the Crop? I nodded slowly and Aria gasped, her hands clasped across her mouth and her eyes wide in horror. She wasn't the only one who gasped. There was a similar noise from the crowd, and a sea of faces turned to look at me.

"What's the matter with him?" I asked.

As Aria opened her mouth to speak, the voice of the Farmer boomed out.

"Take him away. I don't want him dying in here. Your choice is made, it seems." He looked at me briefly before standing up. The room fell instantly silent.

"The trial is over. Bring the two girls to me."

This just gets worse. The Crop has been bred to be fatal to the Aboves. If Will has been bitten, he'll surely die.

Someone swung the ladder back into place and I carefully made my way backwards down it, trying not to stumble. My palms were still slippery so I had to hold on tightly. As I reached the bottom I felt hands trying to help me, but when I looked at people they wouldn't hold my gaze. I couldn't see what had happened to Will.

"Please, my friend – can you see if he is OK?" I asked the man nearest to me, but he just turned away.

Someone took me firmly by the arm and started to

223

lead me through the crowd that was jostling around me. Some of the women had worked their way up from the back and were staring at me. One reached out a thin hand as if to touch me, but she fell back as the man leading me pushed her out of the way.

As we reached the low tunnel leading out of the chamber, my guard caught up with Aria. She was also being held in the firm grip of a guard.

"I'm so sorry…" we both started at the same time.

I grasped her arm, pulling her close for a quick hug. She hugged me back.

"I didn't mean to get you into all this trouble," I said.

"I still can't believe that you came to rescue me. Thank you."

"What have they done with Will? What's going to happen to him? It wasn't a huge cut…"

"It doesn't take much. I'm so sorry. The bite is supposed to be fatal. That's why the Farmer thinks that he can take over. Apparently we're immune."

Fatal. How was this happening? I had to do something to help him. He couldn't die, he just couldn't!

Our guards pulled us apart but continued walking in line. I craned my neck to look around, but I couldn't see Will.

"Can you see him?" I called to Aria, who was just ahead of me.

"They've taken him away," she replied over her shoulder before stopping. "This isn't the way back to the cells," she said to her guard. "Where are we going?"

"The Farmer wants to talk to you in his rooms," he said gruffly, dragging her on. "And you don't ask the questions."

My guard thrust me ahead as the tunnel narrowed. I was directly behind Aria, and it might be the only chance I had to speak with her properly.

"We need to talk, before we get where we are going," I whispered. "We just need a minute."

"OK, try to look a bit ill, and I'll see if I can get them to let us go to the toilet. It's just up here."

"I won't have to try hard for that." I gulped under my breath as Aria tapped her guard on the shoulder.

"I think she's going to be sick or something, Lance. Please – we need to go to the toilet."

"Don't be stupid, girl, she's fine," snapped the guard.

"Please," I said, doubling over and groaning. "I don't feel good. Is there a bucket or something?"

"Look at her, she's terrified, and so would you be in her shoes. No wonder she's sick with fear."

As I listened to Aria's words the reality of the situation settled over me like a cold, clammy blanket. My friend was dying, I was on my way to talk to a man who had just agreed to keep me as a slave, and the chances were that we were all going to be killed horribly in the very near future. The fear took hold of my stomach and I started to retch.

"Argh, not here, not in the tunnel! You, you take her

into there and sort her out. Be quick, mind; the Farmer will be waiting."

The guard holding my arm thrust me towards Aria and she pulled me through a doorway on the left. We went round a corner and I was suddenly aware of the sound of running water.

We were in a long room with a big basin in the middle. A stream of water was pouring out of a spout and into the bowl, but that wasn't the source of the noise. Along one wall was a knee-high stone bench with large holes carved into the top. The water was running beneath the bench. I had to raise my voice to be heard.

"Is this your loo? Do you all sit together in a line?"

Aria nodded, leading me to the basin.

"It's a sociable place. And the river provides everything we need – we have one stream to take away the waste, the other to drink. Here, wash your face, you look terrible. That was impressive acting – I thought you were actually going to be ill."

"It wasn't an act. I feel horrible." I splashed the water on my face, hoping that it really did come from a different source to the water swirling under the toilet seats. "But I needed a minute to talk to you. I have to help Will. What can I do?"

As I spoke there was a rustling noise on the other side of the big basin. Aria darted round. A small child had been crouched down behind it, listening to us. Aria hauled her to her feet. She looked about eight or nine and was wearing an old-fashioned pinafore dress.

"Penelope! What are you doing hiding down there?"

"I'm sorry, Aria, I didn't mean to be eavesdropping. I was in here already and I just wanted to stay to see the Above for myself." Her huge eyes were glued on me.

"Well, here she is. Lily, this is Penelope. Now, go; leave us alone."

The girl pouted as she turned, her long dark plait swinging round in an arc. Then she turned back to face me, clutching her hands nervously.

"I'm glad you're staying. I hope you'll be able to help us."

"I hope so too," I said, not knowing how else to respond.

"Go on now, Penelope. Off you go," said Aria in an annoyed tone, her hands on her hips. The girl darted round me and was nearly at the entrance when Aria suddenly shot towards her.

"Wait!" she hissed. "Come back here. I need you to do something."

Penelope turned and smiled up at her nervously. "All right. What can I do?"

Aria knelt down and took her by both arms. "Can you fetch Carita for me? Stay here until after we've gone, then run and find her. She might know how we can save ourselves."

She chewed her lip, her big dark eyes darting towards me. "Will I get into trouble?"

"No, not if you only talk to Carita. Now, hide again, and as soon as we've gone, run to find her."

"Who is Carita, and how can she help?" I whispered as Penelope hid back behind the basin.

"My sister."

"Oh yes, I remember."

"I don't see her much, not now she's a Breeder. She's just had another baby." Aria paused for a moment. "The Farmer is the father."

"But he's ancient! That's really gross."

Aria turned towards the basin and washed her face, so I barely heard her reply.

"It's her third child too. The others died. If many more die she'll be re-Assigned…"

"We've got to help Will and stop this." I stood up straight and shut my eyes, pressing my fingers hard into my temples and breathing deeply. "We have to make the Farmer see sense."

"If there is a way to appeal to him, Carita will know."

"Hey, you in there. Don't make me come in and get you!"

The gruff voice of the guard made us both jump.

"Coming!" called Aria. She reached for my hand. "Let's go and see if we can save Will."

We walk along the tunnels towards the Farmer's quarters. I've never been there, not even to see Carita. I hope that Penelope can find her in time for me to speak with her.

Ahead of us Lance has Lily by the arm and I'm being led by Mason. I don't know where Dane has gone. Maybe he is with Will.

We reach the unfamiliar corridor, and Lance and Mason make us stop.

"You have to wait here until he is ready for you," says Mason in a very self-important voice. Lily is still shaking and I can see the fear in her eyes. I reach over and squeeze her hand.

At that moment I hear someone coming along the tunnel behind us, walking so fast that they are nearly running. It is Carita, and she has baby Reilly in her arms.

"Aria, what have you been doing? Whatever possessed you?"

"I'm so sorry. I should have…" My voice fades. Would I have done anything different if I had spoken with her? I don't think so.

"The Farmer has said that we can have a few minutes together. Mason, you can come too, and wait outside – make sure she doesn't run off."

I'm surprised at the command in my sister's voice. She has obviously learned something from being the Farmer's Breeder.

Carita reaches for my hand, glancing briefly at Lily. She doesn't speak with her.

"I'll be right back," I say over my shoulder as my sister pulls me down the corridor and round the corner to a small side room.

We step inside and she pulls the drape across the doorway.

The room is bigger than I expected, with a crib, a chair and a few things that I recognise as being Carita's – a brown hairbrush, a tiny silver box and a threadbare stuffed toy. She places Reilly in the crib and he immediately begins to howl. Carita drags me to the far side of the room.

"Quickly, Mason won't be able to hear over the noise. What are you doing? How have you got yourself into this mess?"

"It isn't safe to tell you everything. A few of us decided to try and find someone who can help us to bring down the Farmer, and the plan went wrong. I never meant to go Above."

"So it's true? That's where you've been? Is it as horrible as they say?"

"It isn't horrible at all. They have some very strange customs, but the people I met were all really kind. And it's so, so huge. The sky is so far away – you would never believe it. And there are so many people. You have to try and talk with him, Carita. His plan is just ridiculous. There are far too many Aboves for him to be able to attack them."

"But do they have medicines?"

"They seem to. Everyone looked healthy, even the really old ones. Some of them get to be a hundred years old."

She believes me. She can see it in my eyes.

"They must have something that will help then," she mutters, turning and pacing across the room. She looks at her baby but doesn't pick him up to stop the crying. Then she is back beside me.

"I think Reilly might be sick."

I feel fear clutch my stomach.

"What's happened? How can you tell? Is it…" I let the word hang, unspoken.

She nods briefly, her eyes damp.

"It started in exactly the same way with Mary and Daniel, and the other Breeders say the same. He won't have long if he does have it. He needs help."

"But how are—" Carita silences me with a finger to my lips. She pulls a piece of paper from her pocket and I step back in surprise.

"What are you doing?" I lower my voice to a whisper. "He'll have you sent to the Crop if he knows you have some writing!"

"This is what Reilly needs. This is the name of the medicine that the Listeners can't get."

I look at the paper in her fingers. It's a long word starting with an "A", but I can't read it.

"Lily can read that. She taught me some words but that's too difficult."

Carita leans in close, desperation in her eyes.

"Do you think she can get it? If I can get her back Above, will she bring back some medicine?"

"I'm sure she would help, but do you really think that the Farmer will let her go?"

"I know he's getting desperate too. By the time Reilly can be Farmer – if he lives that long – our Farmer will be really old. Maybe too old to control the Crop. All his other children have died."

"There isn't one?" I ask, horrified. She shakes her head.

"No, I've checked with all the Breeders."

I look at the paper again. "How do you know this will work? Where did this word come from?"

"It's a secret among the Breeders. Years ago," she says, keeping her voice low, "when the infection first started, a sick baby was taken up Above. The Aboves gave the baby this medicine and it started to get better, but the mother couldn't answer their questions and had to run away. The baby was stolen by the Aboves."

"I'm not surprised she had trouble. It's really hard up there."

"The mother managed to get away and come back down with a bottle of the medicine, and that cured another child, but it all got used up. The Breeders asked the Listeners to go and get more, but the Farmer heard about it and had everyone he thought was involved re-Assigned to Feeder. He doesn't want help from the Aboves.

"Another one of the Breeders kept the bottle, though, and someone who knew how to hold a pencil copied out the name. We've been waiting for our chance to get someone to bring some down."

"And the Listeners who the Breeders asked to help never came back," I add as she pauses.

She looks at me in surprise. "You know the story?"

I nod. "Some of it. I didn't know that you had the name of the medicine though."

"The Breeders have been waiting for years, and now finally we have a chance." She stops for a minute and looks over at Reilly. "The problem is, we have to get your friend to go up Above but then come back down again."

"That's not a problem. She'll do it, I'm sure," I say confidently.

"Really?" Carita looks back at me in surprise. "And will she definitely come back?"

"Of course. The medicine is the only thing that can help her friend Will right now. She'll come back to save him."

DON'T LOOK BELOW the SURFACE

CHAPTER 18

A low bench had been cut into the wall outside the Farmer's chamber, and I sank down on to it gratefully. The man who had been leading me by the arm must have decided that I wasn't going to run off so he left me there and walked up the tunnel a short distance. He reached the corner where Aria had been taken and stopped. The other guard was there too, and the pair of them leaned against the wall, talking in voices too low to hear. The one watching over me glanced in my direction every few minutes.

I was grateful for some time alone to gather my thoughts. I had to try and do something to help Will, and quickly too. I just had no idea what. I was sitting with my head in my hands when I heard the heavy curtain across the Farmer's doorway being pulled back. Dane stepped into the corridor.

He saw me there and stopped, glancing up and down the long, smooth tunnel. I saw him wave at the men and they leaned back against the wall and carried on talking.

He took a short step towards me.

"The Farmer seems to have agreed to our deal – I wasn't sure that he would really go through with it. He's going to want to talk with you in a minute though."

"Why? What on earth can I tell him?"

"I suggest telling him that you won't be any trouble – that'll keep you alive longer."

"But what about Will? I must see him! What's wrong with him?"

"If he was bitten by the Crop then there's not a lot anyone can do, not down here anyway."

"There must be something we can give him."

"Look, Lily, the Crop – whatever it is – carries an infection. It's part of the Farmer's plan for when he takes over. The Crop will infect the population and they'll die, but we'll be all right as we're immune. If Will has been bitten, then…" he paused and shrugged his shoulders, "nothing will help. It's put the Farmer in a good mood though. I think he's pleased that Will has succumbed so quickly – it's a good test for him."

"No, that can't be right," I cried, leaping to my feet. "There has to be some way that you can help Will. He can't die! He just can't!"

"Calm down," he said, grabbing me by the shoulders.

The guard, looking puzzled, started walking towards us. Dane glanced at him and shook me slightly. "Listen," he hissed in a low voice. "You need to keep your wits about you. Stay alive for now, and then we can worry about your future. OK?"

"But…"

"Just do as I say! I can't tell you anything else now."

As he spoke the guard reached us. I didn't understand what Dane meant, but when I glanced at him he was looking stonily ahead.

"Bring the girl." The echoing voice made me jump. The guard took me by the arm and led me through the ornately carved doorway.

The room inside was unlike any of the others that I had seen in the Community. On one side there were soft chairs covered in a grey, velvety material, each with some colourful cushions. Opposite was a beautifully carved wooden desk with one high-backed chair behind it. Behind that was a tall cabinet criss-crossed with iron bars. I could just see the spines of some books inside. Instead of the usual single light bulb on a trailing lead, this room had several lights built into the walls. In the third wall was a doorway, its heavy red curtain pulled back with a fancy gold tie. Beyond the curtain I could see into another room with a large bed on the far side.

The Farmer was sitting at the desk, leafing through a small, leatherbound book. The guard led me towards him then turned and left the room. The Farmer continued turning the pages, ignoring me completely. There was nowhere close enough to sit down, so I stayed where I was, standing tall and trying to keep breathing evenly. I had to stay calm, whatever he wanted from me.

Finally he looked up from the book and fixed me with a penetrating stare that sent a shiver down my spine. I looked away quickly.

"So, you're going to be a Breeder then."

I glanced back at him and he was looking me up and down. I stayed silent, hoping that he couldn't see me shaking.

"It seems an odd request. You don't look strong enough, and I don't see why your children would bring the immunity we need. It could be a fascinating experiment though – maybe they will gain it from their father." He sat back in his chair before he continued, tenting his fingers and raising his eyebrows. "You have no immunity either."

"I … I've not been bitten."

"No," he said, smiling slightly. "You haven't. Not yet."

A cold cloak of fear settled over me. Not yet? What did he mean? I tried to speak but nothing came out. Swallowing hard I tried again.

"Farmer, please. My friend is sick. I need to help him."

The laugh was cold and made me jump.

"He is beyond your help. Tell me, how long ago was he bitten? I'm curious about how long it takes."

"I don't really know. My watch was stolen by one of your men."

"Guess." This time it was a command.

I thought back. We had started down the stairs in the morning, but that had taken hours, then we had wandered around the tunnels in the dark before getting thrown in the cells. I had no idea how long we had been in there. With no natural light it was really hard to keep track.

"I don't know how long ago it was, but it happened about lunchtime."

The Farmer nodded briefly.

"It'll be interesting to see how long he lasts."

"Can you let me see him, please?" I was happy to beg if that was what it took.

Before he could answer there was a noise outside in the corridor. I caught an unfamiliar voice.

"...don't care what you say. I'm going in there now."

I turned to see Carita marching into the room, her baby in her arms. The guard was hurrying after her.

"I'm sorry, Farmer, she wouldn't stop..."

"We need to speak," she said to the Farmer, her head held high.

The Farmer sighed and shook his head. "It's all right, Lance. I'll deal with this." He turned to look at Carita. She wore a long, dark skirt and a baggy jumper that couldn't conceal her skinny frame. Her dark hair was swept up into an elaborate knot, emphasising her thin neck. She looked exhausted.

"Really, Carita, couldn't you have waited? Why have

you disturbed me?"

She looked at him stonily, then her gaze fell to the baby in her arms. When she looked back up her eyes were damp.

"He has a temperature."

"So? Babies get temperatures all the time." He sounded nonchalant but I saw his knuckles whiten as he gripped the arm of the chair.

"I know what it is."

"Are you sure?"

"Of course. But this time our baby doesn't have to die."

"What are you talking about?"

"This girl here," she said, pointing at me but not taking her eyes off the Farmer, "she can get what we need. She can get the medicine that will make him better."

"How do you know what he needs?"

"We've always known. We just need the chance to get it!"

The Farmer pushed back his chair and stood up slowly. His voice was low and menacing. "How dare you speak to me in that tone."

Carita held her baby closer to her chest. "If he dies I have no future here anyway. I can't keep doing this. Don't you want him to live?"

"Of course I want him to live, but he needs to be strong. A weak Farmer will be no good to the Community."

"Strong? You want him to be strong? Look at him!"

As she spoke she thrust the little bundle towards the Farmer, and the blanket fell back. The baby was tiny, his thin little arms and legs sticking out of an oversized vest. As he started to cry, his tiny hands made tight fists. Carita swiftly wrapped him up again, holding him tightly. "He's just a baby, only a few weeks old. And it looks as if he's never going to have the chance to get strong. But *you* can be strong. You can admit that – finally – we need to get some help. Let her help us!"

"What are you talking about?"

"She can get us this." Clutching the baby close with one hand, she slapped the other on the desk. A scrunched-up piece of paper fell out of her palm.

"What is this?"

"Why don't you read it?"

"You are crossing the line here, Carita. You know the punishment."

"Don't you understand? Have you not been LISTENING? If he dies I don't care! Read it."

The Farmer picked up the paper and turned it over before letting it flutter back down to the desk.

"Where did you get that?"

"It doesn't matter, but it's what he needs. Let her go and get it for me. For Reilly."

"If we did that, why would she come back? She'll tell everyone about us and this will all be over."

"She'll come back. If she gets the medicine she can save her friend too." Carita spun round to face me.

"That's what you want, isn't it?"

Stunned at this unexpected twist, it took me a moment to get the words out.

"What … what do you expect me to do?"

She grabbed the paper from the desk and thrust it towards me. "If you go back Above, can you get us this?"

I took the crumpled sheet and turned it round. One word was written on it:

Amoxycillin

The "y" was written back to front but otherwise it was readable.

"Is this what Will needs?"

"Yes." Carita nodded fiercely. "It will stop the infection if he gets it quickly enough. It's the same medicine that will save my baby."

"You will get this and come back." It wasn't a question from the Farmer, but a statement.

I looked again at the word, rubbing the letters on the paper with the side of my thumb, and for the first time in hours I felt a spark of hope.

"Yes," I said, standing up straight and looking him in the eye. "Yes, I can get this."

"How?" he demanded, his eyes narrowing.

"If I tell you that, you won't need me. I will go and do this, and come back, but I have two conditions."

My heart was pounding with fear. What if he said no?

It was my only chance. I clenched my fists, willing myself to stay calm. Eventually the Farmer raised an eyebrow. I swallowed hard before I could speak.

"This is the deal. I will bring medicine for your babies if you let me treat my friend, then set us all free."

I folded my arms and looked at him, trying to appear confident. The Farmer regarded me for a moment.

"If you don't come back, Aria will die. Your other friend is already dying. You won't be able to save him."

"But you'll let me try?"

The Farmer nodded.

"I'll be back as quickly as I can. Can I see him before I go?"

The Farmer turned to the guard. "Lance, take her to him and meet me by the lift. And get Mason to find a Listener."

Lance took my arm and led me towards the door. I glanced back to see the Farmer picking up his book again. In the split second I had before the curtain fell back, I could have sworn that he was holding it upside down.

We walked for a few minutes before reaching a doorway covered in a thick, dirty cloth. Lance pulled it back and ushered me inside. It was really gloomy, with only a single dim light bulb. There was no furniture, but a body was propped up against the far wall. Shaking off Lance's hand from my arm I ran across the room.

My heart lurched, but Will was still alive. He was

deathly pale with large dark circles under his eyes and covered in a sheen of sweat. His T-shirt was filthy from the blood that had dripped on it and a dark graze was smudged across one cheek. I touched the other side of his face gently.

"Will? Can you hear me?" I thought I saw a brief nod, so I carried on. "They are letting me go to get some medicine for you. Hang on until I get back, eh?"

His mouth moved but only a dry croak came out.

"Water, please," I begged Lance. He hesitated for a second before giving a curt nod and disappearing outside of the room. I heard him calling to someone else.

I looked around the room for something – anything – to make Will more comfortable, but it was completely bare. Lance hadn't returned.

"Will, I'm not sure if you can hear me, but I've got a plan. They're going to let me go back up Above to get some antibiotics for you. It'll be no problem – I know where I can get them easily, but I need you to hang on, OK?"

As I finished talking I heard the heavy cloth over the door being pulled back, and Lance appeared with a battered tin mug of water. I jumped up and met him.

"Thank you," I said, and he met my eyes for the first time. "Thank you. I really appreciate it."

He nodded and returned to his position at the door.

"Here, Will, try this," I said, sitting down next to him and putting the mug to his mouth. Tipping slowly I wet his lips. His eyes fluttered open.

"Take a sip," I urged, tipping the mug again as his eyes closed once more. He drank a tiny amount then opened his eyes again. His head swayed a little but finally he was able to focus on me.

"Go," he gasped, reaching up with his hand as if to push me. "Don't … come … back."

"I'm not going to abandon you, I promise."

As I reached forward to touch him his head fell on his chest, his arms limp by his sides. But he was still breathing.

"That's enough," said Lance. "I need to take you to the lift."

Standing up I gave Will one last look. "I'll be back," I called over my shoulder as we left the room, making a promise to myself as well as to him.

DON'T LOOK BELOW the SURFACE

CHAPTER 19

Lance hurried me along the corridors and as we swept past tunnels and doorways I caught a few glimpses of women's faces, all of them drawn and tired-looking, but all obviously keen to sneak a closer look at the trespassing Above. One stepped out as we approached. She put up her hand and Lance slowed a little.

"Can you really do it?" she called, pulling her ill-fitting cardigan more tightly around her as he led me past. "Can you stop the sickness?"

"I hope so," I called back, trying to smile encouragingly, but she just nodded and melted away.

At one point we crossed the tunnel with the warm breeze and I glanced down it. The long line of dim light bulbs seemed to stretch forever into the distance. Turning my head I saw that the tunnel did the same in the other direction, and I wondered just how many people were living down there, and how many more there used to be. It was an immense complex and I still couldn't believe that no one from my world had ever noticed that it was buried under their feet.

Finally I smelled the canteen again. Whatever the Community was having for dinner didn't smell the least bit appealing, but it reminded me that I was absolutely starving. I couldn't be sure how long I'd been down there, but I'd certainly missed plenty of meals. My stomach growled loudly.

Being near to the canteen meant that we were also close to the lift, and as we turned a corner I saw an entrance I thought I recognised – the stone archway leading to the stairs. It seemed so long ago since Will and I had sneaked out of there with Foggy, and I had another pang of guilt as I wondered where Foggy had gone. Was someone looking after him? It didn't seem likely, given Aria's reaction to dogs. Maybe he'd found a way back up to the surface. I didn't allow myself to think of any other options.

Just past the entrance to the stairs we turned a corner and there was the lift, ready and waiting, and completely unguarded. I was surprised for a moment but I guessed the Crop guarded me more effectively than anything else – both down and up. It looked quite different to the one in the warehouse. Up there it had just seemed old-fashioned, with the concertina doors but otherwise like a standard lift. Down in the Community it somehow had a more sinister air. There was no call button, just a grubby brass plate with a single large keyhole. The wall surrounding the lift, like every other wall, was made of stone, but there seemed to be a number of horizontal scratches scored into it. Fingernail marks? It couldn't be, the stone was too hard, but for a second I wondered, and shivered.

At that moment Dane appeared from another tunnel. Dane, who had made a deal to keep me as his breeding slave and who had tried to slit Will's throat. He gave a thin smile.

"Thank you, Lance, I'll take her now. The Farmer is just coming."

Lance released his grip on my arm, and as he brushed past I thought I heard him murmur "good luck, lass". I turned, but he was already walking away.

Dane grabbed my arm and swung me round to face him.

"Watch it," I started, but he interrupted.

"Right, Lily, this is what's going to happen. You and I are going to go up in the lift to Above, and I will let you out of the warehouse. Then you and I will go and get the medicine."

"Hang on a second," I said. "That was never part of the deal. I can't take you with me – I've got to get my hands on the drugs and it won't be easy. You must know that – I'm sure you've tried."

"Don't argue, he'll be here in a second, and that's what he needs to know." There was an undertone of steel in his voice and I bit back my retort.

"And I do need some insurance that you will come back," he added. "I'm not convinced that your boyfriend will be enough for you."

"I promised!" I hissed, unable to contain myself. "What sort of friend do you think I am?"

"I'm hoping one who doesn't want to die," he said, pulling back the heavy iron grille and pushing me inside.

I have been allowed to wait with Will. Mason is outside and I know that it's hopeless to try and get away. I have nowhere to run to and I can't leave Will. I wait, and with every moment that passes he looks closer to death. It's as if he's literally fading away before our eyes. Carita comes and helps me try to keep him cool with the water, but he's still burning up. He's not even complaining any more. If Lily doesn't get back soon it will be too late for all of us.

I had barely looked around the rickety old lift when I heard footsteps outside. The Farmer was standing there holding a key on a long chain that was connected to his belt. He didn't look at us as he leaned over towards the brass plate outside. I heard the key slide into the lock, then he turned to Dane.

"I'll send the lift back up after you've been up there for

an hour. No longer."

"That's nothing like long enough," I spluttered.

"No longer," he repeated, pulling the inner concertina grille across from a recessed panel at the side. Then he reached over and hauled at the heavier, outer grille. It made an oily scraping sound as he slammed it into position.

I heard the key squeak as it turned, and the light in the lift went out. The Farmer was briefly silhouetted by the dim light from the corridor, and then he was gone. The lift started to shake, then lurched into life. Everything went dark.

"Exactly how old is this thing?" I shouted over the din of the machinery and the horrible noise the cage made as it laboured its way up. Something was hitting the wall as we moved, scraping like fingernails on a blackboard.

"No idea!" Dane shouted back. "But it generally gets us to the top."

As he spoke the last few words the scraping stopped and all I could hear was the rattling of the chain and some distantly whirring machinery.

I turned on Dane, furious, unable to see him in the pitch black.

"What exactly does he think I can do in an hour?" I cried. "And why has he turned out the lights?"

"Why do you think?" he sighed as if it was obvious. "There's stuff up there that he doesn't want us to see."

"I made it past the Crop once already, remember?"

"Did you actually *see* them?"

"Well, no, not exactly. With the torch I could see the shapes of things moving in the dark, but I didn't see one clearly."

"The lights are out for your protection."

"So I can't see the Crop?"

"So the Crop can't see *you*! No one but the Farmer gets to see the Crop. It's a rule we've had for hundreds of years."

"So your people don't actually know what sort of animals they are?"

"No, as I said, the Farmer thinks it's for the best."

So no one had any idea what they were going to be eaten by until they were about to be eaten. Whatever it was, the people would imagine something far, far worse.

"So what is this all about, Dane? Why do you really want me to stay with the Community?"

"Have you thought why the Crop didn't kill you?" he asked, surprising me. "No one has ever got past them before. They didn't kill you when Aria found you either, did they?"

He paused for a moment and I was suddenly aware that he was standing much closer to me, his voice low.

"There are things that you don't know yet, and I know it's frustrating. But you have to trust me, and know that all I want is to help you."

If I had been looking at him I would probably have believed him – he'd have been looking at me with those big, dark eyes, brow furrowed, his expression begging me to accept what he said. But in the darkness I only had the words, and something about them just didn't ring true. I didn't know why. What I did know was that none of it was a coincidence.

I was wondering how to respond when the lift slowed.

"That was quick," I said, but Dane hushed me.

"Shhh, don't say anything until I tell you. It's best if they don't know we're here."

His hand was firm on my arm as he manoeuvred me towards the back of the lift, and I strained to hear what might be going on. All too soon the noise was clear enough and getting far too close for comfort. And suddenly there was the smell, that dead, half-rotten smell that made me gag. Without warning the lift lurched and I let out a small yelp of surprise.

Within seconds there was a great thumping noise as something hurled itself at the lift gate. The metal grille rattled and squealed in protest.

"Damn it, they're here," Dane whispered. "Try to keep quiet as we pass."

I could barely hear him over the rattling of the heavy metal grille as animal after animal attacked. The smell was atrocious and I pressed myself against the back wall of the lift to be as far away as possible. In my mind's eye I could see the lift lumbering past the Crop level, and listening carefully I could sense the noise moving from above to below as we moved upwards. But what was it?

The only real noise was of something hitting the lift cage but there was no howling or roaring, just that strange slithering in the background. What sort of creature made no noise? Snakes? But they wouldn't hurl themselves at the grille. My imagination was working overtime, but I couldn't think of anything that fit what I was hearing.

Dane's voice cut through my thoughts.

"So come on, Lily, you can tell me. Exactly where are you going to get the medicine from? I know that it's difficult. Where are you going to go where they won't ask questions?"

"Honestly, Dane, you really can't expect me to tell you that. It's my only bargaining chip. Where have you tried in the past?"

"All the chemist shops, but they insist on a prescription, and I can't get one of those unless I see a doctor. If I go to a hospital they ask too many questions because I don't have any symptoms. We've been going in circles for years."

"Why don't you just bring the babies up here when they get sick? Wouldn't it be worth it?"

"You don't understand, obviously. There's no way that it would be allowed."

I shook my head. "You'd rather that they die, that you face extinction as a community, than risk the world finding out?"

There was another silence, broken only by the rattling of the slow-moving lift.

"I wouldn't," he said finally, "but it's not my choice, not yet."

"What do you mean?"

"I mean I would do it differently, that's all." It was another answer that didn't ring true, but from his tone it didn't sound as if he was going to say any more about it.

"And why are they all dying anyway?" I asked instead. "Where has this sickness come from?"

I heard him shift his weight and I wondered if he was going to answer me. When he did speak it sounded as if he were telling a story.

"Years and years ago," he said, "before my grandparents were born, there were hundreds more of us, but it suddenly got very hard to get food from Above, and huge explosions at ground level were forcing more and more of the Aboves underground."

"That must have been the war," I said. "There was lots of bombing and people slept in the Tube for safety."

"Whatever it was, the people displaced a lot of rats down to our level, and they brought with them an illness. The Great Sickness wiped out over half our people, so many that we realised we were going to have to ask Above for help. The Farmer at the time sent up a deputation of people to speak to an official, but he wasn't interested in talking to us, never mind helping. We were told to stop wasting his time. So our people returned home, and watched more of our children die. That Farmer vowed that we would never, ever ask the Aboves for help again, and that one day they would be made to pay for what they did to us. Every Farmer since then has felt the same."

"That's so awful. I can't believe they didn't help you. I guess that in the middle of the war things were much more difficult."

"Whatever the excuse, the Aboves showed us no compassion that day."

"And the people who were left after the sickness?"

"We bred a community of people immune to it, and everything seemed OK. But then a few years ago it all started to change. One by one almost all the newborn babies seemed to catch it, and it's just got worse."

"But you must ask for help! No one up Above will want to see your children die!"

"Someone tried that in desperation, sneaking a baby Above, but they took the child away. When the Farmer found out he was furious, and has been all the more determined since then that you all must be punished."

Moments later the lift finally shuddered to a halt. I heard Dane opening the gate, and with eyes accustomed to the dark, I could see the faint outline of the warehouse door across the room.

"Stay there for a moment," he said.

I could just see him as he walked towards the door. There was a click and then a handful of fluorescent light tubes hummed into life. The light was dazzling and I blinked briefly. The can was still crushed flat under the shutter where Will and I had left it a lifetime ago. To the left was the door, which had a number of substantial bolts.

Dane was being briskly efficient.

"Right – there's no point in arguing, Lily. I'm coming with you and that's all there is to it. If you want to save your boyfriend it's your only choice."

"He's not my boyfriend," I mumbled. "I still can't see why you have to be so difficult. Why would I not come back?"

"We're already wasting time. The Farmer is the only one who has the key to send the lift up and summon it back down again. If we miss his schedule we'll be punished. It's how he manages us. And if we miss it today, we won't get the medicine to Will fast enough."

As he spoke he had been pulling back the bolts, then he clicked the latch before throwing the door open. I had lost track of time and had hoped it might be dark, but bright sunlight streamed into the room. I cursed under my breath. Sneaking about in the darkness would have been much easier.

I stepped out into the sunshine, squinting at the brightness. Without another word Dane slammed the door shut behind us, and the entrance to the Community was instantly anonymous again. Deliveries were being made at the restaurant next door, and shoppers passed by the end of the cul-de-sac. I could hear mobile phones ringing, and somewhere an old Queen song was drifting out of an open window. Standing on the little cobbled street, listening to the world I knew go about its daily business, it was hard to believe that I'd been deep below for – how long? I must have been gone for over twenty-four hours.

"We have to be back in the lift in exactly an hour," said Dane, pointing to the church clock tower. It was just finishing chiming for a quarter past twelve.

"Come on then, this way," I called as I set off.

We jogged through the streets, past all the delivery drivers and mothers with their pushchairs, and within ten minutes we were at the end of my road. My heart sank as I turned the corner and saw the police car parked outside. I caught Dane's arm and hauled him to a stop.

"We're in trouble. That's the police. If you don't want to answer a pile of difficult questions you'll have to make yourself scarce."

"What are we doing here anyway? This is your house. We're supposed to be getting the medicine."

"And I need something from in there to do that! You're going to have to let me sneak in there somehow."

"And have you expose us to the police?"

"Look," I said as patiently as I could. "I'm not going to do that, but I have to get in there. Alone I can probably convince them that I'm OK. With you we're doomed. You have no identity, no address, nothing. They'll arrest you for kidnapping me and then everything could unravel. Let me do this and I'll see you at the warehouse. I promise I'll be back in time. I want to save Will more than you know."

He lifted up his hands in protest but then the door of our house was wrenched open. I could see the familiar figure of Nan moving surprisingly quickly down the front steps.

"Lily Blackthorne, you get in here this minute!" she shouted as I ran up the road. "Where have you been? And who's he? Do you have any idea at all of what I've been through?"

When I reached her she grabbed hold of my arm tightly, and then, as she ran out of breath, she pulled me into a bear hug. For someone who looked so frail she had quite a squeeze on her.

"Don't you ever do that to me again. I thought you'd gone, that I'd lost you…"

I realised with horror that she was actually crying. Nan never cried, ever, not even at *Titanic*. Over her shoulder I could see a policewoman speaking into her radio.

"It looks as if she's home, Sarge. Yes. I'll do the necessary." She snapped the radio off and looked at me sternly. "I take it you're Lily? Care to share with us where you've been all night? You've frightened Mrs Wakefield half to death."

She stood in the hallway with her arms folded, wearing her sensible police-issue shoes, and for the first time I really didn't know what to do. I had to tell them about the Community, about the wild animals living just under the Tube network. It wasn't safe to keep it all secret. But if I did I was going to be hours, and the longer it took, the less chance I had of saving Will. Thinking about it like that made the decision easy.

I patted Nan on the back and faced the policewoman, letting Nan compose herself before she turned round. I knew she wouldn't want me to see her crying.

"I'm sorry, Nan – Officer," I added, nodding at her. "I guess I didn't really notice the time. I've been out with some friends."

"So not on the choir trip then?" The policewoman picked up the note I had scribbled so hurriedly. "And it's Constable Clark."

"No," I whispered, hanging my head.

"When the school rang this morning to see where you were, your poor Nan was frantic and called us. Do you not think a call home might have been in order? I assume you have your mobile?"

"I know, and I'm sorry. There wasn't any phone reception where we were and I fell asleep."

The policewoman reached for her little notebook.

"So who are the friends you've been with? Do we need to go and tell their parents too?"

"It was just one friend actually. We lost track of time, that's all."

"And the name of this friend?" She had her pencil poised over her book.

"It was Will from up the road. Will Dempsey."

"What have you been doing, Lily?" Nan said, shaking

her head. "Why have you been lying to me?"

"I haven't…" I started before remembering about the note.

Constable Clark stepped towards me, hands up in a calming gesture.

"It's OK, Lily, you're home now. Why don't you come and sit down and you can tell us exactly where you've been."

"Oh, Nan, I'm so sorry!" I wailed, grabbing her close again.

I felt her stiffen in surprise. We really weren't into overt displays of affection. I hugged her tighter, making sure my mouth was close to her ear.

"Please get rid of her. I'll tell you everything but I have to be quick."

She gave a barely perceptible nod, then patted me on the back.

"Now now, dear, don't fret. You're home safely now, that's what matters."

"All I really want to do right now is to go to the bathroom and then get a bit of toast," I announced as I relaxed my grip.

"But—" started the policewoman.

Nan interrupted her.

"I think I can take it from here, Constable. Thank you for coming round so promptly, and I can assure you that I'll be having a word with her."

The policewoman looked uncertain.

"All right, I'm just pleased that we have you back safe and sound, Lily. Please think of others the next time you want to stay out all night. Your antics have caused a lot of grief and you've wasted a lot of police time. Are you sure there's nothing else you'd like to tell me?"

I remembered the phone call I'd made to the emergency services. Had they put two and two together? If so I had no chance.

"No, nothing. I just made a mistake, that's all."

I held my breath, looking down at my scuffed Converse and the jeans splattered with Will's blood. Luckily it looked more like mud.

"Honestly," said Nan before the policewoman could say anything. "I think I'm OK to deal with her now. But thank you again for coming to see me. Next time I'll leave it a little longer before I call you – I don't like to waste police time."

Nan looked at me with her eyebrows raised and I looked back at the floor again.

The policewoman turned to Nan and handed her a card.

"I'm glad she's home safely, Mrs Wakefield. Here are my details – please call me if you want me to have a chat with her, OK?"

Nan was backing her up to the door.

"That sounds very sensible, Constable Clark, thank you. And I'll be sure to talk to her now."

The rest of the conversation was lost to me as I shot

down the corridor into the bathroom. I shut the door behind me and turned to open the cupboard.

I had no idea why Nan kept all those medicines, but I was grateful that she did. All I had to do was to work my way through the boxes and find the amoxycillin. I was standing on my toes trying to see to the back of the shelf when she started pounding on the door.

"Right, she's gone. I want you out of there NOW. And I want some proper answers."

What was I going to say? I had no idea, and even without a watch I knew I was running out of time. I could hear her standing outside the door, fingers drumming impatiently. I was going to have to tell her something, and the truth was probably easiest. I turned the key and stepped back. She pushed the door wide and saw the open cupboard.

"What are you looking for?" she asked sharply. "What have you done?"

I took a deep breath. "I need amoxycillin, as much as you have."

Will is fading fast, his breathing slow and shallow. We can't keep his temperature down, and he's been unconscious now for ages. The walls of the little room seem to be closing in on us and I long to take him up into the open air. I remember the park where he walked with his dog, and wish for the same cooling breeze for his face. Every so often I hear Mason walk up and down outside. Sometimes there are voices, but no one is allowed in but Carita.

I'm holding his fingers tightly, willing him not to go. I realise that I'm rocking and rocking, as if my movement could pump the life back into him. My friend is dying and I have no more tears.

We wait.

Nan put the cup of coffee down on the table in front of me, next to the various packets of amoxycillin, and then turned back to the toaster. The clock on the cooker said 12:53.

"Really, Nan, I don't have the time. I just mentioned the toast to get rid of the policewoman."

"I've already told you, young lady, you're not going anywhere, particularly not with those," she pointed at the boxes of drugs, "until you tell me what's going on."

"I want to but there's no time. All I can say is that someone's life depends on me getting those medicines to where they need to go, and in getting them there quickly."

I took a sip of the coffee and shut my eyes briefly, enjoying the fleeting moment of normality.

"And is 'Amox-i-cillin' really the same as 'Amox-y-cillin'?" I asked. "It's important that I get it right."

"They're the same," she said. "The one with the 'Y' is an old spelling, that's all. But that's irrelevant. These are strong medicines, and there are a lot of them.

You have to tell me who they're for. They might not be the right ones for the infection, and anyway, the person really must see a doctor. Can't you take them to casualty?"

I shook my head. "I'm sorry, Nan, that's just not possible. I've tried."

"Can you bring them to me?"

I looked up from my mug and into her eyes, eyes that were old but still missed nothing. There was something else there too, something I couldn't place.

"It's a good idea," I said, "and I'll mention it, but right now I have to go back."

"What if I say no?"

She was only asking all these questions because she loved me, I knew that. The effects of not sleeping for twenty-four hours were catching up with me, and I felt almost too exhausted to speak. I took another mouthful of the coffee, finally feeling the caffeine starting to mop up the cotton wool that seemed to be stuffed in my brain.

"You know you've always told me to do what's right? Well, that's what I'm doing. And I have to go now."

Nan opened one of the kitchen drawers. Pulling out a carrier bag, she put the medicines inside.

I took a final swig of coffee as I stood up. "Can you please do me a favour? Can you call Will's mum and tell her that he's with me? I don't want her worrying too."

She nodded, holding out the bag towards me. "You'll

get in trouble if someone sees you carrying all that. Here."

"Thanks, Nan. Oh, do we have any Calpol too? That's what Mum used to give the twins, wasn't it?"

As I reached for the bag she grabbed my wrist in a vice-like grip. "Are these for the babies? Is it still going on?"

"What? What do you mean?"

"Who is this really for? I'm not letting you go until you tell me."

Her grip tightened around my wrist. I knew that I could get away, but it would mean pushing her hard and I couldn't bring myself to do that. She knew it too, and we stood there for a second, nose to nose, waiting for the next move.

"Nan, I don't have time to argue – it's an emergency. I really need this stuff. What else have you been stockpiling it for if it wasn't for an emergency?"

"I've been keeping it in case it was needed," she said, dropping my arm and turning away. "In case the immunity wore off."

"What? What do you mean?"

"There are things you need to know before you go. I'm going to call—"

She stopped as the doorbell rang, and seconds later rang again, much more insistently.

"You sit there. Let me just get rid of whoever that is. I'll be quick."

She made her way to the front door and I heard her conversation. It was Will's mum, who had obviously just had a visit from the policewoman. There was no way I could look her in the eye and say that Will was fine. Grabbing the bag, I ran towards the back door, and before they arrived in the kitchen I was gone.

I ran through the street, searching for clockfaces as I went. Everything had taken so much longer than I thought, and it was taking more long minutes to get all the way back to the warehouse. I clutched my precious cargo close to me, determined not to drop anything. There seemed to be a huge number of people on the streets, office workers milling about getting their sandwiches, couriers whizzing around on their bikes delivering parcels, and packs of pensioners, walking slowly along the pavement chatting. I swore under my breath as I dodged one particularly leisurely group, and ended up sprinting down the road itself.

I thought that I knew how long the trip back would take me, but as I ran past the church I could see the hand move on to the three. I was cutting it fine – too fine. As I sprinted towards the last corner I heard the bells begin to strike the quarter hour. I ran so fast that I felt as though my heart was going to jump out of my chest. I had to get back to Dane before the lift went down without me – I couldn't possibly fail when I had got so close. Looking up I saw the door of the warehouse closing.

"Noooo!" I yelled. "Dane, let me in!"

"Have you got it?" His voice was low as he threw open the door.

"Of course I do! But we're wasting time…"

I had to pause to suck some more air into my protesting lungs. All I wanted was to slide down to the floor and collapse in a small heap, but there was no time. I pushed past him.

"Come on then, let's go and get these drugs to him," I gasped, racing across the warehouse towards the lift, which stood open.

Dane turned to bolt the door. He hesitated.

"Are you sure, Lily? If you go down and Will dies, you might never come back. Give me the medicine and run while you can."

"My deal with the Farmer was that if I saved Will and brought medicines and instructions on how to use them we could all go free."

"Exactly, so stay here and I'll send him back to you – if he lives. You have nothing to lose." The lift machinery started to clank into life. "But if you come down and the drugs don't work, then what's to stop the Farmer going back to the original plan?"

I didn't trust the Farmer for a minute to send Will up. Why would he? But if I returned and joined my friends, then I had to deal with the consequences of whatever happened.

"I'm not abandoning my friends. They wouldn't

abandon me so I'm coming back down. Let's go."

I stepped into the lift and started pulling across the outer gate.

Dane flicked out the lights in the warehouse and jumped into the lift as it started to move. He finished shutting the outer gate and I heard him haul the inner one into position. Everything was completely dark.

"Are you sure you have exactly what we need?" he asked.

"Yes. There's more too, other drugs that will help quickly."

"That's OK then. And it's good you know how to use them. You can teach the others."

My heart sank as I realised what that meant. I had automatically assumed that, as they knew which drug they wanted, at least one of them would know how to use it. If they didn't, what was I going to do – guess? Why hadn't I asked Nan?

It was a stupid, stupid mistake. I turned to face the wall, slapping it in frustration. Not enough of the drug and the children would die. Too much and they could also die. The babies were also far too little to take a tablet, and I prayed that whatever Nan had put in the carrier bag it had included some instructions.

"You OK?" asked Dane, surprised.

"Just nerves I guess."

"Remember to keep quiet this time and they'll ignore

you, OK?"

I was about to ask him what on earth he was talking about when I remembered the Crop. He must have thought I was nervous because of them.

"Why are you doing all this, Dane? What's in it for you? If you wanted girls from Above to become Breeders, why not just grab one outside the warehouse?"

He gave a tired laugh.

"This wasn't actually the plan, you know. I had something rather more subtle in mind, but you girls really made life complicated."

"Aria mentioned a plan. She was really upset that she had failed you."

"Did she tell you what it was?"

"That you needed someone special from the Tube platform and were going to take them down to the Community using the old crop tunnels."

There was silence, and in the darkness I couldn't see if he was surprised that I knew so much.

"Did she tell you who we wanted?" he asked eventually. "Do you know what her mission was really about?"

Something about his tone chilled me, and I took half a step backwards.

"We were planning on bringing you down the secret back route through the Crop levels," he said. "But it had to be done quickly, while they were still feeding, and Aria didn't make it back in time. Instead she went Above with you."

"Me? You wanted me?"

"It had to be you. No one else could do what you can do."

"What are you talking about?"

He didn't answer immediately, and I thought maybe he wasn't going to, but then I caught the musty dead smell again. We were passing the Crop. I stayed silent, the questions backing up in my brain. What could they possibly want with me?

"On the way up I told you about the baby who had been taken Above," he said eventually. "The one who didn't come back, remember?"

I nodded, confused. "Yes, what about it?"

"She was the Farmer's child. All the other children he's had have died of the infection. Every single one apart from her. He has no one else to take over from him. No one except for that baby. No one but you, Lily."

His meaning was clear.

"Me?" I asked with an indignant squeak. "You think the Farmer is my father? That's rubbish!"

"It is you. Why do you think that you got past the Crop? They know you have the Affinity. With you we can overthrow the Farmer, get rid of the Crop and rebuild a proper community."

There was no doubting the excitement in his voice. He truly believed what he had just told me.

"You've got everything wrong. I've got parents, they've just moved away, that's all."

"You've been lied to, Lily. There's no doubt it's you. It's going to be great!"

I stopped listening to him, appalled. It couldn't possibly be true. He and Aria had to have made a mistake. There must have been another girl on the Tube platform. They just got the wrong one, that's all. It was all just a horrible coincidence.

Dane was still talking. "It's the Crop that's the key. It's how he controls everything – he breeds it, he nurtures it and he feeds it, and he is the only one who can do it. If anyone else were to get into this lift without the protection of the gate, they'd be dead in minutes. And building up the levels to use it as a weapon – that was the final straw."

He paused for a moment, and when he spoke again his voice was softer.

"But you'll be able to take over, Lily. We can overpower the Farmer and then you can control the Crop for us. We need them as protection, that's all. Not as a weapon."

I shook my head, forgetting that he couldn't see me in the dark.

"You're wrong, Dane. It can't possibly be me."

"It's OK, I understand that it'll take a bit of getting used to, but now we have an excuse for you to be down here, so we'll have plenty of time."

He really believed it; that was clear from his voice. How was I going to convince him before he took me up to the Crop for a test? That was never going to go well.

Before I could speak again his hand found my arm and he squeezed it. "Not a word to anyone, all right? If he hears about this we're all dead."

I was about to reply when the greasy smell of fried food hit me, adding to my general feeling of nausea. We were nearly at the bottom. As the lift shuddered to a halt, the dim light from the corridor reached us. Dane peered at me.

"You don't look well," he said. "I hope that I've not upset you too much?"

"Why would I be upset? He's obviously not my father – it's a ridiculous suggestion. Come on, I want to get back to Will."

"OK, OK, just let me get this – mind your fingers."

He unlatched the gate and it sprang back, closing tightly into a recess in the lift wall.

There were no guards this time, and Dane set off down the corridor with me right behind. He knew that I wasn't going to try to escape. I jogged alongside him.

"We need to run faster, Dane. Get a shift on."

It's too late. Will is lost, his body limp. I can't let his passing go unrecorded so I'll make the mark for him as he joins our others, the long, long list of children who never really were. Before he is taken away I will cut my own thumb, and cover his hand in my blood. His handprint will be left on the wall alongside Carita's lost children, their cousins and the other children who would have been their friends if things had been different. It will be all that is left to show that he was ever here at all.

The race through the tunnels seemed endless, but finally we made it back to the miserable room where Will was being kept. There was no sign of Lance or any other guard. I threw aside the thick curtain and burst through the entrance, desperate to get the medicine into Will as quickly as possible. Aria was sitting on the floor leaning back against the opposite wall, her eyes closed, cradling Will's head on her lap. Carita was also there. She looked exhausted.

"OK, I've got the drugs. Let's get them in him!" I said as I dropped to the floor next to Aria.

She opened her eyes slowly and looked at me. I remembered reading a book once where someone was said to have "dead eyes" and never really understanding what they meant, but looking at Aria's face it became clear. All the life, the emotion, the fight – everything was gone.

I rocked back on my heels.

"Are we too late?" I whispered.

She just turned her head away. I looked down at my friend and reached over to touch his head, to say goodbye, to wish I had been quicker. I was expecting him to be cold, but he was very, very hot. I grabbed his hand and found a weak pulse.

"He's not dead! Come on, we can still help him!"

"It's no use. Once they get to this stage they always die."

Aria's voice was flat, beaten. I tapped Will on the cheek to try and get a response.

"That might have been the case before, but it isn't now. Come on, I need your help. COME ON!"

Finally Aria seemed to snap out of her trance-like state. Carita hovered around, nervously watching everything. I looked around. The tin mug that Lance had brought earlier was nowhere to be seen.

"I need water – some in a cup for drinking, some for more sponging. Is Dane still outside? Can he get something quickly?"

Carita shook her head, biting her lip. "I'll go. Dane will have gone to report back to the Farmer. I'll be back in a minute," she called as she turned and ran down the corridor.

The carrier bag I'd brought from home was beside me on the floor. I tipped everything out of it.

"Let's get the temperature down," I mumbled, wishing that Nan was with me.

He was unconscious so there was no point in giving him a tablet.

"What can I use?" I asked myself out loud.

I sifted through the packets, finally spotting something that looked like a fat pen. Nan must have added it to the bag. It was an emergency pre-filled syringe, the type that you just had to press on to the skin and it delivered the jab. Without worrying about anything else I stripped off Will's shirt. His skin was burning hot under my fingers as I found the right bit of his upper arm. As I was about to shoot the needle home I looked more closely at the writing on the side. Adrenaline.

"No!" I shouted, throwing it aside. That wasn't what I needed. I picked up some more of the packets, thinking hard. There were capsules and chewable tablets, and bottles with powder in to mix up to give to children. There was nothing I could give him without water. I sat back.

"What's wrong?" asked Aria. "Why are you waiting?"

"I need water, and I need it now! Tell Carita to hurry."

Aria leapt up and ran to the doorway. I turned back to Will, frustrated that there was nothing that I could do. There was a damp cloth next to him, so I laid it on his chest, hoping that it would feel cool to him.

"Come on, Will," I urged. "Hold on. I've got the medicine for you – just hang on while I work out how to get it in you."

I wished that I could move him to somewhere more comfortable than the stone floor. The thin cloth he was lying on was next to useless. I knelt down next to his head and stroked the hair back from his face, then rolled his shirt up into a ball and put it under his head.

"Fight, Will, fight!" I whispered. "I can't bear the thought of losing you. You mean too much to me."

"I'm here! Where do you want this water?"

Carita was back with an old-fashioned glass bottle full of water, a small cup and a bowl, with Aria right behind her. She brought them over to me and I sat up quickly, reaching for the medicines. I found some capsules of the amoxycillin and dropped the powder from inside into the water, scanning the leaflet in the dim light to check the dosage information. I did the same with some paracetamol capsules too. I had no idea if I was supposed to mix them, but there was no time to waste. Then I stirred it all with my finger, trying to get as much as possible dissolved.

"Right, you two try and sit him up a bit," I said, absently-mindedly licking my finger. "Yuk! That tastes vile. I guess the taste might bring him round if nothing else does."

Between them, Aria and Carita hauled Will up into a sitting position. "What do you need us to do now?" asked Aria nervously.

"Just keep him steady while I try and get some of this medicine into him. Ready?"

As they lifted his head up, Will's eyelids fluttered.

"Come on, Will," I soothed. "Here, try this."

I touched his lips with the cup and he opened his mouth. I carefully tipped in some of the mixture. He immediately jerked his head back and spat it out.

"Hey, Will, don't do that. You need to drink this."

I held it up again and he tried to move his mouth away.

"I mean it! You have to take it now."

His eyes opened a tiny crack.

"Bossy," he croaked, but opened his mouth and drank the rest of the medicine without complaint, only grimacing once it was all finished. He opened his eyes again and slowly focused on me. "You came back. Thanks."

"No problem," I said, smiling. "Just keep taking the medicine and we'll be out of here in no time, I promise you."

There was a slight flicker at the corner of his mouth before his eyes closed and his head sank back down on to his chest. I motioned to the others to lie him back down again. Aria smoothed the hair off his forehead as she made him comfortable.

"Is that it? Does he get better now?"

"Not that quickly. He needs more water, so we have to keep getting that into him, and we have to keep him cool. If we're in time his temperature will start to come down in the next few hours, so the only thing we can do is wait."

"And all this stuff – where on earth did you get your hands on this?"

Something told me not to say anything, just in case someone was listening. If the Community knew that Nan had a stockpile of prescription medicines they might be ruthless in getting it off her.

"You need to know the right people," I said vaguely.

"Now Will is all right, can you help Reilly?" Carita reached out towards me, hope on her face at last.

I rummaged in the pile of medicines, reading the sides of the packets until I found the one I wanted.

"This one is for babies. The bottle has powder in it. Fill it up to the line with clean water and give it a good shake, then feed him two of these tiny spoonfuls three times a day," I said, reading the leaflet and fishing out the spoon from the bottom of the box.

"Thank you, I'll take it to him now. One of my friends is looking after him for me. I didn't want to bring him in here." She gave me an apologetic smile.

"Does anyone else need medicine right now? Do you want to take more?"

"No, Reilly is the only one who might be sick at the moment. The Farmer will want to see this before anyone else has any, I'm sure."

With Will comfortable, all we could do was wait. Aria and I sat and watched Will, taking it in turns to sponge him down. It was slow going though, and nothing we could do was going to hurry it up. Hour after hour we sat there, barely speaking. Eventually Carita arrived back with some food, a mostly tasteless sort of stew, but as none of us had eaten for hours we ate it greedily. I tried not to think about what the slightly stringy meat might be. Shortly after that we could hear a distant bell ringing.

"We heard that before, Aria. Is it some sort of lights-out warning?"

She had started on another round of sponging, trying to help keep Will's temperature down, but paused and turned towards me.

"Yes, that's the warning to return to the sleeping quarters. People don't walk around while we are sleeping; it's not allowed." She looked around our room. "I guess they're not going to make us go to the dormitories. The Farmer told me earlier that I can stay here with you two."

She looked at Will for a moment.

"We may be winning, Lily. He seems quieter, don't you think?"

She smiled at him briefly and sponged his shoulder tenderly. It was almost heartbreaking to watch, and I had to swallow hard, unable to speak.

Along with the stew, Carita had brought a tiny candle so that we could watch Will in the dark. It had only been lit for a moment before all the overhead lights blinked out. Aria was still next to him, sitting on the floor with her chin resting on her knees.

"As you're stuck here now, Carita, why don't you and Lily try and get some sleep?" said Aria. "I'll look after him for a while."

"There's no way I'm going to sleep. I'm far too wound up," I said.

"Well, lie down and rest then. Who knows what'll happen tomorrow?"

She had a point, so I stretched out on the hard stone floor, and as I shut my eyes I felt the need to sleep crashing over me like a wave. Within seconds, I was gone.

Lily is asleep at last. She must need it; she's been up for hours and hours. Days maybe. I still don't know what she did to get the medicines, I think she's worried about talking in front of some of the others, but they've all gone now. Everyone is asleep apart from me. Even Will.

He is lying almost motionless on the thin sheet. He always seemed so strong but I'm not sure that their medicine was in time. Despite what I said he doesn't look any better to me, but then he's not dead yet either, so we have to keep trying.

In the dim light of the candle I can see the outlines of Carita and Lily, and I think about the events that have brought us all here together. And I think about Dane and his new plan for Lily. I can't believe that he had the nerve to suggest it, or that the Farmer would actually approve it. If the drugs work though, what will they do? With the right drugs we can save the babies, and won't need new Breeders from Above. Will Dane – and the Farmer – let her go? The questions go round and round my mind for ages until I hear a noise. Carita is waking up.

"Hello, Aria. Let me take over for a bit. I was able to get some rest earlier so I'm not so tired now. You must be exhausted."

"I'm all right for a while." I nod towards Will, who looks nearly dead in the flickering light. "Do you think he looks any better? I'm not sure I do."

"It's impossible to tell in this gloom. How long was I asleep?"

"Not so long. We've got ages before the lights come back on."

Carita stretches and looks over at Lily, who is sleeping up against the far wall.

"Good, she looks as if she needs the rest."

"Lily said that we'll have to give him some more medicine in a bit, but I can do it. I don't think we'll need to disturb her."

"How does she know all this stuff?" Carita whispers to me. "It's as if she was a Breeder and had a child of her own."

"She told me that she had baby brothers – twins – and that she used to help her mother with them."

"And where on earth did all the medicines come from?"

"I don't know. I remember her telling me that Nan had a lot of medicine, but why would anyone have all this?"

"Who is Nan?"

"She's the woman Lily lives with, but she's not a relative. Apparently that's very odd up Above. All her family have moved away, or that's what Will told me. I think they left her behind and she went to live with Nan, and all Lily's old friends now hate her."

"Oh, she must be upset about that. Is she Assigned to Will?"

"I don't think so. I did ask him that and he just looked

uncomfortable. I think it's time for the next dose of medicine, don't you?"

I had only heard the last few sentences, but it was clear that Aria and Will had been talking about me. It was also clear that the thought of being with me wasn't something he was enthusiastic about. I swallowed hard as an unexpected surge of emotion overwhelmed me.

They were leaning over Will, giving him the antibiotics that I'd left out and looking at him as if he were the most important person in the world. Just like Mum used to look at the twins. The thought slipped out before I had the chance to squash it, and a tear of self-pity suddenly dripped on my cheek. I had no idea why my own parents preferred my brothers to me, or were so ready to abandon me and move to the other side of the world. When I'd suggested staying in London to do my exams I didn't think for a minute that they would agree with me. I thought they'd want me with them, helping with the boys, being a family. But I was wrong. Mum had leapt at the idea and before I knew what was happening my stuff was at Nan's place and my kitten had been rehomed. I'd barely heard from them since they'd gone – a few Skype calls on the computer and that was it.

Everything finally slotted into place, and everything I felt that I knew and understood blurred slightly. It all made sense if what Dane said was true. If I was adopted wouldn't my parents prefer their own biological children?

Was that man really my father? What would my life have been like if I'd stayed? I couldn't imagine growing up under the rules and constraints of the Community.

Nothing about who I was and where I belonged made sense any more, and I felt an icy hand clutch at my heart. I was utterly alone.

Watching Aria tenderly looking after Will was too painful, and I didn't want any more responsibility. I curled up into a small ball on my side and let the tears flow silently until I cried myself back to sleep.

It must have been quite a long time later when I woke. The room was nearly in darkness, the candle burned down to a tiny stub. Across the room I could see Aria slumped up against the wall, sound asleep. Carita was curled up next to her. Will was lying perfectly still in the middle of the room.

I struggled up, instantly awake, and scrambled over next to him. He looked peaceful in the shadows, the dark smudges cleared from under his eyes and the sheen of sweat finally gone. I had been too late with the antibiotics.

Will was dead.

I couldn't find it in myself to cry; he looked so much better now his long battle was done.

Rocking back on my heels I took a deep breath. I couldn't believe that I was never going to talk to him again, never going to feel his kiss. I had to get back Above to tell his mum, as I'd promised, to let her know that her brave son had died trying to help someone else. I had to escape. I turned back towards Will to say goodbye, to memorise his face before I had to leave it forever, and suddenly the tears came, blurring my vision. Unchecked, the hot, fat tears streamed down my cheeks, and I sat next to his body for a while, weeping silently for my friend. Finally I leaned over to kiss his forehead, and a tear dripped on to his cheek from mine.

He twitched. Stunned, I wiped my eyes and looked closer, leaning over and stroking his cheek just once. He stirred, and opened and closed his mouth a couple of times, before giving a distinct snore.

"We did it," I breathed to the sleeping room. "We saved his life."

CHAPTER 20

Since returning to the Community I'd come to a strange sense of acceptance. It was pointless to try and come between Aria and Will – all I would do was make both of them hate me. We'd been through so much together, and if that was how it was, so be it. I didn't know how much time any of us had left and it seemed stupid to waste any of it.

The candle was practically burned out when Aria stirred. As she sat up I motioned to her to be quiet because Will was asleep. A broad grin spread across her face.

"Really? Is he honestly all right?" she whispered, looking between Will and me.

I nodded, my hand hovering over his. But I couldn't bring myself to touch him so I let it fall back. "He's sleeping like a baby."

"I can't believe it. I've never seen anyone recover from the sickness. I wish we'd had those medicines before."

She turned and shook Carita. "Wake up," she hissed. "The medicines have worked! You must see if Reilly is better!"

"What?" said Carita. "It really works? Let me see!"

Jumping up she leapt over towards Will, placing one hand on his forehead and feeling for his pulse with the other. Without waking up he shook her off and turned over, exhaling heavily.

"It works," she breathed, picking up one of the packets of pills and turning them over in her hands. "Reilly is going to live."

"I hope so," I said. "Why don't you go to him?"

"It's curfew until the lights come on. None of us would dare to walk around in the dark."

As she spoke there was the sound of a distant bell and the light bulb hanging from the centre of the room started to glow dimly.

Carita stood up immediately.

"I must go. Thank you, Lily, for everything – for saving my baby."

"Here," I said, jumping up and handing her a bottle of Calpol. "Take this too. If he gets a temperature, give him one small spoonful, no more than two times a day. He shouldn't really have it until he is two months old, but it's worth you taking it now, just in case of another emergency."

"Thank you." She turned to Aria and the pair of them held hands for a moment. "I hope that I see you again, sister. Fight hard."

Aria nodded, her bottom lip caught between her teeth. "Look after Reilly. Keep yourself safe."

They dropped hands and nodded at each other, then Carita was gone. A single tear ran down Aria's cheek and she brushed it away quickly.

"The Farmer will be here soon. We must be ready."

"What do you mean?" I asked. "What do we need to do?"

"We have to save our lives," she said simply, gathering the boxes of antibiotics together and giving them to me.

As we spoke, Will stirred, turning back over and sighing. Finally he opened his eyes. His skin was no longer that horrible grey colour but a healthy pink, and his still-damp hair was sticking up in all directions. To me he looked absolutely gorgeous, and it was all I could do not to reach out and touch him.

"Hi," I said, trying to sound brisk. "How are you feeling now?"

He sat up, stretching out his shoulders and back, and I had to look away before I went completely beetroot.

"Back's a bit stiff," he said. "Feels as if I've been sleeping on a stone floor."

He caught my eye and smiled, tapping his palm down on the smooth rock beneath his thin sheet. As he looked down at the stone he stopped suddenly.

"Um, Lily, I don't seem to be wearing my shirt. Any chance of getting it back?"

I scrambled up quickly so he couldn't see my cheeks, which were burning.

"It's just over here. We had to take it off to sponge you down, keep you cool. Sorry."

He took the shirt from my outstretched hand. "Hey, don't apologise. I don't remember too much. What happened?"

I was working out where to start when Aria leapt in.

"You got the sickness, Will, the one that kills our babies. You got an infected cut, probably from something that bit you. It's really dangerous for people who aren't immune."

She moved over and sat down next to him The two of them looked so comfortable together, and I could feel myself welling up. I didn't want to cry – he was getting better, it was all good, and I had to focus on that.

"I remember being in the big room," he said, "then it all gets a bit hazy. I had a strange dream about you, Lily. I thought you might have escaped."

"She volunteered to go up and get the medicine to save you," said Aria. "Without her you'd be dead by now."

"Really? Wow, Lily, thank you."

He turned towards me, but I looked away.

"You'd have done the same for any of us," I said,

shrugging as I busied myself arranging the medicine boxes in the bag.

"So where exactly did all those come from?"

I glanced towards the opening into the corridor. I still didn't know who was out there, and I couldn't risk exposing Nan to anyone else.

"I'll tell you later; it's not important. What's good is that you're well and that they now have something to give to the babies."

At that point there was a brief commotion outside in the corridor, and the Farmer swept into the room, followed by Mason and Lance, and three other men I'd not seen before. Behind them were several women. Within seconds the place was packed, and I was glad that Aria had suggested getting everything together – we were in danger of getting trampled. Will and I turned so that we were facing the crowd.

"We should have run the minute you woke," I whispered to Will from behind my hand. "I'm not sure I like the look of this."

As I spoke the Farmer looked Will up and down.

"Are you fully recovered?" he demanded.

"Much better than I was, thank you."

There was a hushed silence as everyone waited to hear what the Farmer was going to say.

"Where is the other? Bring her here."

The crowd parted as if it had been unzipped, and Aria was nudged forward. Someone got hold of my arm too,

thrusting me forward so hard that I nearly dropped the carrier bag.

With a brief glance at Aria the Farmer turned his back and started walking towards the door, scattering the crowd of women at the back who were peering over the men's shoulders, trying to get a glimpse of Will.

"Bring the girls to my rooms," he called over his shoulder as he swept out.

Mason and Lance took Aria and me by the arms and led us back down the corridor to the fancier rooms we had been in the day before. I craned my neck as we walked but I couldn't see Will.

"Are they bringing Will?" I whispered to Aria when we were close enough to speak. "Do you think that he'll be OK?"

She shrugged, her face white and her eyes full of fear. I had been feeling quite confident that I could talk us out of the mess, now that Will was OK, but seeing her face all my bravado deserted me. She looked as if she was on her way to a firing squad.

The sick taste is back in my mouth. There's no way that the Farmer is going to let us all go, not when he needs Feeders. Lily is clutching the bag of medicines, the only thing that stands between her and the end. The Farmer sweeps ahead of us into his personal chamber and sits in his special chair behind the desk. We stand facing him. I look at Lily, who is still looking around frantically. Dane and Will are not with us.

I want to see his face again before the end. Whatever deal Lily thinks she's negotiated, there's no way they are letting me go. I'm done for. Lily seems confident, though, as she stands there, facing the Farmer.

We wait, the blood pounding in my ears. The Farmer opens his book before looking up at Lily.

"How can we be sure it was your medicine that cured him?"

Lily stands up a little straighter.

"No one can be sure that it was the antibiotics. But Aria and Carita believed that Will was as good as dead before I gave him the medicine."

Lily turns to look at me so I nod quickly, not daring to speak myself.

"And how do we know that it will be the same for the children?"

"I gave Carita some medicine for Reilly. Has he improved?" asks Lily. She pauses, but there is no answer. "Look, I've kept my side of the bargain. I've brought you medicines you couldn't get for yourselves and saved my friend. The three of us should be free to go."

"The three of you?"

"Of course. Me, Aria and Will." She hesitates and looks around. "Where is Will?"

The Farmer puts up his hand to silence her.

"Enough. Show me the medicine."

Lily hesitates for a fraction of a second before walking

forward with her bag. Then she reaches into it and starts pulling out the packets, transferring them into the crook of her arm.

"OK, so what we have here is a whole range of amoxycillin, in different formulations. Some of them are branded, others are generic, and obviously the dosage varies. There's tablets, filled capsules and some bottles of the powder for the paediatric suspension. Those need reconstituting with the appropriate amount of water. We've also got an emergency treatment for anaphylactic shock."

She sounds as if she is talking in code, and as she talks she's piling up the boxes in her arm, creating a tottering mound.

"And to be really effective you also need a good paediatric analgesic such as paracetamol, and that's here. I need to be careful with some of that as it's pre-diluted in glass bottles and I don't want to drop them."

She sets the bottles on the table, then stops and looks at the Farmer.

"All clear then? Here they are."

He stares at her.

"And how exactly do they all work?"

"I've just explained all that. Now, where is my friend?"

"You'll get your friend when I get my information."

"I've told you everything I'm going to. When Will is back here I might remember a bit more."

There is a silence in the room. No one has ever spoken

to the Farmer like that. I see his knuckles whiten, then he reaches for one of the bottles on the table. He glances at the label and puts it down again.

Everyone is still, waiting, then Lily steps forward and drops all the cardboard packets on the desk. They sit in a pile between her and the Farmer. The seconds seem to last forever.

"Bring the boy!" he commands.

Lily continues to stand there, making no effort to clear up the boxes. We wait, listening, and finally there is the sound of hurrying feet. Moments later, Dane and Will appear in the room. My heart leaps as I see him and I heave a huge but silent sigh of relief that both of them seem all right.

"You OK?" he mouths to Lily.

She nods. "You too?"

He looks at me and I nod as well. Dane is leaning against the wall, as if he doesn't care what's going on, but he keeps glancing over at us. No one speaks. The Farmer sits back in his chair.

"Continue," he orders, waving an arm in the direction of the medicines.

Lily picks up the first packet.

"I'm going to need a pen and paper."

The Farmer looks towards Dane, who is closest to the door. "Paper then, and quickly. It's time to get this finished."

Lily flicks a quick glance at me, and then at Will. I see

THE BENEATH

her hand is shaking. What does the Farmer mean?

After a few minutes Dane reappeared and handed me a lined pad of paper and a cheap biro.

"Write down what we need to know," commanded the Farmer.

I started working my way through the packets. Using my best, clear handwriting I made a list of the different types of antibiotic, most of which were just varying brands of amoxycillin. I couldn't believe that all the stuff Nan used to go on about had sunk in enough to be useful. Then I wrote down exactly what we'd done for Will, and what they ought to do for a baby. As I wrote I was conscious of a couple of the other men in the room edging closer. I froze for a second then realised that they were just watching me put pen to paper. When I had finished, I straightened up. The Farmer was looking at me too.

"None of this will be of any use to anyone who can't read. Please make sure they know what to do."

He said nothing as I handed the pad and pen to Dane along with the medicines, which I'd repacked in the bag as I went. As I stepped back next to Will the Farmer relaxed further into his chair, placing his elbows on the arms and tenting his fingers under his chin.

"So, we have the medicine we need, and you have saved your friend. Your time here is done."

"Does that mean we can go?" I asked, incredulous.

He gave a sharp incline of his head.

"Thank you, but I'm not going anywhere without Aria," I said, folding my arms. "That was our deal – all three of us, remember?"

The Farmer sighed. "You dare to challenge me again? You are a very foolish girl." He stood up, and all the people in the room took a step backwards. "There will be no arguments from any of you. Dane, take Aria back to the cells. Mason, escort these two back to the lift. I will join you there shortly."

"But I can't leave Aria," I protested, whipping round in time to see Dane catch her arms up behind her back. She gave me a tiny smile.

"Please go, Lily. You've done all you can, and now we have medicines. The Breeders will be forever grateful."

"Enough!" called the Farmer with an edge of steel in his voice. "Dane, take her away now."

"No!"

I stretched out to reach Aria but Mason grabbed me and held me back. Dane led Aria to the door. For a moment her slim frame was silhouetted between the heavy drapes.

"Goodbye, Lily. Thank you for everything."

And then she was gone.

CHAPTER 21

I found myself staring at the empty doorframe, a hollow feeling in my chest as I fought down the rising panic. What were they going to do to her? I glanced sideways at Will, trying to gauge if he was up for a fight, but he still looked exhausted. The sound of Aria's footsteps faded.

"What's going on?" he asked in an undertone as we turned back round to face the Farmer. "Do you think…"

"I don't know," I answered out of the side of my mouth. "I really don't."

As I spoke the Farmer lifted his hand.

"Silence. Take these two to the lift."

Mason, who still held my arm, tightened his grip and started manoeuvring me towards the door.

"But Aria…" I began, trying to turn back. Will grabbed me by the arm and helped lead me out.

"Shh! Come on, let's get out of here before they change their minds."

"What? Are you just going to leave her? Aren't you going to fight?" As I spoke, Mason continued hauling on my arm. Will was only just able to keep pace behind us. He looked quite white again. As our eyes met he raised his eyebrows and nodded towards Mason, then lifted his finger to his lips.

"Oh, I mean, yes, there's no point," I blustered loudly, hoping that Mason wouldn't realise that Will and I were having quite a different conversation.

"What's your plan?" I mouthed at him as we marched down another endless tunnel.

"Secret weapon," he mouthed back, smiling.

We reached a big crossroads in the tunnel. Air blew across our path from the larger tunnel coming from the right and Will stopped dead in the middle of the junction. Mason dragged me a few paces further on before he realised that Will had stopped.

"Come on," Mason growled. "You're going up. You don't want to be late for the lift."

Will turned round so that his back was to the wind, then raised one hand to his mouth before producing an ear-splitting whistle.

Mason turned around in anger. "What'd you think you're doing, disturbing everyone like that? You're lucky it wasn't rest time or it'd be right back to the Farmer for you." He let go of my arm but shoved me in the back, forcing me down the tunnel ahead of him. "Come on, I've got better things to do than this."

Will stayed still for a moment, scanning down the tunnels, but nothing happened.

Mason stopped and went back to him. "I'm supposed to get you two to the lift. Don't you want to leave?"

As he spoke I could see Will clenching his fists and rising up slightly on to the balls of his feet. He was going to try and fight Mason.

"Will, no, you're not fit enough!" I called as he dropped into a boxing stance.

Mason stopped dead and crossed his arms with a sigh. "Look, lad, you have to come with me. There's nothing here for you now. It's time to go."

Will started to move around him as if he was looking for the best angle of attack when we heard footsteps. Three Community men appeared out of the mouth of the main tunnel, stopping dead as they saw us. One began to laugh.

"Come on, Mason, are you going to fight the boy? One solid blow and he'll be down."

Will looked around then dropped his arms, outnumbered. "OK, you win. Just take good care of them, won't you?"

Mason hustled him up next to me and we started walking again.

"Them?" I asked in a low voice. "What on earth were you planning on doing?"

"I hoped that Foggy might come running. He'd scare these guys, and then we could go and get Aria. We can't leave them both behind!"

Foggy. With everything else going on I had forgotten about him again. But I knew that Will really loved him and would be horrified at the thought of leaving him down with the Community.

"I really thought he'd come if I whistled," he said, his voice breaking. "What am I going to tell Mum and Dad? We've had Foggy since I was ten. He's a member of the family."

"Do you think he'll have made his way out already? It's possible, right?"

"Possible but not very likely," he said, looking back over this shoulder. "I mean, how would he have got past the Crop? They'd make mincemeat of him."

"I'm not so sure," I said. "When we were up there the things definitely backed off, and I thought that was because of Foggy. He must be really frightening to whatever they are. I guess they've never seen a dog before."

As I spoke I realised that I could be quite wrong if what Dane told me was true. If I was the Farmer's daughter, perhaps they didn't attack because I was there and unwittingly controlling them. If that was the case then Foggy would never have survived alone. I tried not to think of that horrible smell as the Crop advanced, of my fear that, whatever it was, it was about to finish us off.

"And without Foggy," Will continued, "we've got no hope of rescuing Aria. How can we live with ourselves if we leave her behind?"

"In here." Mason's voice cut across us.

We had reached the lobby by the lift.

This time it wasn't so dark and I was able to see the lift more clearly. It was entirely ancient, with every bit of exposed metal rusted. The floor was the least rusty-looking part, which was a relief. I turned to Will as we were hustled inside – he looked white and strained.

"We can't leave them, Lily, we just can't!"

But it was clear we didn't have any choice. Three of the men were standing in a loose semicircle around the lift, and Mason was standing guard by the archway into the main tunnel. We would never get past them all.

"You're right," I whispered very quietly in his ear. "We'll just have to find a way to get back down again."

He nodded once but didn't turn to look at me. Snatching a glance at his profile I could see the tears glistening in his eyes. Reaching for his hand I gave it a quick squeeze, hoping that it might comfort us both. He squeezed it back and then dropped it as the men suddenly stood up straight. The Farmer swept round the corner and each of the men stepped back slightly, dropping their eyes. He stopped in front of the old brass plate on the wall outside and stuck his key in the lock. There was the sound of clicking as the key turned, and then the Farmer stepped into the lift with us, pocketing the key as he went.

One of the men pulled the heavy outer grille across the gap, and as soon as it clicked into place the lift groaned into life. Far above us I could hear the machinery whirr into action and the lift lurched upwards, making us stagger. The horrendous noise of the lift scraping against the wall hurt my ears, and I could see Will wincing too.

I knew what we had to do. As soon as the lift got us to the top, and we got out of the warehouse, we were going to go straight to the police. It was the only sensible choice, and the only way left for us to save Aria. If we could persuade them really quickly then hopefully the Farmer wouldn't have time to find her and drag her back up to the Crop.

I was a bit surprised that the Farmer hadn't considered we might do that, and the more I thought about it, the odder it seemed. It was hard to think though, with the awful scraping noise. I glanced over at Will, who had his fingers in his ears. The Farmer seemed completely oblivious to it, watching the stone wall race past, and as I watched too, the hair on the back of my neck started to stand up. Something was badly wrong.

The Farmer wasn't there to save us from the Crop, to protect us as the lift sped upwards.

The screeching of metal on stone abruptly stopped. There was only the comparative silence as the lift carried on clanking, working its way up the shaft. Will caught my eye then turned to see what I was looking at. He realised the problem immediately.

"He's not letting us go, is he?"

"I don't think so. There's no gate – nothing to stop them swarming in."

"How do we stop this thing?"

He spun round again, staring at the walls before turning on the Farmer. Grabbing him by the arm, Will pulled him round to face us.

"Where on earth are the buttons?" yelled Will.

The Farmer smiled slightly and shook Will's hand from his arm. "It was very naive of you two to think that I was ever going to let you go. You know far too much. It's time to accept your fate."

CHAPTER 22

Dane is walking me towards the cells. He's not talking because too many people are watching us – watching me. The women all look distraught, and Maria reaches out for my arm as we pass her. She is very pregnant.

"Is the rumour true?" She looks between me and Dane, who nods.

"He's let them go but she's to be punished." He is using his Listener voice, trying to sound commanding, but Maria knows better. She steps forward, barring my way down the tunnel.

"Thank you for the medicine, Aria. That was unbelievably brave. I'm so sorry that … this had to happen. I wish it could be different."

"It was my friend who got the medicine, not me."

She gives a tight smile. "But it was you who found the

friend." She rests her hand on her round belly. "This one has a chance to live now."

Before I can reply I hear the sound of running footsteps, and I see Lance coming round the corner, very red in the face. Dane sees him too, and I hear his sharp intake of breath. Lance reaches us and stops, bending down for a moment as he gasps.

"He hasn't, has he?" Dane's question is urgent.

Lance looks up and nods miserably, still unable to speak

"NO!" Dane slams his fist into the wall.

This is bad. I feel the cold fear racing down my spine.

"Tell me!" I shout, grabbing at his sleeve. "What's happened?"

He turns towards me and I see the water glistening in his eyes. "The Farmer has taken them up himself."

My knees turn to jelly. The small crowd of women in the tunnel are silent, mouths open in horror. There is only one time that the Farmer takes anyone up in the lift, and they never come back down.

I want to fight, to scream, to lash out, but instead I run. Dane doesn't try to stop me as I dodge everyone and race down the familiar tunnel, trying to run away from my own thoughts.

They will be sacrificed to the Crop, torn to pieces and eaten alive. I can feel the bile rising in my throat as I think about it. Is it already done? Has the lift delivered them to their end? We all know roughly what happens – the rumours tell us that, but none of us knows the truth.

Does Lily have the Affinity? Will she know what to do?

It was our plan that brought her here, but we didn't expect this. It's my fault that she's in that lift, waiting to be delivered to the Crop.

The tears in my eyes make it hard to see, and I stumble as I misjudge a corner. As I fall I catch my shoulder on the wall. The force spins me round and I end up in a heap on the floor. All I want to do is curl up into a ball, but as I sit there hugging my knees I hear an unexpected noise. Something is whining and scraping in a room a little way ahead. I get to my feet and creep along the tunnel.

The room is gloomy. This part of the Community is where we store things now, and people rarely come this way. Most of the rooms are full of boxes or are unfinished. I peer round the edge of the door and then start back in surprise.

"Foggy! What are you doing here?"

The dog is wearing a belt as a lead, and it's wedged between two rocks. The more he's pulled, the tighter it's got, and he's desperate to get past me and away. He looks even bigger in this tiny space. I've never noticed the teeth before, and I don't want to get anywhere near them. He starts to whine. I know that I'm going to have to go into the room. I feel my heart pounding as I start to edge my way round the wall. The smell is terrible and I breathe through my mouth to stop me gagging. As I get closer I see the knot on the collar.

I'm going to have to touch the dog.

All I want to do is run, and I feel cold and clammy. My hand is shaking as I reach forward. The dog jumps up and licks my hand, and I yelp and leap backwards, rubbing my hand down my trousers to get rid of the lick. Foggy sits down immediately, almost as if he knows I don't like it. Taking a deep breath I edge closer again.

First I try to loosen the lead from between the rocks, but it's wedged fast. I pull with all my strength but it won't budge. Now I have no choice. I reach out for his collar, feeling the fur on my fingers. It's more slippery than I expect, and that makes it worse. There is something horribly creepy about fur.

I concentrate on the collar and the lead that is knotted tightly on to it. It takes me a moment to work it loose, finally releasing the dog, and with an astonishing burst of power he's gone. With a single bark he shoots down the corridor and disappears round a corner. I slump back against the doorway, drained.

"Find them, Foggy," I whisper to the walls. "Help them."

The lift shuddered to a halt.

Will was looking at me in absolute horror as the Farmer's words sank in, and both of us stepped backwards in the lift, away from the gaping cavern. The dim light from inside the lift lit up a small circle of the space and I could see the closest columns, rough-hewn from the rock. On the floor at one side was the stick we had brought from Nan's, abandoned during the race to get away from the Crop.

The Farmer strode out of the lift and picked up the stick, shaking his head. He walked to the closest column and reached up, where a small recess was carved out of the rock at about head height. He lifted out a small box, and seconds later I heard the rasp of a match. He lit an old-fashioned oil lamp, adjusting the wick before he lifted it out of the recess. Then he turned towards us.

"There is no point in trying to run. The Crop will find you. Follow me and it will be over with quickly." He turned and walked away.

Both of us were pressed against the back wall of the lift. I remembered the journey up with Dane and what happened when the Crop arrived, and I could feel my whole body shaking.

"No, no, this can't be happening," I whispered, almost paralysed by fear.

"What can we do?" cried Will, staring around wildly and feeling the walls for some controls. "They have to be somewhere!"

"Shh! Don't let them hear you!" I hissed, shaking myself into action. "There was a huge gate – you know, one of those concertina grilles – across the doorway before. Where is it?"

We lunged for either side of the lift doorframe, both trying to find the concealed grille. I could just see it, pressed back into the lift frame, but although I could get my fingers to it, it wouldn't budge.

"It's locked into place," I said, trying and failing to prise it out. "We're never going to move that."

Will joined me, peering into the dark recess. He tried too.

"It's no good," he said, standing back, "and we're wasting time. We can't go down as the lift is blocking the way on to the ledge. Maybe we could make a break for the stairs going up – just run for it."

He spoke in a whisper, even though the Farmer was too far away to be able to hear us. I could still see the pool of light as he walked further into the cavern full of columns.

"I'm game for it," I said, taking a deep breath. "Count of three?"

He nodded and reached for my hand.

"Three!" he shouted.

We leapt out of the lift and darted to the left. We hadn't gone more than a few steps when the light from the lift went out.

"Damn! Did you see where we needed to go?"

"No, just that it was this general direction, around the back of the lift shaft. Let's keep walking, but keep your hands out in front in case we hit something."

I looked around but could no longer see the Farmer's lamplight, and within a few seconds there was a grunt and Will's footsteps stopped.

"Ran into a column," he said. "Keep going left and we'll find the wall."

We turned, but at that moment the lift groaned again and started to move. In the darkness it was impossible to tell exactly which direction the noise had come from.

"Will, stop! With the lift gone there's a huge hole to fall down. We must be more careful."

"I'm glad to see that you two are putting up a fight." The booming voice made me jump. "The Crop do like a chase. It improves their appetite."

I put my hands out in the dark and found Will. Grasping hands tightly we circled around, desperately trying to see where the Farmer was standing. Eventually I glimpsed a small puddle of flickering light. The Farmer was bending down as if he was talking to someone. Or some*thing*.

"Look, he's over there." I pointed using the hand that was clasped to Will's so he would know where to look.

"What's he doing?"

"It's difficult to tell. Whatever he's looking at is still in the dark." I hesitated for a moment. "Could we rush him and grab the lamp? If we had that then we could find the way out."

"And risk walking headlong into whatever he's got over there? I don't think so!"

"We have to try something!" I cried. "I don't want to just stand here and wait for those things, whatever they are."

As we spoke the lamplight was getting closer, but

we didn't know where to run. My breath was coming in short, sharp bursts and I could feel Will's fingers tighten hard around mine.

"Would you two like to see our secret before you die? I don't often do this, but I think for such special guests I could make an exception."

He was nearly on us. I wanted to run and hide, but the light was mesmerising, and somehow I was rooted to the spot. And then he was there, just a few metres away from us.

"Let's see what we have here," he said with relish.

The Farmer raised the lamp and fixed it to a hook on the nearest column, then turned a knob on the side. The flame shot up, making everything much, much brighter. Will and I were side by side, facing him, but he was watching something behind us. Smiling, he put his hand to his lips, but I couldn't see clearly what he was doing.

There was a moment of silence before I heard the horribly familiar slithering noise. Seconds later the smell of rotten meat washed over me and I felt my legs turn to jelly. Was this really it? Was this how I was going to die?

I was shaking so hard I could barely move. I was suddenly icy cold, and every breath was a shallow gasp. Whatever the Crop was, it was right behind me. If I did have any sort of "Affinity" for it, as Dane believed, now was going to be the time to test it.

I felt Will's fingers circle around mine as he swore under

his breath. He took a step closer, pressing against me.

"Don't turn round, Lily, please. Just keep your eyes shut."

I dragged in a deep breath and closed my eyes tightly for a second. But I had to know. I had to confront the truth.

I turned to face the Crop.

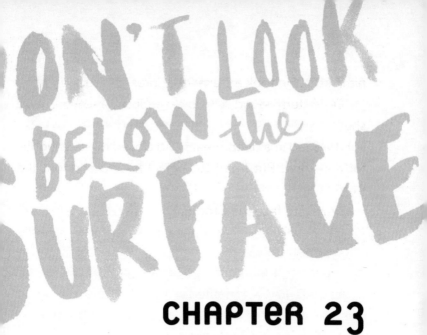

CHAPTER 23

Rats.

A seething sea of hundreds and hundreds of huge and hungry-looking rats.

They stood in a semicircle around us, teeth bared, sheltered between the columns. Some were still shaking their heads a bit at the sudden light, and all were swishing their snake-like tails. Hardly daring to move my head, I scanned around. They ranged in size from fairly normal-looking to monsters the size of small dogs with long, thick tails.

They made no sound except the creepy slithering of the tails on the stone floor; no squeaking or growling, just silence. Their yellow eyes watched us without blinking, mirroring the hideous yellow colour of their teeth – some of which were nearly as long as my fingers. The thought of what those teeth were about to do crystallised the fear inside me. I couldn't speak or move, and I was having trouble breathing. Everything was starting to go black around the edges and I could feel that I was beginning to sway. If I fainted, maybe I wouldn't feel the teeth. It wasn't much comfort.

I shook myself and tried to focus. Blacking out wasn't going to help Will, and if Dane was right, I had the ability to control these beasts.

I looked at their horrible eyes and picked one of the larger ones. *BACK*, I shouted in my head. *Leave us alone!* But, as I expected, absolutely nothing happened. How on earth was this Affinity supposed to work?

"Get back!" I shouted out loud, hoping that they would respond to my voice, but that did nothing either.

"Lily!" called Will, tugging at my hand as the Crop edged towards us. "Come on, we have to run for it!"

The Farmer laughed.

"And where exactly do you think you'll be running to? You can't deny the Crop their meal, not now they're expecting you."

That was an odd thing to say.

"What do you mean, expecting you?" I asked. "Was that why they didn't attack before?"

"Maybe not as slow as we thought," he said. "Exactly right. It really wasn't so surprising that you got down to us, not when they can be anywhere in their tunnels. But no one can escape once I've called them. Now they're just waiting for the command to feed."

I looked at him closely in the lamplight.

"But you don't have an Affinity with them, do you? No secret power? You just have a way of controlling them."

I pointed to his hand, which was still clutching something.

"Keep him talking, Lily," hissed Will. "They're not coming any closer."

"So what is it?" I asked, bargaining on the fact that he would like to brag. "Have you trained them from birth to obey your commands?"

"Training is the domain of the Farmers."

"So all you're doing is ensuring that your offspring remain in control!" interrupted Will. "There is no 'Affinity'; you're just running a dictatorship, and passing on the secret from father to son."

"Very clever," said the Farmer. "None of my people have made that connection, and you'll not live long enough to tell them."

"Another reason for keeping them ignorant and contained," I said.

I shook my head and looked out across the sea of rats that were poised just metres away. There must be something I could do to stop them, to stop the wave of fur and teeth and long, slithery tails that were waiting to engulf us. All the Farmer had to do was … what? Whistle?

I knew what I had to do.

I grabbed at my necklace, hidden as usual beneath my

T-shirt, scrabbling along the familiar trinkets until I came to the small silver whistle. It had never worked, not on human ears anyway.

I saw the Farmer's eyes widen in shock as I lifted the whistle to my lips. He groped for his, but I was quicker. I blew through the tiny mouthpiece as sharply as I could, and the effect was electrifying. The rats instantly stopped their fidgeting and turned, and hundreds of beady yellow eyes fixed unblinkingly on us.

"Keep going, Lily!" cried Will, leaping towards the Farmer as I took another deep breath.

The Farmer got his whistle to his mouth but Will was there, knocking it out of his hand. It skittered sideways, chinking on the stone. The rats were standing perfectly still watching us, waiting to do what they had been trained to do.

"Back to me, Will, quickly!" I cried.

Will leapt back beside me, and I blew again and again. I just didn't know what command I was giving. One of the largest rats sat back, lifting up its front legs, nose quivering in the air.

"Attack them!" screamed the Farmer, flapping his arms towards us. "Them! Over there!"

"Stay absolutely still," I whispered to Will.

I gave another swift blow on the whistle, which was obviously making sounds that only they could hear. The big rat that was sitting up sprang up on its back legs and started racing towards the Farmer. A wave of others followed. The Farmer turned and ran, a swarm of scuttling bodies chasing after him. I grabbed Will and held him close as the sea of stinking rats pushed past us, their bodies horribly warm against my legs and their tails whipping us. The noise of those slithering tails grew to hideous levels as hundreds – thousands – of rats shot in and out of the circle of light. Their sheer volume was mind-numbing, and Will and I stayed as silent and still as possible as the swarm disappeared into the dark, following the Farmer wherever he had gone.

My heart was hammering and my legs began to shake uncontrollably. I had to sit down before I fell.

"That was horribly, horribly close," said Will, helping me down. "How on earth did you know how to do that?"

"Just a sec," I breathed.

I put my head between my knees to stop myself feeling so sick. In a few moments the nausea passed and I sat back, pulling the hair back off my damp face.

"Nan always tells me that if you're in trouble, you should whistle, and I remembered this." I lifted up the chain to show him the little silver charm. "I used to blow it as a child but it never made a sound. I guess the pitch is right for their ears."

"Wow. That's a bit freaky."

I thought so too.

"Where would Mrs W get a whistle like that?"

"No idea. She gave me this necklace years ago."

"I can't believe you remembered it. That was so close."

He sat down beside me, giving me a weak smile. "My legs don't seem to be working so well. Shaking a bit."

"That's not all she gave me," I said, thinking aloud. "She had all the medicines too."

For a second we were both silent.

"So she happened to have the exact antibiotic you needed?" he asked.

"Uh-huh. Exactly. She always has a huge cupboard of medicines. For emergencies, she says. She buys them off the Internet."

"Your Nan knows too much."

I was thinking the same. So did that mean Dane was right after all – that I was in some way destined to be here?

"Let's get back up there, then ask questions, I think."

"Good idea."

He stood up and held out his hand. I took it eagerly, testing my wobbly legs as he pulled me to my feet. Once I was upright he stepped closer, folding me into his arms.

"No more heroics, Lily. I don't think my heart can take it."

He obviously saw the confusion that flashed across my face. "Sorry," I mumbled, looking away. He reached for my chin and lifted my face up to his again, then stroked my cheek briefly.

"When we get home can we have a normal date or something? Get a coffee or go to the cinema? Somewhere people aren't constantly trying to kill us?"

I couldn't believe what I was hearing.

"I ... I thought you liked Aria?"

His hands were still warm on my back and I didn't want him to move.

He laughed. "I do, but not like that. I like you, Lily, I have for ages. Why else do you think I came all the way down here with you?"

I looked up into his eyes and could see that he was telling the truth. He leaned down, brushing his lips across mine before burying his face in my hair.

"You still smell good. I don't dare kiss you properly yet. I must smell disgusting."

My lips still tingled where he had touched them, and I couldn't think of anything sensible to say. I just held him tighter, enjoying the moment.

"Now," he said, pulling back and giving me a smile, "do you think we could get out of here before those monsters come back for more?"

I finally found my voice.

"OK, good plan. Can you get the lamp?"

We started working our way back to the lift and then around towards the stairs.

"Do you think that he's dead?" I asked as we searched for the right way to go. "I mean, if he is, what are the Community going to think? Who will lead them? Who will contain the Crop?"

"Let's get out of here first and then worry about that."

We were so busy talking and peering round the

columns that we didn't notice the change in atmosphere until it was too late. Violently bright lights snapped on, blinding us and stopping us in our tracks. A voice thundered around and bounced off the walls.

"This is the police. We are armed. Put your hands in the air NOW!"

Will carefully put the lamp down before he raised his hands. As he did, a small canister was thrown past us, and rolled into the dark, hissing.

"How many more of you are there? Come on, out with it!" barked the voice.

"Here? Just the two of us," I yelled back.

"We're the ones you're looking for," called Will, ducking as another hissing canister was launched over our heads.

I could feel my eyes begin to sting, so I shut them tightly for a moment. Not being able to see was even worse, so I opened them again, just a tiny crack.

"Is that tear gas?" Will shouted. "Do we look like we're about to make trouble?"

As he spoke a figure moved forward from the light, the silhouette clear.

"Lily, I'm Detective Inspector Harding. You talked with my colleague Constable Clark yesterday at your house. Are you OK?"

Her voice sounded odd, but relief washed over me – we no longer had to do any of this alone.

"Yes, we're fine."

"You're going to need these," she said, holding something out to me.

She moved closer towards us and I could see that she was wearing a gas mask, and in her hand were two more. The mask was muffling her voice. I put one on and it helped my eyes adjust to the brightness of the two banks of lights. Will took the other.

"Is anything else here?" she asked, scanning around behind us.

"No, not now. But there are rats – lots and lots of rats. Big ones. They will eat you, given half a chance."

I was suddenly too weary to worry about the fact that it all sounded mad.

"So we heard. It's one of the reasons why we brought the tear gas."

"And the guns," muttered Will.

She was wearing body armour, a helmet and a holster.

"We've been very worried about both of you, Will. Your mother is frantic."

"She's not here, is she?" There was panic in his voice. "Please tell me that she didn't come down? It's not safe!"

The police officer put her hand on his arm.

"We know, Will. No civilians are with us, not even your guardian," she added, turning to me, "which really upset her."

"I'm not surprised," I said, imagining the argument.

As we were speaking, the area around us had filled up with more and more armed police in gas masks, and more of the lights on tripods had been moved further into the chamber and around towards the lift. Cables snaked across the stone floor. The clouds of gas streaming out of the canisters were quickly spreading away between the columns. In a few moments the air cleared and Detective Inspector Harding took off her gas mask. Will and I loosened ours too.

"How did you know we were here?" I asked.

"Mrs Wakefield told us everything you told her, and then directed us to the entrance above. She warned us about the defences too."

That puzzled me – I'd not told Nan anything.

"What are you going to do now?" Will asked. "Where are those guys going?"

"We need to control the rats. They've got motion and heat detectors that will find them pretty quickly."

"I'm not sure you have enough men," I said dubiously, thinking back to the sea of rats that had surrounded us not long before.

"We know what we're doing. We have other means of dealing with the rats," she said. "And the people. We just need to get them out."

"Hang on a sec, you can't go barging in there. They won't be happy about it."

"People can't live underground commanding packs of flesh-eating rats."

An edge of steel was just detectable under her friendly and comforting tone.

"But what if they don't want to come? They've been down there for generations. You have to understand that they feel let down by us, the Aboves, and they're living their lives quite independently from us."

"Well, that's not quite true, is it? They send raiding parties up every night for food, I believe."

"Food that's been thrown away by the supermarkets and the fast-food shops, that's all! The only person who was dangerous to us has gone, and is probably dead by now. The rest of them aren't doing anyone any harm, are they?"

Detective Inspector Harding stood with her hands on her hips, shaking her head at me.

"Lily, their leader sounds like a megalomaniac. We can't leave them living down there. Who knows what they might do next? Now, enough arguing. We need to know how we get down to the lower levels."

As she spoke, a policeman appeared by her side. She stepped back as soon as she realised he was there.

"Status report, please, DI Harding. And quickly."

He was obviously the one in charge.

"These are the missing kids, sir. I was just about to get some intel from them about the set-up down here."

"What do we know so far?" he asked sharply.

"This is the rat level, sir. I believe that the people are further down. They may offer us some resistance, from what these two are saying."

"Well, let's execute the plan then, shall we? Get the

children back up top immediately."

Will pulled himself up to his full height and looked the new police officer in the eye.

"What plan? We have friends down there. Will they be safe?"

"I'm sure they'll be fine if they do what they're told, if the leader down there is sensible," said DI Harding. "The guns will be just a precaution."

"Before you do anything you'll need to deal with the rats," said Will, pointing in the direction they had gone. "The leader of the Community may well be dead – he's just been chased in that direction by several thousand of them."

He paused for a moment until the policeman looked back at him.

"I think they might be eating him," he added in a deadpan voice.

There was a moment of silence. The man's jaw dropped.

"What? Which way?"

"Down there." He pointed towards the back of the cavern. "And whatever you do, don't whistle. It's a sign to attack."

He shouted the last bit at their backs as they raced into the depths, calling for the lights to be moved. In the momentary confusion Will grabbed my arm.

"We have to go and warn them. If these guys burst in with guns it could be a bloodbath."

I nodded, too shocked to talk but realising instantly that he was right. Looking around we could see that we weren't being watched, so we made a beeline for the lift shaft. There was just enough light from the trail of lamps across the cavern to see the edge. Will swung around to the ladder and jumped down without hesitation, then turned to catch me as I followed him.

This time I didn't stop to consider the yawning drop, stepping straight on to the ladder and then down on to the ledge. Within seconds we were through the big metal door, running down the stairs as fast as we could, racing to warn the Community that their enemies were on the way down.

DON'T LOOK BELOW the SURFACE

CHAPTER 24

I run through the corridors of home, reaching out to touch the familiar, smooth walls as I pass, trying to memorise the stone before I leave forever. There is only one choice left to me, and I need to see Dane before I go back into the secret entrance to the Crop to escape back Above. I'm still numb at the sudden turn of events. I wonder if the Farmer had seen something familiar in Lily and realised she was a threat.

We are being led by a madman, and the medicines were not worth the price that we paid for them. I think about Lily and Will facing the Crop, and I have to stop and steady myself, feeling the bile rising in my throat. I swallow hard. What do we do now? Can we save our Community for the future? Should we?

Are we worse than the Aboves?

I can't answer all the questions that are spinning around my head. I have to speak with Dane to find out if he will come with me.

As I turn a corner I see Dane running full pelt towards me. He barely slows down, just grabs me by the arm as he passes.

"Quick, Aria, we don't have much time. We have to get to the Rotunda!"

"The Rotunda? Why?"

I gasp as he drags me along with him, struggling to keep to my feet as we race.

"The Farmer – Carita said she saw him running past, muttering the name. She said he looked crazy. We have to stop him."

"From what?" I gasp as try to keep up.

"He didn't come down in the lift. Maybe Lily was able to use the Affinity to beat him and escape. He's going to be very angry."

"You think they're not dead?" I finally drag him to a stop.

Dane turns to me, his dark, brooding eyes looking more worried than I have ever seen them before.

"Something has gone wrong for the Farmer, and we need to get to him before he does something stupid."

We start running again. Lily has beaten the Farmer! But why is he going to the Rotunda? It doesn't make sense, but my heart is singing. My friends are OK! I run faster to keep up with Dane.

He pulls me through tunnels that I've barely visited since I was a child learning the map. It's an area we rarely come to now that we don't need the space, and what they used to do here is a mystery to me.

"It's the only thing he can do now," says Dane, slowing down as we get close to our destination.

"I don't understand."

"I'll show you."

As he speaks we arrive at the entrance to a thin, low tunnel. Crouching down, we creep along it until it opens out into the Rotunda – an old circular room, a couple of steps lower than the tunnel. On the far wall is what looks like an immense gate, built in two semicircular halves. I had forgotten that it is here – the whole place is some ancient relic from the Aboves. It's something they built years ago and then abandoned. Instead of stone walls it is built in red brick, just like the ones up Above, only cleaner-looking.

The Farmer is hunched over some machinery by the gate, examining wheels and cogs. Dane puts his fingers to his lips and slips to the side behind a huge iron cylinder with thick pipes coming out of either end. The pipes run into a line of iron boxes. Once he is out of the Farmer's line of sight, he waves at me to speak.

"What are you doing?" I call.

He whips round and sees me, his eyes glittering with anger. His clothes – usually immaculate – are ripped and bloodied. He has a cloth wrapped around his hand.

"This is all your fault. If you hadn't gone Above none of this would have happened. I was so close!"

He slaps his palm on to the machinery before returning his attention to a huge, cogged metal wheel. Taller than me, it is connected to a pipe that goes into the wall.

I can see Dane on the far side of the room.

"Keep him talking," he mouths at me.

"So close to what?"

"To paying them back! Releasing the Crop and watching the havoc it would play on their smug faces. They are so nearly ready – just one more breeding round and I would have had enough for it all!"

"Are Lily and Will dead?" I ask, desperate to know for sure.

"She's a witch," he says icily. "I should have had her killed immediately. There was no need for what they did."

I've known the Farmer for my entire life, but I've never seen him look so dangerous. I can't see a hint of reason left in his eyes, and I have no idea what he might do next. I take a few steps towards him, wanting to keep his attention until Dane can get closer, but careful to stay out of reach.

I can see the tendons on his arms, taut where he is pulling at the wheel.

"What exactly did they do, Farmer?" I ask.

I am trying really hard to keep my eyes fixed on him and not glance behind him towards Dane.

"She has turned the Crop against me. There's no protection for us now. There is only one thing left that I can do for my people. Here, pull hard on this."

He is trying to turn a wheel on the machinery. I must obey to keep his focus on me. I wish I could see where Dane has gone. I take a firm grip on one of the rusty handles, pulling on it with all my weight, and very slowly it starts to give.

"Perhaps the Aboves will help us, Farmer. They all seem very reasonable to me. We can ask them."

"It's too late for that," he grunts as he continues to strain against the rusty old wheel.

"I don't see why. Once we've explained to the Aboves about our lives and they understand, then we can live a bit more openly. Above is a strange but beautiful place – I'm sure the others would like to visit."

I see a movement out of the corner of my eye. Dane is edging closer. I must keep the Farmer talking until Dane can do whatever he has planned.

"You really don't get it, do you?" the Farmer is saying. "That was our last chance. Once we're breached, this is the only solution."

He gives a final heave. The wheel groans loudly and suddenly starts to inch round. There is a dull clanking noise behind me and I look round to see the huge gate in the wall moving slowly upwards.

"What are you doing? What do you mean, it was our last chance?"

The gate continues to move as he wrenches at the wheel again, and a tiny trickle of water appears at one side. With another wrench the gate inches up again, and the trickle turns into a torrent as a gap opens up across the wall. Water is spraying out in a wide waterfall, splashing on to the floor close to my feet. I realise with horror what I have helped the Farmer to do.

"No! Stop him!"

As I shout I look over towards Dane. He is nearly in reach, but the Farmer sees my glance and turns. He grabs a long metal rod and in a single movement swings it round. It connects with Dane's head in a sickening crunch. Dane drops to the floor where the water swirls around him. He doesn't move.

"No!" I scream. "You've killed him!"

The torrent of water has turned into a river of evil-smelling scum, which is already lapping up towards my knees. Within seconds it will be up over the steps and down the corridor. Our world is flat, and flooding has always been one of our big fears.

"No, you can't do this! All your people, the women, the babies – you're going to kill them all?"

"It's for the best, believe me."

The water reaches my thighs. It's cold and nearly takes my breath away.

"For whose best?" I shout over the roar of the waterfall now cascading through the opening gate. "I don't want to be a sacrifice!"

He catches me by the hand as I try to pass him to reach Dane.

"We pay the price, Aria. You let the Aboves follow you in, and you must suffer the consequences. You can see that it's the only way."

"You're mad!" I scream.

I try to shake off his hand, but his grip is too tight. He is too strong for me. The water swirls around my waist. It's already pouring through the tiny entrance into the Community tunnels. I grab the wheel and try to wrench it closed, but he drags me away from it.

"No, Aria, there's no use fighting. We must be the first to pay."

He pulls a length of rope from round his waist and loops it over my head and shoulders.

"Don't struggle," he says. "You'll only make your death more uncomfortable."

He wraps the rope round my hands and ties it to the machinery next to the wheel. Struggling makes the rope tighter.

"Please don't do this," I beg. "Think of Carita and Reilly, of your family. Reilly is your son – do you really want him to drown?"

His voice is calm.

"We can't live up there, you know that. They fight and kill each other, abuse the women and the children, let people starve… We're better off like this."

He gives me a twisted smile and turns away.

"Please, untie me," I beg again. "They're not that bad. They can help us!"

The water has pushed Dane's motionless body up towards me. I strain across, trying to lift myself up so that I can reach him with my feet. He's so close! But I lose my grip and sink under the oily water. Spluttering, I pull myself back up and try again. I catch his arm with my foot and pull. He bobs towards me. In the noise and confusion in the shadowy, echoing room I can't tell if he's alive or dead, but I manage to wedge him between my body and the machinery. He is on his back in the water, and I fight against the current to get my face close to his to see if I can find any sign of life.

On the other side of the wheel the Farmer is smiling calmly as the water rises, swaying gently as he turns to watch the torrent. I think he has lost his mind. I shout over the thunder of the water.

"Have you realised why Lily was able to control the Crop? Why Dane sent me up Above to bring her down?"

I see him stop swaying, his back to me. He is listening.

"Do you remember the Breeder – your Breeder – who sneaked a baby Above to stop the sickness? Do you?"

He doesn't turn.

"The baby lived. Lily lived, and she came back down to help us."

"That girl is no daughter of mine," he says.

"She is! Let her help! The Aboves are kind – they don't want to hurt us!"

He turns round, and his gaze is as icy as the water churning around us.

"She's not my daughter. My Breeder made a big mistake. She took another's child Above for medicine, thinking I wouldn't punish her, but she was wrong. When she came back I sent her to the Crop, and disowned our child. I didn't want her filthy blood contaminating my line."

"So who is it? Who is your daughter?"

He laughs.

The swirling torrent is at my chest. If I wasn't tied on I wouldn't be able to stand.

Fighting the current, the Farmer grabs another rope and lashes himself to some huge pipes leading away from the wheel. The water is now close to the top of the tiny tunnel, which is the only way out. He shouts over the roar of the water.

"I should have got rid of you then!"

Then he disappears under the spray and foam. I pull against the ropes but they are too tight. There is no time to think about what he's told me. Dane's face is next to me as the water rises, and I try with every last ounce of strength to keep him close. I wish that I could stroke his cheek. But by bending over I can just reach his lips, and I kiss him gently.

"Goodbye, Dane," I whisper as the water rises over my chin.

It's time to die.

* * *

Will and I tore down the spiral staircase and shot out of the doorway at the bottom. I struggled to run in a straight line.

"Wait," I gasped to Will. "There's no point just running off; we need to know where to find people. Why don't we shout?"

He took a deep breath, lifted his fingers to his mouth and gave a deafening whistle.

"HEY! COMMUNITY! We need you here – NOW! This is an EMERGENCY!"

People started appearing at the ends of the tunnels and from doorways, then a large group of men came running round the nearest corner. Among them were some of the group we had first run into. They didn't look happy at being disturbed again.

"What do you two think you're playing at?" spat the one with the beard. "You're supposed to have gone."

"There's no time to explain," I panted, still trying to get my breath back. "I don't know how, but there are police from Above up by the Crop, and they are going to be coming down here at any moment."

"What!" The man nearest to me stepped back in indignation. "You've let the Aboves down here? That can't happen!"

"It's true," said Will, "and they'll be here any minute. You mustn't fight them. They have guns."

"Now you're talking nonsense. If there are Aboves

down here looking for a fight, then they're going to get one." He smashed his fist into his palm and looked around at his friends. "Who's with me?"

There was a clamour of hands and raised voices as they jostled forward.

"WAIT!" bellowed Will.

He whistled again so loudly that everyone fell silent.

"Please let us negotiate for you. No one needs to get hurt."

As he spoke, a howl echoed down the corridor to our left. Everyone froze. Two short seconds later the men leapt back as Foggy stampeded through them, practically bowling Will over. As Will hugged him there was another sudden noise from the right. It was women screaming.

Everyone spun round.

"Can they have got in already?" I asked the nearest man.

"They have to come this way," he replied. "Something else has happened."

The screaming became more distinct.

"Run!"

"Get to the stairs!"

"Water! The water is coming!"

At the word the men looked at each other then turned and most of them ran, scattering down different tunnels.

"Get the women!" called one of the older men. "They must get up the stairs."

"Where's the Farmer? Is he down from the Crop yet? He needs to be here."

The bearded man who had talked to us the day before rounded on me.

"What did you say about the Crop? And where's the Farmer? What have you done with him?"

"The Crop turned against him. He ran, and I don't know what happened to him. That stairway is full of armed police who'll be here any minute. What's the problem with the water?"

As I spoke, a dark stain on the floor spread around the corner, and just ahead of it, running hard to keep ahead, was Carita with a bundle in her arms.

"Carita!" I yelled. "What's going on?"

"We're being flooded. Drowned like rats in a bucket," bellowed the man with the beard. "This is all your fault!"

He towered over me for a second, fists raised, and I thought for a moment he was going to hit me, but then he turned and ran too.

Carita reached me, gasping for breath, just ahead of the water. It was only a few centimetres deep but it was already thick with dirt, rubbish and belongings.

"You have to help me. I need to get Reilly out of here, but Aria is in trouble."

Will was by my side, his hand on Foggy's head. Carita looked startled as she saw the dog, but swallowed hard and carried on.

"Dane was looking for her. The Farmer has gone to

the Rotunda and opened the sluice gates. If they go there to try and stop him they'll die."

As she spoke, the filthy water rose up over the edge of my Converse. It was astonishingly cold.

Will grabbed Carita by the arms.

"Get the baby up the stairs. You'll find some people coming down, but tell them you have to evacuate – tell them it's an emergency. Lily, go with her, tell the police what's happening. I'll get Aria."

"No way – you're still ill. I'm coming with you."

There was no time to argue. I could see more people wading through the ankle-deep water towards us.

"OK, Carita," said Will. "Please, get up the stairs now, tell the people that the Crop is gone, there's no danger. Just get up there!"

I grabbed her by the arm as she turned.

"Which way, Carita? How do we find Aria?"

She nodded down the tunnel, tears streaking her face.

"Follow the water. There is a low, narrow tunnel leading into the Rotunda. That's where it's coming from."

I grabbed Will by the hand and we set off down the corridor, running as fast as the water would let us. It was easy to tell the direction, but increasingly difficult to go at any great speed. Foggy kept up behind us, nuzzling our hands whenever he could. The water was treacherous. It was full of things it had picked up from the floor, and all sorts of rubbish was banging against my legs.

When the water reached my thighs, I knew that there

was no going back. Either we found Aria and Dane and managed to shut off the water, or we would drown. There wasn't time to get back to the stairs.

We rounded a corner and saw the water roaring out of a tiny, low tunnel. The water level wasn't quite up to the top of the tunnel, but it was impossible to see what was at the far end.

"How the hell are we going to get through there?" I shouted at Will over the thunder of the water. "It's way too hard to swim through."

"I don't know," he shouted back.

We had to get in there. The water was already over our waists, and Foggy was doing a doggy paddle behind us. Will felt around the edge of the tunnel entrance.

"If there was only something we could hold on to," he said, "we could pull ourselves through. But there's no handrail. I'm going to have to try swimming. Stand back …"

He launched himself forward into the foaming water. I could see his legs thrashing against the current and for a moment I thought he was making headway, but then he tumbled back, disappearing under the surface. Foggy barked – a shockingly loud noise in such a confined space – and dived under the water.

I felt suddenly alone.

Seconds later, both emerged. Will managed to step aside from the main torrent and stand up, pushing the hair out of his eyes.

"It's no good. The water is just too fast, and I'm still weak," he gasped, grabbing for Foggy's collar and pulling him close.

"What's that you've got there, Foggy?" I asked.

As he had surfaced a rope had caught over his back.

"Where's that from?"

I pulled on the rope briefly and it went taut. Following it along under the surface, I realised that it disappeared into the tunnel.

"Will! Look at this – it must be tied on to something inside. We can use this!"

Will pulled on the rope and nodded.

"You stay here, Lily. We don't know how long the tunnel is. I'll go through and shut it off."

"Yeah, right," I said, hands on my hips. "You just swim in there and flick a switch and the Farmer will be happy with that. No problem."

"Crap. You're right. Both of us have to go. At least let me go first, and if there's any trouble just let go of the rope – the current will take you out here again."

I took a deep breath. I could feel my heart pounding and realised that the shivers running down my spine had nothing to do with the cold water.

"I'm good to go," I said.

"Right, Lily Blackthorne, let's do this."

He grabbed me and kissed me hard before breaking away to look at the dog.

"You stay here, Foggy, OK? Stay."

As we spoke, the water reached the top of the low tunnel. Then Will was gone, kicking his way into the tunnel. I counted to five, took several more deep breaths, and dived in after him.

The cold hitting my face nearly made me take a lungful of water, but I pressed my lips together, concentrating hard, and started to haul myself along the rope. I tried opening my eyes but I could see almost nothing. The buffeting of the water was vicious, and my knuckles scraped along the wall as I was pulled backwards by the torrent. Slowly, slowly I dragged myself hand-over-hand along the rope. My lungs began to burn. How long could I hold my breath? How long did I need to try for? The pounding in my ears was deafening, and the urge to breathe in was almost unbearable.

Another grab and pull, another stretch along the greasy rope, trying to get and keep a firm grip, time and time again. What if I had already died and this was my punishment for what I had done to Aria, to be pulling myself forever along an endless rope, gasping for air? I could do no more, it was impossible. But then the rope pulled me forward, and Will was hauling me up and into the air.

I struggled to suck enough oxygen into my lungs as I grabbed at him, gasping.

"Quick," he shouted, shaking my shoulder. "Over there! Keep hold of the rope."

We were in a big circular room with a huge sluice gate

at one side. The water level in the room was almost up to the opening in the gate, but it was still pouring in. Next to the gate I could see mostly submerged machinery, wheels and pipes. Several dark shapes were bobbing around in the water near the biggest wheel. We pulled ourselves along the rope, reaching the other side in a few moments.

The wheel had a turning handle just above the level of the water.

"Here," gasped Will. "Got to turn this."

With one of us on each side we managed to turn the wheel a small amount.

"Is that the right way?" I called, unable to tell if the gate was closing.

"No idea. Do more."

Half the wheel was submerged, so to turn it we had to sink under the water and brace ourselves against the machinery. As our heads broke the water again the gate groaned.

"Yesss!" shouted Will. "Again!"

As we started getting some momentum on the wheel, I had time to look around. The shapes in the water were bodies bobbing lifelessly on the waves. I recognised Aria's shirt.

"Will, we have to stop, look!"

"No! Just need a few more turns."

I had to look away as we made the last few turns of the wheel, which got easier as the water volume reduced.

Finally it was down to a trickle and the roaring of the water was replaced by the roaring of blood in my ears.

"I can do this now," said Will. "Go and see."

I waded and swam around the mechanism as quickly as I could.

Aria's long hair was floating out around her head, her eyes shut. Dane's motionless body was in the water next to her. Blood was streaming out of a wound on the side of his head. He had been wedged up against the machinery with his face clear of the water, supported by Aria, but it looked as if her efforts to save him had been too much for her. I hauled her up but couldn't get her free – she was trapped by her hands. I felt along her arms until I got to the rope round her wrists. It was tied tight, the knot a hard ball. I looked over at her face – was I too late? She was floating limply, her face nearly submerged under the surface of the water. We needed to help her, but until I could get her free it was going to be impossible.

I dived under the water, desperate to get closer to the knot. The water was dark and murky, which made it really hard, but I could see and feel just enough to work out what to do. Surfacing for air I worked at the knot, pulling and twisting, digging at it with my fingernails, and at last there was a tiny amount of give. Aria still hadn't moved. I tore at the rope until finally it was loose enough to wrench her hands free.

I turned Aria over so that she was on her back in the

water. Will was back by my side, leaning over. "Aria, come on, you know you can hear us. Open your eyes!"

He gently slapped her face but there was still no response.

"Get behind her, Lily. Let's see if we can pump some of the water out of her."

I knew exactly what he wanted me to do. Remembering my school first-aid class, I got behind her and clasped my hands around her middle, just under her ribcage. Then, bracing myself against the machinery, I pulled back and up sharply. A stream of water flew out of her mouth.

"That's it, Lily, that's what she needs! Again!"

I squeezed her hard, and more water shot out. Then I did it again. And again. Nothing was happening.

"We need to give her mouth-to-mouth now, Will. I can't feel her breathing. Hurry!"

Will leaned over but then Aria gave an almighty cough and started to thrash about, arms lashing out. Will dodged out of the way. She coughed again so violently that I thought she would be sick. I stayed behind her, rubbing her back and talking to her gently.

"Come on now, Aria, just breathe. That's it, breathe…"

The coughing slowed a little.

"We need to check the others," said Will, pointing at Dane and the person who I assumed was the Farmer.

The Farmer hadn't moved. The water was now almost still, only swirling around by the entrance to the tunnel where it was still flowing out.

Leaving Aria propped up against the wheel I waded over towards the bundle of wet clothes that were floating in front of the huge pipes. Taking a deep breath I pulled at them, turning him over. His face was nearly as grey as his jacket. The rope that he had used to tie himself on was wrapped around his neck, trapping him below the high-water mark. The Farmer was dead.

CHAPTER 25

It seemed as if a lifetime had passed. I was curled up in the armchair at Nan's house with Will's back resting against my knees. A tray of steaming mugs of tea was sitting on the little table, and I breathed in the familiar smell, finally beginning to relax. Nan was trying to usher the last of the social workers out of the house.

"They'll be perfectly OK with us, I assure you, and as soon as either of them asks to go back to the rest of their people I'll call you and let you know."

The short, friendly-looking woman turned in the doorway of the small sitting room and smiled at the figures wrapped up in a huge duvet on the sofa.

"Are you two sure you'll be happy here on your own?"

"We're not on our own," Aria mumbled, snuggling deeper down into the folds. "We're with our friends."

"All right then, Mrs Wakefield…" Her voice faded as Nan led her down the corridor and the door closed.

I could see through a tiny gap in the curtains that the policeman outside was keeping the press further down the street. They descended on the social worker as she reached them, and I turned away, thinking back to earlier in the day.

There had been endless policemen and doctors, and hundreds of photographers desperate to get pictures. Everyone from the Community was led, blinking, into the light. They had lost everything in the flood, but there had been only one fatality – the Farmer.

Dane had regained consciousness just before we got him to the stairs, and although he had to go to hospital to be checked over, he had insisted on coming back and was by Aria's side, a large dressing bandaged to his head. I couldn't see, but I would have bet that he was holding Aria's hand under the duvet.

My phone buzzed again. The news was racing like wildfire. We were already booked for breakfast TV in the morning. Nan hadn't been sure, but the police public relations person had persuaded her that it would be useful to have our version of events aired, to show that the Community people could be trusted. All the messages on my phone were from my classmates, desperate to be friends again. Jenny had even sent me a Facebook request.

Nan walked back into the room and sat down on the

only remaining seat. For a moment there was silence, and then all of us started talking at once.

"I don't understand…"

"So how did you know that…"

"Where on earth did you…"

"I suppose I should start at the beginning."

Nan's voice was so calm that the rest of us stopped talking in surprise. Having got our attention, she paused for a moment as if she was trying to decide how to start.

"About forty years ago I had a son. He was destined for big things, and at quite a young age he became the leader of our people, the Community. But he was not a good leader. He was too keen on looking after what he wanted and not worrying too much about anyone else."

I felt the hair on the back of my neck stand up. Could this be real?

"His first partner was the prettiest and most talented girl in the Community," Nan continued, not looking at me, "and she soon became pregnant. But her son died almost as soon as he was born, and other babies got sick and died too. And the more children died, the angrier my son became. Our people had been through it all before, you see.

"We agreed as Breeders to take the next ill baby Above for help. It happened that my son's partner – Marit – was next. Luckily her labour came early so we kept the birth secret, but a few days later her little girl did get sick. We knew that we had to take her to get treatment.

"My partner, the previous Farmer, had told me all about the Crop and the whistle, so I was able to smuggle them out in the dead of night.

"We had heard stories about the world outside, but weren't prepared for how different it was. As soon as we arrived and asked for help we were taken to a hospital. The baby was saved very easily, and we realised how much better our lives would be if we were allowed to talk with the Aboves."

My world was spinning. *Nan* had been in the Community? It didn't make any sense to me.

"So you were a Breeder too? Is that right?" I asked, leaning forward.

Nan nodded. "It was a long time ago now. But let me tell you about the baby first."

I sat back uneasily, suddenly frightened about what I might learn. Will took one of my hands and held it tightly.

"Marit wanted to go back and persuade the Farmer that things could be different, but I didn't think he would listen. Then, before we could decide what to do, the Aboves told us that we couldn't keep the baby because we couldn't prove who we were.

"Marit slipped out of the hospital and ran back to the Community with some medicine. I stayed, unable to leave my grandchild unaccompanied. As I had no papers, no history and nowhere to go, I had to watch as they arranged the adoption. But the couple who were adopting seemed kind, and agreed to allow me to have some part in my grandchild's life."

"Hang on a minute," I said. "Are you telling me that I'm adopted, and you're my actual grandmother? I'm that baby?"

Nan gave me a tiny smile.

"The authorities couldn't charge me with anything, so I got an identity and I learned to live in the world of the Aboves. I helped your new mother take care of you, and after a while I got enough education to be able to work at the chemist's stacking the shelves and secretly learning which drugs would help in the future. I started leaving them outside the warehouse, hoping that one of the Listeners would find them, but it doesn't sound as if any made it down.

"My life was happy, you were happy, but then everything changed. Your adoptive mother got pregnant, and it was clear when the twins arrived that things would be different. So when it all went so horribly wrong with your dad's job and they moved to China, I offered to have you stay with me here."

She gave me a rueful smile. "I thought that you wanted to stay, you see, but I'm not sure if I was right."

"Do you think that they love me at all?" I asked in a small voice.

Will squeezed my hand even harder.

"I know it doesn't seem like it sometimes, but they do, in their own way," she said. "They're on their way back right now, actually. They've been worried sick."

She stopped for a moment to sip her tea before taking a deep breath and continuing.

"So, there we were, minding our own business, when one of the Community suddenly appeared in my home."

She looked over at Aria, still huddled in her duvet.

"You can imagine my surprise," she added drily. "How did you find me?"

Dane sat up a little straighter.

"It's my fault. I found you," he said. "There were rumours, and I did some investigating when I could. I never thought to ask you about getting the medicines though. That was really stupid of me." He shook his head and then winced when it hurt.

"But I knew we had to do something," he continued. "The Farmer was sending more and more people to feed the Crop so that he could use it to attack London, but he couldn't be made to see how ridiculous that idea was. If anyone tried, he had them killed. We had to find another way. We needed the Farmer's descendent to take over. We needed you, Lily."

He paused for a second and turned to Aria.

"I'm sorry for dragging you into all of this too. It was a mad scheme to kidnap Lily. I can see now that we should have just come and talked."

"That would have been simpler," said Nan with a small sigh. "Much simpler."

"It would have worked if the Crop hadn't chased us

Above," said Aria, fighting her way out of the duvet. "But once I got up here and saw how wonderful everything was, I couldn't bring myself to leave straightaway. I thought Dane would be cross that I had mucked things up and didn't know what to do."

"I got that wrong too," said Dane, pulling Aria towards him and kissing the top of her head. "If only I'd spoken with you it would have been so different."

"No, it's my fault," said Aria, her eyes filling with tears. "I can't believe that the Farmer was ready to sacrifice all of us."

"All of us. Even his own baby son," agreed Dane.

"So let me get this straight," said Will, sitting forward. "Lily is the biological daughter of the Farmer, so you and Dane thought that she would be able to control the Crop. But actually, he was only controlling them with a whistle, so anyone could have done it."

"If we'd known that," Dane said, shaking his head, "none of this would have happened."

"And I'm the daughter of a mad mass murderer," I said, still reeling from the news. "Last week I was the daughter of a corrupt banker. I'm not sure this is any improvement."

"No, there's more," said Aria, picking at the edge of the duvet. "The Farmer told me something strange just before he died."

"What did he say, dear?" asked Nan.

"He told me that it wasn't Lily, that *I* was his daughter,

but that he had disowned me because of what my mother had done."

"What?" exclaimed Dane. "I don't understand."

We all turned to look at Nan.

"Which of us is it then, Nan?" I asked. "Why would he lie about that?"

Nan sat back, placing her fingers carefully together in an eerie echo of the Farmer.

"When Marit left you here," she said, looking back at me, "she took some drugs with her to help another baby. You *are* his daughter, Aria."

Aria stared at her, an appalled look on her face. "What do you mean? Are you saying that my mother wasn't really my mother? And that Carita isn't actually my sister?"

Nan nodded. "That's right. But the Farmer *is* your father."

"Oh, that's a horrible idea," she said shuddering and shrinking back into the duvet as if to get away from the thought.

"But you just said that I was—" I stopped, confused.

Nan smiled. "You are both right. You were raised Above, Lily, and you, Aria, were raised below."

She looked over at Aria and then back at me.

"Lily, Aria is your twin sister."

I sat back on the sofa in shock, my mind whirring with all that information. Glancing over I could see that Aria was still looking stunned, her mouth hanging slightly open. Then she turned towards me, and a slow grin spread across her face.

"We're sisters – Lily, you're my sister!"

I looked around the room at every face – Nan, Will, Dane and Aria – all looking back at me. A few short days ago I was being bullied and was alone with no family and no friends, hiding out on Tube platforms. So much had changed. Now I had friends who would risk their lives for me – including a gorgeous boy who might be my boyfriend – and a sister, plus a whole Community of people I could call my own.

I started to smile.

CHAPTER 26

The police had finished clearing the Rat Cavern, as someone had unimaginatively called it, the lights had been mostly dismantled and the wires reeled in. Dozens of specialist officers had swarmed through the tunnels, bagging evidence and making maps.

The Police Commissioner had asked for the tour before the caves were sealed up.

"What I don't understand," she asked the junior detective who had been assigned to show her around, "is how this much tunnelling had gone unnoticed when it is so close to the Tube network. Don't TfL have engineers checking these things?"

"I'm sure they do, ma'am," said the officer. "But from what I've heard, these caves are all pretty old, so they might have been here long before the Tube tunnels were built."

"Perhaps," said Commissioner Vijh, sighing. "It's not going to stop the Mayor asking awkward questions at the emergency assembly tomorrow though, is it?"

The two of them continued walking along the narrow string of lights until they came to a section where the floor was littered with small white tags, each with a number. Commissioner Vijh bent down to look more closely at the nearest few, reaching out to touch the ground but pulling back just millimetres before her fingers grazed the rough surface.

"How many was it?" she asked, her voice so low that Detective Sergeant Rooney barely caught her words.

"We've not had the full forensic report through yet, ma'am, but from the number of teeth we found piled up here it's hundreds of people, probably over a thousand."

"Genocide on an unprecedented scale right here in London." The Commissioner shook her head as she looked at the tags stretching away towards the far wall. "I can't imagine why those people put up with him for so long."

Detective Sergeant Rooney wasn't entirely sure what to say to that, so stayed silent apart from a murmured "No, ma'am". The pair then continued walking until Rooney coughed gently.

"There really isn't much more to see, ma'am. We've searched every inch of the caves, clearing out all the bodies of the rats. The gas was very effective. I didn't see a single live one."

"I heard a rumour, Rooney. Someone said that they weren't just ordinary rats but something much bigger. Can you verify that?"

"We've tried very hard to keep those rumours down, as we don't think it would be helpful for the public to know the truth. Some of the ones I saw were the size of foxes or small Labradors. Huge." Rooney shuddered just thinking about it again.

"No, you're absolutely right – this really mustn't get out. The Mayor would go ballistic."

The Commissioner stopped and touched one of the sturdy supporting columns. "I've seen enough, thank you. It's time I left."

"Right you are, ma'am," said Rooney, turning round gratefully. "Let's get back above."

Much further into the caves, through a tiny crack and beyond the reach of the paralysing gas, something stirred. Beady yellow eyes pierced the dark to watch over the litter of newborn rats, each considerably larger than a man's hand.

They could wait.

ACKNOWLEDGEMENTS

The Beneath has been a long time coming, and it has only made it this far with the help of some fabulous professionals at Nosy Crow. A great team of editors has helped to knock it into shape – Rachel Moss, Hazel Cotton and chief whip-cracker Kirsty Stansfield. I might not have seemed grateful at the time, but I can see now that you helped to tease out the book which was hiding in the early drafts – so thank you all. Dominic Kingston has also been a key part of the team, driving the publicity machine and introducing me to some brilliant librarians and booksellers.

While I've been writing I've been constantly amazed by the blogging community, with their boundless enthusiasm for new books and their continued support of old ones. I'm really looking forward to hearing what you think about this one. My writing friends from Twitter have also been invaluable, keeping me going when the end was nowhere in sight, offering virtual coffee and cake at every opportunity. Twitter has also given me access to experts in a whole range of subjects, and I'd particularly like to thank Jenny Rees for her advice on police procedure.

One other person whose name I must mention is Lizzie Wakefield. Lizzie gave a whopping donation to Authors for the Philippines after the devastation of Typhoon Haiyan in order to have her name in this book – I hope that you like being Nan, Lizzie! Sorry it's taken so long.

I must also thank all the readers of *Small Blue Thing* I've met and spoken with at school events, on the blog, at *Queen of Teen* and on Twitter. Your enthusiasm and encouragement has been humbling and inspiring – please keep writing!

And finally I have to thank my family – Pete, Jake and Ellie – for their patience and unstinting support. I couldn't do any of this without you.